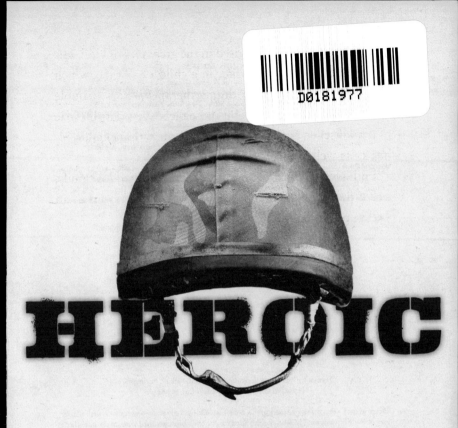

HEROIC

PHIL EARLE

PENGUIN BOOKS

PENGUIN BOOKS

Published by the Penguin Group
Penguin Books Ltd, 80 Strand, London WC2R 0RL, England
Penguin Group (USA) Inc., 375 Hudson Street, New York, New York 10014, USA
Penguin Group (Canada), 90 Eglinton Avenue East, Suite 700, Toronto, Ontario, Canada M4P 2Y3
(a division of Pearson Penguin Canada Inc.)
Penguin Ireland, 25 St Stephen's Green, Dublin 2, Ireland (a division of Penguin Books Ltd)
Penguin Group (Australia), 707 Collins Street, Melbourne, Victoria 3008, Australia
(a division of Pearson Australia Group Pty Ltd)
Penguin Books India Pvt Ltd, 11 Community Centre, Panchsheel Park, New Delhi – 110 017, India
Penguin Group (NZ), 67 Apollo Drive, Rosedale, Auckland 0632, New Zealand
(a division of Pearson New Zealand Ltd)
Penguin Books (South Africa) (Pty) Ltd, Block D, Rosebank Office Park, 181 Jan Smuts Avenue,
Parktown North, Gauteng 2193, South Africa

Penguin Books Ltd, Registered Offices: 80 Strand, London WC2R 0RL, England

penguin.com

First published 2013

001

Text copyright © Phil Earle, 2013
'The Brothers' copyright © Michael Wagg 2012
All rights reserved

The moral right of the author has been asserted

Set in 10.5/15.5pt Sabon
Typeset by Palimpsest Book Production Ltd, Falkirk, Stirlingshire
Printed in Great Britain by Clays Ltd, St Ives plc

British Library Cataloguing in Publication Data
A CIP catalogue record for this book is available from the British Library

ISBN: 978-0-141-34627-4

www.greenpenguin.co.uk

Penguin Books is committed to a sustainable
future for our business, our readers and our planet.
This book is made from Forest Stewardship
Council™ certified paper.

ALWAYS LEARNING   **PEARSON**

To my brother, our Jonathan, our kid.
I wrote this down for you.

We could see them through the trellis,
From the pit where we sat,
Framed,

Two boys swapping stickers.
The two of us
Talking of battlefields and bedrooms,

And swapping stickers.
And how the faces are now changed,
The frames frayed

But become something mirror-familiar –
Each other's heroes, perhaps.
And, even across enemy lines,

Brothers, being there.
And how paths part, criss-cross
Through sanded pits and poppy fields,

Then meet again,
At a point somewhere solid,
Framed, like a medal.

At its heart two boys

Swapping stickers.

'The Brothers' – Michael Wagg

SONNY

Talk is cheap, which explains a lot. Explains why every day of my life has been a shouting match, why, even with the phone held away from my ear, all I could hear was banter. White noise.

We might not have the money for much else, but we can always afford an argument.

The problem was, this noise was stopping me from focusing when I needed to be doing just that. We all stood to cash in here.

My patience stretched tight then snapped. I barked at them to shut up, or words to that effect, and was met by a moment's silence, then . . .

'OOOOOOOOHHH!' Three voices, each one thick with sarcasm. I could imagine them, thirty floors below, all holding imaginary handbags in the air, waving them in my direction, before falling about laughing.

Idiots, I thought, pushing a smile off my lips, before straining back into the distance.

Where is it?

It's late.

I'd been sussing this out for ages, since before Jammy and

Tommo left for Afghanistan. A chance to have some fun and make a bit on the side. Not just for me. For all of us.

But we had to get it right. No mistakes, because whichever way you looked at it, there was risk involved.

I didn't let the thought settle, but not in case it made me change my mind. I mean, it wasn't the first time, or the last either.

It's not breaking the law that gets to me, it's breaking the rules. Jammy's rules.

Never steal from your own.

Sounds like one of the Ten Commandments, doesn't it? Felt like it too, although Jamm has laid down way more than ten over the years. Sometimes I struggle to keep up with them.

But that's the beauty of this scam; we're not breaking the rules. Not really. We're taking, but not from our own. None of that stuff in the van belongs to Mr De Mel till he signs for it. And he won't sign for it, because it won't ever reach him. Not all of it, anyway.

It's a beautiful thing. And it'll work as long as the idiots downstairs manage to keep their minds off passing girls and on the game.

I was starting to twitch: I knew I needed the van soon to keep the lads focused on the plan, so when the silver Transit rolled off the dual carriageway and towards the Ghost estate, I hoped we were in business. A check of the logo on the side – *Fat Barry's Cash and Carry* – and bingo. Game on.

'Right, lads,' the urgency in my voice surprised even me. 'Target is three minutes away. Get in position and stick to what we said.'

A series of whoops and laughter came back, but I didn't have time to wind them in. I had thirty floors to cover before I reached the ground and, unsurprisingly, the pee-stinking lift was still out of order.

By the time I piled through the front door, skipping over a collection of drunks and smackheads, there was no time for even the briefest of pep talks. The van was turning the corner, only thirty metres from the front of Mr De Mel's corner shop. Sucking in a lungful of air, I powered along the kerb, only skipping across the road when I'd passed it.

Look calm.

It wasn't difficult. I wasn't nervous, I was pumped with the knowledge that we could pull it off. Positioning myself a dozen paces behind the van, I walked slowly after it, waiting for it to draw to a halt.

The plan wasn't difficult. Not really. Just needed a bit of play-acting and fortunately we had Wiggy to do that. Never been on a stage in his life, but I swear the boy had movie star written all over him. There wasn't anyone he couldn't charm or scam.

I just couldn't believe I hadn't thought of this earlier.

As the van approached him and slowed, all Wiggy had to do was step into the road, pretending to be drunk. If he timed it right, the impact would be nothing more than a kiss, but with his acting skills, he could turn it into something much more special.

I waited, heart thumping, not daring to look around the vehicle. But then it happened: a thud, the sound of Wiggy's arm slapping the bonnet, a horrendous groan, then shouting from two other voices as the van braked.

Hitch and Den.

Perfect. Their part was simple: turn the drama into a crisis. Make the driver feel so guilty that by the time they'd finished with him, he'd never want to drive again. But most importantly, they had to buy me time.

And that's exactly what they did.

'WHOOOOAAAAH!' shouted Den as he jumped into the road, arms outstretched in panic. His eyes, wide as dinner plates, flitted to Wiggy, who I guessed was writhing about like a fouled centre forward. 'Didn't you see him, you idiot?'

Peering round, I saw the driver's window wind down, then a shaven head emerged to be greeted by Hitch.

'You were driving too fast. It's twenty down here, you know. The kid didn't stand a chance.' It was a bit on the dramatic side, the guy had hardly been racing, but it was enough to get him out of the van to see what was going on under his wheels.

Keeping low to the ground, I scuttled to his door and leaned in to find the keys waiting for me. *Bingo!* Snatching them from the ignition I crept back to the rear, opened the door and jumped in, pulling laundry bags from the waistband of my jeans.

Man, this was way too easy. And inside? It was Santa's grotto. Packed to the rafters with stuff, all of it sellable.

It looked like half of the shops in the city were waiting for a delivery, but that wasn't my problem, and anyway, I couldn't carry it all. All I wanted was the stuff with value, the stuff people on the estate survived on. Booze and smokes basically.

I found the cigarettes quickly, ramming as many as I could into my bags. I reckoned I had a minute, two at the most, before the driver either got fed up or cottoned on. When that happened, I had to be long gone.

Next was the booze, but I had to be picky. Beer was no good, cider neither. Smooth going down, but no resale value. What I needed was the good stuff: spirits. I wouldn't get face value for it, but we'd get a lot more than we would for a four-pack of lager. I found a box of vodka, branded. Perfect. In a bag it went. I had no idea if I'd be able to carry it all but it was worth a go.

It was only when I tried to lift the bags that I realized it was time to leave. With this weight I'd be lucky to waddle across the estate, never mind run. I only wanted one more thing, and paused by the door when I saw them. Grabbing a handful of lollies, I rammed them deep into my pocket, then lowered myself back to the ground.

As I peeled away, I caught Den's attention, and with a smile, he kicked the plan into its closing phase.

'You got a phone, mate?' he demanded of the driver. 'We should get him an ambulance. I don't like the noise he's making.'

I don't know what Wiggy was doing on the ground, but he'd obviously convinced the driver that it was serious. With no sign of complaint, he headed back to his cab, leaving the lads with their cue to splinter.

I took it in from the entrance to our block.

They ran silently, in three completely different directions, Wiggy having made a miraculous recovery from his life-threatening injuries. It was comedy gold – the poor driver returned to nothing but the dust from their heels. All right, he could see the three of them legging it, but hadn't a clue about which one to follow. Instead he swore loudly before seething in my direction. That was my cue to leave too. God knows how he'd react when he saw what I'd been up to.

I climbed the fourteen floors to the flat, barely feeling the weight I was carrying. We'd arranged to meet and split the stuff once the dust had settled, but after dumping the rest of the booty in my room, I slipped two bottles and a carton of cigs into my rucksack. Time was tight and I needed the cash now. It wouldn't take me long to find a home for these.

Back in the sunlight, I peered at my watch then stepped up the pace. Thirty minutes until it all began, and I still had plenty to do.

Fencing the gear took minutes. Two hundred cigs (minus twenty for me, call it commission) to a bunch of lads on the bench, then the vodka to a couple who were already pickled in the stuff, and my pockets were jangling and heavy. I could've haggled for more, but time was tight.

Instead of worrying, I ran over to the centre of the square and the statue, shaking two smokes from the packet as I stood at its feet. Strange, I'd seen these bronze soldiers every day of my life. It was the first thing I saw when I looked out of my bedroom window, but it wasn't till you stood underneath the statue that you realized how massive it was. Beautiful too.

If ever there was a time for speed, this was it. People looked the other way on the estate, did what they had to do to get by. But no one messed with the statue. It was one of the unspoken laws of the place, separating us from the rest of the town, from the people who'd rather we didn't exist. They'd done their best to hide us away from the fancy marina and the fat wallets who threw their cash about on the weekend. It didn't bother us. We'd rather ignore their existence too.

Flicking a look over my shoulder, I sparked up the smokes, dangled them from my mouth and pulled myself carefully on to the plinth. With one foot on the first soldier's knee and a hand on the other's rifle, I hauled myself skywards, stopping when I reached their faces. Gripping hard with one hand, I reached for the cigarettes and pushed them inside each of the mouths till they held.

'Knock yourselves out.' I grinned, wishing I still had a bottle of vodka I could leave them too.

With a jump, I was back on the ground. Resisting the urge to give them a salute, I headed for town. Twenty minutes left and I had plenty of ground to cover.

 SONNY

Sweat pooled on my top lip as I ran for the town centre. I licked it away, grimaced, and tried to remember if this was how the sea tasted.

I'd swum in it once, but it was so long back I couldn't recall swallowing any. I remember bobbing next to a piece of used bog paper, but little else. Funny that.

Nerves chewed me as I checked my watch – Dad's watch – a big-faced chrome number that had proved far more reliable than he ever had. It was the only thing he'd left behind. The telly and microwave disappeared with him but Mum never bothered pawning the watch.

'If it was worth anything he'd have remembered it along with the remote control,' she'd said, her words emotionless.

Instead it sat on Jammy's wrist for years, then ended up on mine once he had shipped out. It hadn't left my skin since. Kept my brother close and in my head, despite the miles between us.

It told me I had ten minutes till the parade went through and I still had a stop to make. You didn't turn up without flowers. It wasn't what you did.

Our town had been ordinary. In the dictionary, under

that word, there should have been a picture of the place in all its dull glory. In fact, the air base had been the only thing that created a bit of spice. Without the squaddies getting legless and lairy at weekends, there'd have been nothing to put in the local paper. There's only so many car boot sales you can advertise.

Of course, everything changed when the Twin Towers came down. When those planes hit, we felt the tremors all the way over here. We still do.

Suddenly, there were more people in uniform than ever; in town, by the barracks, but especially on the estate: flyering, persuading, filling shaven heads full of dreams. Plenty listened, plenty signed up.

Town got quieter on a Friday night. Our lads were fighting on the other side of the world instead, without the help of booze. It didn't hurt the newspaper though. Columns were filled by the stories of locals coming back broken. Some didn't come home at all.

And that changed everything. Instead of being a nuisance to the town, the air base became this almost holy place. It gave everyone a purpose, because every time a soldier was blown up, they'd parade him through the streets, Union Jack shrouding the fact that inside the coffin bits of him were mangled or missing.

Everyone turned out, the streets were always packed, people came from everywhere, even the south.

The florist had to move to a bigger shop, the undertaker doubled his fleet. The petrol station started selling bouquets of their own, bargain-basement ones that looked like they were already on the way out.

Those flowers died on the forecourt. This wasn't about doing it on the cheap.

My legs twitched as I waited in the queue with a handful of white roses, the ones I always chose out of superstition.

'Lovely choice, darlin',' Mrs Morgan smiled. 'Very tasteful.'

I shoved the money into her hand and broke through the queue behind me; had to be on the lamp post before the trumpeter started.

It took me longer than normal to wade to my space. Two soldiers were coming home today; coaches from Scotland lined the market. Whole communities had come to welcome them back. No one got irritated with me, though. A lot of folk knew my regular spot as I shimmied up the lamp post, wedging my feet either side of the pole. Only when balanced did I retrieve the flowers from the back of my jeans, ignoring the thorns as they dug at my palm.

As always, the clocks chimed before the trumpet cut in and, seamlessly, the hearses crept into view.

It was always this moment that killed me, that stole my breath and mashed my head in total fear.

It could be him. Could be Jamm. I could've missed the phone call or the knock at the door.

How would I ever look Mum or the others in the eye, knowing they'd expect me to step up and be the person he'd been?

I could only ever disappoint them; would only ever fall short of the bloke he was.

I looked for Mum in the crowd, but there were too many

faces, all wearing the same expression. I could picture her anyway, black suit anvil-pressed, hair scraped back precisely with twenty pins. I sometimes wondered if the hair-grips were the only things holding her together.

Her eyes would be scanning the crowd, looking for me. Was I here? Was I all right? Sometimes it felt like she'd never met me. I was hardly made of glass. I *could* get by without him if she gave me the chance.

I didn't let the irritation settle, fortunately didn't have to, as my eyes rested on someone else. And in that moment, none of it mattered, because her eyes found me too. The lines that creased our foreheads disappeared, and although we were separated by hundreds of people and a line of security barriers we couldn't be any closer. It was enough. Had to be.

Only the sight of the garlands through the hearse window brought me back to the street.

Danny

Son

Dad

I allowed myself to breathe when I saw the names on the wreaths clearly, allowed myself a tear as the flowers fell from my hand on to the top of the polished car.

For the past five weeks I'd prayed that I'd never read my brother's name spelled out in poppies.

In the weeks that followed I often wished I had.

SONNY

So you probably want to know who the girl in the crowd was. And that's fine by me. I could talk about Cameron Thompson all day long. Although, inevitably, thoughts of her bring me back to Jammy, and another of his commandments.

Thou shalt not cop off with thy mate's sister.

Keeping to this was proving more difficult than the stealing one.

I mean firstly, they wouldn't have got away with this in Jerusalem or wherever Moses was when his hormones kicked in, and secondly, it was clearly aimed at Cam, as there's only Wiggy who also has a sister.

No disrespect to Tina or anything, but she's . . . ample. So big there's a health warning tattooed under her bra strap about the danger of suffocation.

Don't get me wrong, she's a nice girl, big heart, big everything really, but she's not interested in me, and frankly, phew, ditto and amen to that.

Cam on the other hand is . . . well, it's impossible to explain. She's just Cam.

A stupid, gorgeous, tough, quirky mess of contradictions. People who don't live on the estate would tell you she's typical of a girl from the Ghost, that she's brassy and confrontational. But if you actually watch her, I mean *really* watch her, you'll see that she's never the first to speak. All right, she'll fight her corner if pushed, in fact she's tastier with her fists than any of the lads from the west side of town. But you'll never see her strike first, only strike back.

That's *one* of the things that makes her rock my entire world, but by no means all of it.

I mean, the girl is fit. Tall without being lanky or scrawny, everything in the right place, without her ever feeling the need to flaunt it like others I could mention.

She's everything I'm not, basically, and for that reason I always reckoned she was leagues above me. She's Man Utd to my Grimsby Town. If any of us were ever going to stand a chance with her, it was Jammy.

Which is why the whole thing messes with my head on such an epic scale.

No one knows about it of course. Not Wiggy, Hitch or Den, and especially not Jammy or Tommo. Though if it did get out, the news wouldn't take long to reach them. Ghost estate gossip could easily reach Afghanistan, believe me.

I tried to work out who would be most hacked off if they heard, Tommo or Jamm. Tomm's her brother, after all, so you might say him, but the rule belongs to Jammy, so he'd probably try and come down hard to mark his territory.

I thought about it for a few minutes then gave up. It wasn't like I signed a contract or anything, and I didn't chase it either. These things just happen sometimes. And when they do? Well, you just have to roll with it, don't you?

You see, Cam and Tommo's situation is complicated.

Actually, that's not true. It's not complicated at all, they just have a disgrace for a dad. The kind of disgrace who likes to hide behind his drink; the kind who can't hold his beer by the end of the night, because by then his hands have clenched into fists. Fists he can't straighten out until they've had a go on someone who he's supposed to love.

It's when I see his ratty face that I'm glad I don't have an old man of my own. He'd only disappoint me too.

We've known about what Larry does for years, how he rules the house and how the drink rules him, but it's not like we can do anything about it. Police aren't interested unless someone in the family makes a statement, and the chances of that, knowing the beating that would follow? Well, it's never going to happen.

I often wondered if that was the reason for Tommo joining up. He'd never gone on about the army before. Maybe he'd just had one too many pastings from Larry. I don't mean he signed up out of fear. Tommo wasn't scared of his dad. He'd often take one for the team. Two black eyes and a split lip meant his ma and Cam were left alone. No, he might've followed Jamm because he was about to snap and put the idiot in the hospital. And if he did that? Well, Larry would have no problem dialling 999.

The issue I had with him going to Afghanistan was Cam. I mean, if she was my sister, there's no way I'd leave and put her next in the firing line.

But Tommo had his reasons, and he's sound. One of us. An Original.

On the day he left with the rest of them, I saw his face.

What it meant. I could see some of the other soldiers, all screwed up out of fear for themselves, wondering whether they'd ever come back. I'm sure Tomm was feeling that too. But the way he held on to Cam, the way their bodies shook without a word? It said everything I needed to know, and what I needed to do.

I know what you're thinking when you hear all this. That I engineered it, me and her. But that's not how it happened. First week I dropped her a few texts:

how u doing?

Nothing heavier. Responses were brief.

Fine.
All gud.

Then everything changed with a knock at the door about two and a half weeks in. Listen to me being vague. I know exactly when it was. Eighteen days after they left. It was a Wednesday. Three in the afternoon.

I'd not been in long, still burning up after a run in the heat. It wasn't a clear-your-head-and-keep-fit kind of run, more the if-you-stop-you'll-have-your-head-caved-in variety, but either way, I was sweating. Shirt off and Coke in hand, I'd collapsed in front of the box and was surfing for something to watch. The knock was irritating, but not for long. Not when I saw who it was through the frosted glass.

'Can I come in?' Her words were out before the door was

fully open, before I had time to stick my pecs out and pull my stomach in.

'Course,' I said, resisting the urge to sniff my pits.

'Sorry to barge in,' she went on, turning to face me.

Her cheeks and eyes were red, the top of her chest above her vest was blotchy. Instantly I thought of Larry, of rearranging his face.

'What's up?' I offered her the chair but she wouldn't sit. 'Is it your dad? What's he done?'

Reaching for my phone I scrolled for Den's number. He was the biggest of all of us, the one you wanted at your shoulder when it all went down.

'It's not Dad. I haven't seen him for days. He does this, goes under for a week or so then pitches up like nothing's happened. Longer he's face down in a pint, the better.'

'Then what's up? What's going on?'

Her face dissolved. Not in a pathetic way. She could never be that.

'It's the telly. The news. I've barely switched it off since Tommo went. It's on twenty-four hours. Always about bombs and shootings. I want to turn it off and leave the house, Sonny, but I can't. I keep thinking if I leave it on I'll catch a glimpse of him, and be happy. But he never shows up, and now there's reports of another explosion. One of those improvised ones. The worst yet. Then they said where it was and I couldn't remember if it was the same place that Tommo and Jamm went . . .'

No more words came. She just swayed and looked at me, so scared she couldn't even manage to wipe the smudged tears that fell to the carpet.

I didn't know what to do. Hold her, calm her, stick the news on myself? I daren't do any of them for very different reasons, but had to pick one, so I stabbed at the remote until I reached News24.

As the camera settled on a raging cloud of smoke, I felt nerves prickle across my chest.

It summed up why I'd been resisting the news ever since they left. It was bad enough the scenarios playing out in my head without being confronted with it on the TV too.

I thought about others on the estate going through the same thing. Young mums little older than us, their kids screaming as Daddy left for Helmand. They told me about stuff they did to keep the little ones calm. Jars full of sweets: a Smartie for every day Daddy was away. And when the jar was empty? Then Daddy would be home.

It seemed so simple. Made me wish I was ten years younger and a hundred times more innocent.

It was clearly getting to Cam. She wasn't blinking as she stared at the screen. She didn't even react when the newsreader told us that the family of the blown-up soldier had been informed. All she did was pull the phone from her pocket and jab at the keypad before pushing it to her ear.

'Mum?' Her voice was calmer than when she'd been talking to me. 'Anyone been in touch?'

I presumed the answer was no as she exhaled loudly and slumped on to the settee, hanging up in the process. Immediately I checked my own mobile. Couldn't face the prospect of a missed call from Mum.

'I never understood why they always said that stuff about

families being informed,' she gasped. 'I do now. It's so idiots like me can stop bricking themselves 24/7.' She looked angry at herself, which I wasn't going to have.

'Give yourself a break. It's not easy, I know that.'

'I can't help it, though, Sonny. I can't walk past a newsagent without looking at every page in every rag, just in case I've missed something. If there's a telly in a shop, I'll watch it till the news rolls round to the start again.'

'I understand. I do. But you've got to try not to worry. It's not like we can do anything about it, except trust they'll look after each other.'

I thought for a second that her face had softened from panic to mild dread. But it didn't last long.

'Do you ever find yourself Googling Jamm's name? In case it's leaked on to the web before it reaches the news on TV? I try to stop myself but it's . . . '

'*Hey!*' I interrupted, then let my voice soften. 'It's OK. I get it.' I really did, but had no idea how to make it any easier for her. So I did what I always do and winged it.

'Look at us. All of us, and the scrapes we've got through to be here. All right, it's not easy, but we're still in one piece despite it all. That's why I reckon they'll be all right. There're as many knives here as there are guns over there, and there's none sticking out of us yet, are there? They'll be all right if we are.'

I made a joke of it, patting for an imaginary blade across my shoulders and hers. My fingers turned pure electric as my skin touched hers, especially when she didn't flinch. I left them there, squeezing gently as Jamm disappeared from my head for the first time in weeks.

'And we are all right, aren't we?' she asked, eyes all the more magnetic for the make-up smudged around them.

I felt brave. Don't know why or how, but for once, around her, I felt invincible.

'You tell me? I reckon so.'

And that was it. The gap between us disappeared. Not because I lunged or took advantage. It just happened. And happened. And happened. The footage on the news disappeared. Jamm and Tommo were looking the other way, for now at least.

Breaking a rule had never felt so good.

SONNY

No one knew the estate like us. That's why we were The Originals.

It wasn't a name we bandied about, or sprayed wherever we could.

We weren't a crew, in fact that was the point. We were anything but. An anti-crew.

People talk about living on the Ghost, reckon there's only one thing you need to have straight in your head to survive.

Are you in or are you out?

Know that and you're set.

We knew different. We blew that theory up every day. And, mostly, that was down to Jammy.

He just *got* this place, knew how to play it.

Step in far enough to keep face without ever wading out of your depth.

That's how the commandments came about.

It's not like I don't listen to them or to him. It's more that I could never live up to everything that he was.

Jamm's taller than me. Broader, blonder, better looking, brighter, smarter (there's a difference, apparently), and after a while, standing in that kind of massive shadow gets to you. Stops you even trying to match up. I'm short enough as it is, I don't need people knocking me down any further.

So I play with the commandments. Shave the edges off some, fold others without ever quite ripping them in half.

You see, that's what Jamm isn't always so good at. Being creative.

And that's why no one knows the estate better than me.

Because I always need somewhere to hide.

The day after we turned the van over, though, it wasn't just me who needed to be invisible. It was all of us. Seemed like on every pavement there was a sign asking, 'Have you seen these scumbags?'

I was surprised to see them, the signs. They were those Crimestoppers' ones that demand witnesses come forward and spill the beans. They didn't appear very often on the estate. If there was a sign for every shonky deal that went on around here, then we'd be reduced to walking on the roads. Fact.

But for some reason, our little scam had taken the interest of the authorities, or maybe Fat Barry was slipping the coppers a bung to try and get even with us. Either way, we were reminded of our van scam every time we stepped outside. And as a result? Well, I was beginning to feel paranoid. Seemed like it was only a matter of time until someone matched the description on the signs to one of our mugs, and we couldn't have that. It wasn't like I could pay back what I took. The money was already well spent, and to make matters worse, I'd broken another of Jamm's more important rules:

Don't fence goods on the estate.
It's not our patch to sell, only to buy.

Simple, but I'd managed to break it straight after the robbery because I didn't have time to flog my stash anywhere else. Not if I wanted flowers for the parade, and anyway, I was doing that for Jamm. To prove that I'm not as useless as everyone thinks I am.

Except I must be, because I'd sold stuff where I shouldn't have and now I'm paying for it by having to lurk in every alley and staircase on the estate.

I hadn't had to leg it yet, as no one knew it was definitely me. But the lads from the Cuda crew weren't usually bothered with hard evidence. A rumour's all you need when you run practically every racket on the estate.

The prospect of that confrontation, plus the paranoia of the police closing in, was enough to get me calling the boys together, panicking in a way that Jammy never would.

I'd guessed the others had followed the rules and taken their booty clear of the estate before lining their pockets. Then again, I thought, as I opened the door to Wiggy, maybe they had no need to sell their loot at all.

Wiggy's a prolific smoker. One of the best I've ever seen. Can destroy a cig in seconds. Maybe it adds to that movie star demeanour of his, I don't know. I've known him all my life but I can't really remember a time when he didn't have a butt dangling from his lips. Even as he stepped inside now, he had one on the go and a pack tucked into his t-shirt pocket.

Den, however, is more about the sauce. The boy loves a drink. Not in a sitting-on-a-bench-with-a-brown-paper-bag kind of way. We've all seen enough of them, had too many in our families to fall into that trap. What I mean is, if the party needs starting, Den's your go-to guy for a swig of something special.

Not that he turned up today with a four-pack of anything. I think he knew from my message that I wasn't up for a party.

'What's up, then?' he asked, filling the doorway as he entered.

'Give me five minutes and I'll tell you. We're waiting for Hitch.'

He blew a long breath out. 'Be more than five, then.' His face wore a look that said, *I wish I'd brought some beers after all*.

Hitch, you see, well, he's the real Original among us. Like Den, he'll have a go on anything that's getting passed around, but without ever getting trolleyed.

I don't know, he's a quiet one. Keeps it all in. When the banter's flying about, he'll laugh along and point the finger, but it's not often he'll chip in.

We all reckon it's to do with home. None of us exactly come from a model family: any of us that have two parents, one of them's either a drunk or a disgrace. But none of us really know what the score is with Hitch.

I remember asking him, years ago, when we were kids, 'Who do you actually live with?'

He didn't bother to stop chewing his nails as he answered, 'Auntie.'

'Mum or Dad's side?'

'Neither.'

'How is she your auntie, then?'

'Dunno. Just is.'

'Family friend?'

'Something like that. It's complicated.'

That summed him up for me. Hitch was complicated and simple at the same time.

When it all kicks off, he's there. Well, he was. He's seen me through more scrapes than I can remember and never once filled Jammy in on details he didn't need to know.

We just knew to accept whatever was going on behind his front door.

Had our suspicions that he'd mostly brought himself up. Certainly Auntie had disappeared by his seventeenth birthday, leaving him on his own in a shabby council flat. There were times, watching him destroy a bag of chips, that you wondered when the last food had passed his lips. He was an enigma. He came and went. And since Jamm and Tommo had been overseas, he'd been even harder to pin down.

Wiggs sighed after fifteen minutes had dragged by. 'Call him.'

'I already have. Twice.'

'Rudeness.' Den was twitchy too, so when the doorbell buzzed, we were both on the verge of breaking out the party poppers. Can't say Den's delight lasted when I walked back in with Cam, though Wiggs, as usual, led with a gag.

'You done something with your hair, Hitch?'

'Funny you should mention that,' laughed Cam, waving her bag in their direction.

They looked confused as I shot her a look, *I haven't told them yet!*

'What's going on, Sonny?'

'We should wait for Hitch.'

'He's not coming, is he? He's flaked out like always. So let's have it.'

'Ten more minutes . . .'

'NOW!' Den was on his feet, blocking out every inch of sun. I was out of time.

'Well,' I stammered, 'we've got a problem. Or we did have. The good news is I've got a solution. That's why Cam's here.'

They stared at me, then Cam, then me. I saw their hearts sink as they saw the hair clippers come out of her bag.

Wiggy ran his fingers over his skull, looking nothing like his nickname. 'Couldn't you have given me a number one? You didn't have to take the guard off the clippers as well.'

Cam blew the last of the hair away and looked at me. 'Tell the boss, not me.'

'It *will* grow back, you nugget.'

'Not quickly enough,' he moaned. 'It's nearly autumn, you know. I'll have a cold by the end of the week.'

'It'll be far colder in a secure unit if the police catch up with us, so stop your moaning.'

He lit a cig and smoked it sulkily, going on about being too quick to be nabbed for anything.

Dennis, on the other hand, was chuffed with the result, rubbing his fingers through the mohican that Cam had carved him. It was a far cry from his initial anger when I told him the police might be on to us. If he hadn't promised Jamm that he'd keep an eye on me, I'd have been picking my teeth off the carpet for days.

His new fin was wobbly and uneven, but Den was so tall

it was unlikely anyone would notice. 'Smart,' he said, winking at Cam, sending a jolt of jealousy through me.

I wasn't exactly looking my best either, sat on a kitchen stool with a plastic bag tied round my head.

'Can I take this off yet?'

I'd never been bothered about my hair in my life, but suddenly I needed to look at it. Now I had Cam to lose.

She checked her watch and nodded. 'You should be all right. Just make sure you rinse it properly.' I sprinted for the bathroom, hearing her shout, 'And be careful with the towels. Your mum'll kick off if you trash them.'

I did as she told me, not daring to take my head out of the bath until the water ran clear. Only then did I check my appearance in the mirror, a single word leaving my mouth in surprise. It was the same one that all of them shouted as soon as they saw me.

'Jammy!' they said, almost in stereo.

'Up yours! I look nothing like him.'

'Spitting image,' Wiggy laughed.

But it was Cam's reaction that really got to me, despite not uttering a word. All she did was walk towards me and push a hand through my hair. It was a simple gesture, one that had Wiggs and Den looking at each other quizzically.

I should've been concerned that maybe she'd given us away. But I wasn't bothered about that. The only question in my jealous head was this: whose hair did she think she was stroking? Mine? Or my brother's?

JAMMY

The Chinook banked left, taking my guts with it. I tried to ignore the power of the setting sun as it crashed against my eyes, but couldn't. The effects of its ten-hour barrage clung to my fatigues. It was like the sun had leaned down and licked every inch of me like a dog.

In danger of slipping off the seat, I pulled heavily on my drinking tube, remembering the boss's words when we'd first arrived:

'As many litres a day as you can, gentlemen. Anyone going down dehydrated in the first week will have me to answer to.'

We'd nodded, not really understanding until now exactly what he'd meant. It was too late for Tommo, though. He'd caught a bug within six hours of landing and, judging from the smell rising beside me, was still suffering.

I reached into my pack and handed him a dehydration sachet, which he took with a groan.

'Don't complain, pal,' I shouted above the *whup* of the blades, then motioned towards the boss.

Don't let him see you're struggling. It's too soon.

Tommo understood me. We'd been communicating

27

without words for as long as we could remember. And anyway, he knew I had him, I'd told him that on the day he got over-excited and joined up. The day after me.

'What are you doing?' I'd asked him. 'No need for you to jump in too, was there?'

He'd smiled excitedly, like he'd signed on rather than up: 'You're kidding me, aren't you? You think I'd let you have a clear run at hero status? You're having a laugh, pal.'

He was talking out of his back-end again. He always made out I was the one in charge. They all did, I suppose: Wiggy, Dennis, Hitch, even our Sonny. But that's not how it was. They led us into plenty of stuff we shouldn't have been anywhere near, the only difference was it was always me who dug us out, one way or another. Which is why I was here, instead of on the Ghost, thinking of ways to get among Tommo's sister.

'You're an idiot,' I'd told him. 'It's not like I really had a choice. But you? You can barely handle *Call Of Duty*. What are you going to do with a machine gun?'

He'd laughed again, so I'd fixed him with a look he'd seen a million times in our lives. 'Are you sure? About all this?'

He'd nodded furiously. 'I know you've got me. Me and my back.'

'Course I have.'

What else could I say, regardless of the unease eating me alive?

I turned my attention back to the horizon, the red mountains fading as the sun dived for cover behind them.

My head whirled with how surreal this all was. A Chinook, for god's sake.

I'd reckoned the six of us might have managed a trip to Ibiza one day, if we'd finally got lucky and they'd changed the laws on robbing banks. But this? Well, it wasn't how I'd intended it.

The adrenalin I'd taken off with still gripped hard. Hardly surprising when the boss told us they'd lost a chopper on a previous run to the base.

'Keep your legs crossed until we land,' he'd shouted as we'd got on. 'Second thoughts, scratch that. You won't need to think with your tackle for the next three months at least.'

It was a line he'd obviously delivered before, enough times to realize it wasn't funny. We'd groaned like a bunch of kids in front of their embarrassing uncle, when actually we all knew we'd need the boss more than anyone until we found ourselves back home. Long as we had him and each other, like they'd taught us, we had a chance.

Of making a difference. Surviving.

I understood what they meant as soon as they'd said it. I get the whole brotherhood thing. No big deal. It's how it's always been.

My attention hurtled left as we banked again, and for the first time the Forward Operating Base fell into view. A mash of buildings: some permanent, some temporary, all ugly. I smiled despite knowing this was the dangerous bit: somehow it reminded me of home.

The fury of the helicopter blades couldn't hide the sound of sliding machine-gun catches beside me. I'd no idea how many times these gunners had flown virgins like me into this place, but I couldn't believe they were any calmer than we were. The closer we were to the ground, the closer we all were to the Taliban, to a row of bodybags.

I swallowed the thought before it settled. Not going to happen.

The boss's voice scratched our ears through the headset.

'One minute, gentlemen, then a hundred metre sprint to the gates. No daydreaming, we're not tourists any more. And there's no glory in arriving unless we are complete. Equipment checks.'

There was a chorus of clicks as chambers engaged. I made sure my armour covered everything vital, then checked Tommo was doing the same.

He was sweating like a pig. Leg bouncing on the floor, knee knocking against mine. I pressed my leg against his, the message clear.

Calm. Breathe. Calm.

The shaking stopped momentarily. Then it started again, small tremors this time.

I checked the other lads, their reactions. Some seemed outwardly calm, others had gum clacking between clenched teeth. Only Giffer looked truly focused, but he'd been here before. Iraq, too. There was no twitching from him, no tics. His movements were calm and measured as he loosely wrapped a strip of black material around his gun arm. I wondered what that was about. Superstition? Mourning? I flashed him a look – *Why?* – but only got back, *Later*.

He was in the zone, where I should be. You don't survive as many tours as him without doing things right; without being lucky too.

The ground grabbed the Chinook's feet and held on tight, the boss hollering without hesitation, 'MOVE MOVE MOVE!' arms windmilling madly.

JC was first out, grit etched into his face, too tense to chew any more. Caffeine next, then Pee, El Guido, Boz, Slasher.

I shuffled along, closer to the hatch, but could see only dust and darkness.

There was just Tommo in front of me now, gripping his gun so hard the veins were popping round his knuckles. High blue veins like Helmand contours.

He was terrified, I knew he was. Shoulders twitching, head down, for a second I thought he was crying. Fifteen years and I'd never seen him leak a single tear. This wasn't the time for it. Not now. Not when we hadn't even begun.

'A hundred metres!' I yelled in his year. 'Thirty seconds. It's almost the distance from your front door to mine. Let's have it!'

I don't know if it was the mention of home, or a new wave of adrenalin, but it kicked Tommo forward. I heard him yell as he disappeared into the dust cloud, my eyes flicking to the boss: had he seen what I had? Did he know Tommo was flaking already?

He gave nothing away, every cell focused on delivering each member of his regiment safely, so I sprinted on, feeling the rotors kick pebbles on to my calves, biting like gnats at the height of summer.

The distance meant nothing, nor did time. I could have been running for hours and not noticed. All I could think about was making it inside the gates and sorting Tommo out. Before the boss or one of the others did.

Eventually, quickly, the gates loomed out of the dust and I piled through, almost running straight into Tomm, bent double, laughing like a loon.

Make your mind up, will you?

But I didn't say it. Instead I slapped his pack roughly and drew heavily on my drinking tube.

It was a small step. Well, a couple of hundred of them. But it was a start. We were here. Our war was beginning.

JAMMY

The sun melts everything around here, including time.

From the moment it breaks above the mountains you can feel its anger. It's like the Taliban's had words with it, got it onside to pummel the strength out of us before they get stuck in.

None of us know what to do with the heat, even the vets like Giffer shuffle around, attempt to start something positive like cleaning a gun, then start flagging after fifteen minutes. If the enemy knew how many half-assembled weapons there were in this place they'd be on us in a flash.

At first it was almost funny, like we'd landed in the lousiest campsite on the planet, with the worst-smelling bogs and a distinct lack of totty. But at least it's different, so different to the summer monsoons going on back at home. Anything but that.

Each day the heat sucks you dry. But no matter how much water you drink, it's never enough to stop the dust feeling like it's blown in through your ears and nestled in your brain.

Sleep is patchy, and not just because of the carnival of noises and smells that rip through our digs. The fans whirr and cough throughout the night. By rights, with all that noise we should be frozen to our cots, but we're not. Useless things don't kick out enough chill to dry the sweat on our toes, never mind anything else.

When three a.m. crawls on top of you, though, and you're still not under, your head starts to twist, asks you to name the beds that'll be empty by the end of the tour, describe the reasons each of your friends vacated them: mortar attack, sniper, improvised explosive device, friendly fire; on and on it goes. But I don't let myself, couldn't bear it if one of those messed-up prophecies actually came true. After what we've been taught about what we have to go through together, as family, it would be traitorous to let myself.

I don't even entertain the thought of my own death. Although given half a chance, my mind would be rampant at the possibilities. I've enough people to be strong for here, without even thinking about the idiots I have to be tough for at home.

Instead I let dawn crawl around, feel the fans wave the white flag at the first sign of the sun, then wait for the dawn chorus of yawns and farts to bounce off the temporary walls. I'm up before the smell gets the chance to invade my nostrils.

If it's the heat that's slowly defeating me, for others it's boredom. By eleven o'clock the sun's banished us to kick our heels in the shade, but even that's melting quickly, forcing us together almost into a scrum.

It's too much for Caffeine, his shaven head the same colour now as our berets.

'I've had enough of all this.' It's not the first time he's

34

sounded off since he arrived. If I have to hear this isn't what he joined up for once more, I might go mad.

'Right. Battle bingo,' he declares.

'Do what?' says El Guido, his bare, rubbery gut soaking up a dangerous amount of sun.

'I heard the septics playing it yesterday.'

'The who?' Guido can't cope with sun *and* slang.

'Septics. Septic tanks, Yanks. You know, our American friends.'

'Oh I know 'em,' moans Guido. 'They speak better English than you for starters, you nugget.'

The quality of banter is even suffering due to heat exhaustion, but Caffeine goes on, arms waving madly as he lays out the rules.

'It's a wishlist,' he grins. 'Military Christmas list. The guns you want to fire, missiles you want to launch, number of heads you want to pulp before we go home.'

He says it so matter-of-factly he makes it sound like a game of noughts and crosses.

There are a hundred ways I want to tell him to shut up, that his list should only include doing his job and having two arms and legs left at the end, but I don't have to. Giffer does it for me. Does it better than I ever could.

'Good soldiers, the Americans,' he says.

Why is it the Welsh always sound like they're singing, even if they're tone deaf, like Giffer?

'Skilled. Focused. Machine-like almost.'

Caffeine rolls his eyes as soon as the older man begins, but Giffer doesn't notice, or doesn't care.

'But don't you believe that any of those lads you heard

have seen any more action than you, you hear me? Cos I'll tell you this for nothing, Caff. If you've actually fired a missile that levels a house, and if you've seen the bodies that your missile blew apart, then you wouldn't brag about it. You certainly wouldn't want to shout "house" or "bingo" or any such rubbish. You'd rather not have fired it at all. You'd almost do anything not to have had such an itchy finger. Believe me.'

I believe him. The others do too, though Caffeine can do nothing but pull himself to his feet and declare he's off for a dump.

'Be the most excitement I'll get today,' he declares, his last moan until he realizes there's no paper left in the bog. The thought makes me smile. Giffer lies back, eyes closed, wisdom shared.

He's obviously seen stuff. Plenty of it, and I'd imagine a lot of it is burnt into his head. I try to imagine what that might be, but stop when I see Tommo chewing the inside of his cheek nervously.

I try and cajole him, get him grinning, but give up when he refuses to play. Instead I settle for a call to Sonny, and listen to him gabble like he's chock-full of speed.

'What's the news over there, then? You going all Rambo or what?'

'Hell, yeah. You know me. Never seen without a hunting knife between my teeth.'

'Cracking,' he laughs, though he knows I'm joking. 'I'll tell the lads.'

'How are they? Keeping you out of bother?'

'Totally, they're only letting me out when I'm on a lead.

Though Den said I can lose the muzzle in a week or two.'

'Well I'd better give him a buzz, tell him not to rush it.'

'You'll never guess what happened last week, Jamm.'

Calls are often like this. Random, scattergun.

'Some girl from Pickard House gave birth in the lift. Poor cow was living on the fifteenth and got stuck halfway down. Two and a half hours till they got it moving and when the doors opened it was like something out of a slasher movie.'

'Was the kid all right?'

'Yeah, apart from the shock of what someone had written about his mum on the wall he was fine. Imagine that being your introduction to the world?'

'Enough to make him want to climb back inside.'

'Ha! Too right.'

It was good to hear his voice, even when I pressed harder about what he was up to and the inevitable pushback came.

'You don't need to worry about Mum, Jamm. I'm telling you, she's fine.'

'But you're keeping an eye on her, yeah? Doing your bit?'

'I am when there's nothing on the box . . . ' I heard him sigh with frustration. 'Course I am. I'm not an animal, you know.'

'But I know what Mum's like. She'll run around all day if you let her.'

'Well I'm *not* letting her. Not that you believe me, clearly.'

'Sonny, come on. We can't do this over the phone. I can't reach to give you a slap!'

'You don't need to, my ear's already bleeding.'

And that cut the tension again, letting us get back to the smaller stuff. He told me about places I know, people too, and it settled me. Made me remember I won't be here forever, despite what it feels like now.

The conversation ends like it always does. With the same line from him.

'Look after yourself, you hear? And don't forget to duck . . . '

I can't put the phone down without him saying it. I might not need reminding what could be waiting out on patrol, but somehow it feels like his advice keeps me safe anyway.

#

Shortly after my phone conversation with Sonny, the waiting was interrupted by a call to the briefing room that turned into a stampede, dust kicking up and sticking fast to our damp skin.

'Intel suggests there will be movement inside the town today,' barked the boss. 'Heroin being transported. Large quantities. Amounts that could bankroll Taliban fighters for months, fund an upgrade to weapons, strengthen their dominance in the area.'

Heroin. It's not new to me and Tommo. We've seen plenty of it passing between palms back at the Ghost. Watched it suck the life right out of people. People we knew, schoolmates, family. But we've not been close to the manufacturing end. By the time it's dealt at home, it's cut, diluted, tied up like a bomb in a baggie. Out here you see the poppy fields, can almost hear the crop ticking, waiting to be cut, processed, primed. It's stuff they'd literally die for.

The thought of it was enough to put steel in me, make me do whatever the boss asked.

'What we don't know, however, is the location of it.

Where it's been processed. Intel says if we find the plant, we find the gear. They won't want to move it any more times than necessary. Our objectives today are to reach out to the locals, ask questions, gain trust. The majority of them don't want the drugs in their town either. All we have to do is find one of them who's happy to give the location up.'

I heard a sigh from my left, disappointment from someone who wanted a livelier introduction to their tour. The boss had none of it.

'Not dangerous enough for some of you, eh? Not enough that if we do find the gear, the Taliban will throw every grenade, bullet and rock they can find to stop you getting to it. They'll set IEDs in our paths. Inside boxes, cans, spaces so small you won't possibly believe there could be explosive inside. But they will be the ones to watch: strong enough to take your leg and leave you to bleed out in seconds. You hear me?'

The boss left us with one more shout.

'This all ties in to the hearts and minds conversation, gents. You've heard it at home as well as here. You know this war is about trust, about educating the locals, giving them opportunities to live without heroin surrounding them. But the first step has to be them trusting us, recognizing our aims are about their safety. It all starts with you, gents. Do your jobs, come back safe, come home together.'

We dressed ourselves clumsily, like kids having to tie their laces for the first time. Tomm could barely get his helmet fastened, his hands were shaking so much. I had to fight the temptation to sort it out myself.

As we stepped into the sun, we gasped as one. Immediately,

I pulled my tube round to a better place. I'd need liquid on tap to get through this. Told Tommo to do the same.

As the boss went through radio checks, I noticed Giffer going through the motions with his armband again, just as he had on the Chinook.

'What's that all about, Giff? Not superstitious, are you?'

His laugh rumbled like gunfire. 'No place for superstition this, Jamm. This is my gun arm, and this is my tourniquet ready, see? Any Taliban dares to shoot this arm, there's no way I'm bleeding out. One quick pull, and I can take them down before they finish me. Simple.'

At that moment I'm scared. Scared like I've never been in my whole life. And I know why. I'm never scared at home. Never, despite everything that goes off around me. Because there, I know the rules. If I make a mistake at home, I can get around it. Things might get tasty, but there's always a way.

But here? One mistake, one step too far left or right, and it's over. I'm missing an arm, a leg, or worse. I bleed out.

We paced to the gates as a pack. Armoured, tooled-up, but more naked than we'd ever been in our lives. Once the doors were pulled back we streamed out, two by two, arms lifting in turn to touch a single word painted in red above the gate: DAVENPORT. The name of the first soldier to walk through and not come back. We touched it out of respect, to show him he didn't fall without reason, but we knew, all of us, that it didn't make us immune to the same fate.

I chanced a look at Tommo. He was holding it together – just. He was followed by Giffer, who already had his game face on.

The armband idea might work for him, but it feels like there's not a tourniquet big enough to keep me safe.

We paced to the village in no time, driven down the hill by adrenalin and the naive desire to get things done. After the endless days at the base and Caffeine's mindless banter, even the blandest landscape was eye-popping.

I suppose all of it was exotic, in comparison to the estate.

Days as hot as this back home led to a sea of discarded football shirts, exposed beer guts and the whiff of value burgers burning on disposable barbies. There were no such reminders of home here, although as the market place opened up in front of us we were bombarded with smells that I'd never be able to identify if I lived to be a hundred. It was a mental mix of sewage, then almost candyfloss sweetness, followed by spices so overpowering they blasted a path right through your goggles.

I tried to think about how I'd describe it to Sonny and the others, but it was so dizzying I had to park it and concentrate on the job at hand. One look at the number of people swamping the square demanded that, as did the bomb-blasted windows of the towers above.

'Eyes alive, gentlemen,' buzzed the boss in our ears, 'and remember, tits and teeth.'

I couldn't help but grin. Didn't ever think I'd hear those words coming out of a ranking officer, but the boss loved them, it fitted his whole ethos of dealing with the locals. Charm them, win their trust, seize the initiative.

Trying to ignore the looks from the townsfolk around us, which varied from fear to relief to contempt, we split into groups of four, sharing a local interpreter who was skilled in asking the questions we need answering.

It was slow work, hard enough to make our own way through the crowds, never mind identifying and isolating individuals who we thought could help. Our questions were dismissed quickly by most with shrugs, blank gazes and often anger.

Are we crazy, they'd ask? Sign up to sure execution for drugs that they doubted even existed? Why didn't we concentrate on rebuilding houses flattened by our air strikes? Bring medicine for the kids hit by our shrapnel?

We filled the terp with our words and he tried to calm them, but our notebooks remained as empty as when we arrived. Apart from the dust. That covered every inch of us.

The boss demanded regular updates, the tension in his voice impossible to ignore, but no matter how many times we asked, pleaded or begged, the answer remained the same – nothing.

I was losing the others in my group. Slasher and Guido looked increasingly frustrated, while Tommo's attention was anywhere but on the locals we were questioning. Every time I checked him out, he was facing a different way, eyes skywards or flicking nervously over at the towers. He was pacing around too, jigging from foot to foot like a five-year-old who needed the bog. I left the terp to Slasher for a second and took Tommo by the arm, wheeling him to one side.

'What is wrong with you?' I whispered between clenched teeth. His eyes were wired, unblinking, like he was OD-ing on adrenalin.

'Nothing.' His gaze didn't move, but no sooner was the word out than he changed his mind. 'Everything. There's people up there. I see 'em.' He pointed the barrel of his rifle up at the windows. His fingers were blue with tension, gripping the trigger way too tight.

'Chill out, will you? Of course there's people up there. They live there. What do you expect?'

His head shook, the barrel pointed again. 'I don't like it. It's not safe. We're wide open down here.'

I grabbed his arm, not caring if we were seen. 'What do you expect? People to roll over the second we ask 'em a question? Of course it's not safe. You're not at home any more.'

'Well, I don't like it.'

'You don't like it? Listen to yourself, Tommo. None of us like it. But it's what we joined up to do. So focus on getting the info we need. Get that and we go home.'

His eyes widened at the mention of home and I regretted the word instantly.

'You know what I mean. Do your job.' And with a final squeeze, I let go of his arm and went back to the others.

An hour on and the market teemed with punters. They seemed to crawl from every crack and corner of the square like ants, and as a result Tommo's fears were spreading to us all. We hadn't a clue where the friendly locals ended and the Taliban started. For all we knew we were questioning the leaders of the cell, the very guys we were trying to bring down. We were sapped and confused, but knew we weren't heading back to base yet, not without exhausting every opportunity there was.

The boss's voice jolted us upright, ears straining against our headsets. I wanted to tell the guy selling fruit next to me to shut up. Just for a minute – shut up!

'Gents – move carefully but we have something. Four men spotted humping boxes from building at south-west corner of the square. Slash, Giffer, move your boys over to assist. Move slowly, but with purpose – one whiff of us and this could all kick off.'

My heart leapt as the four us threaded our way through the market, parting the crowd with difficulty, ignoring the pleas from the kids for the pens and sweets that littered our pockets.

Was this it? Was the intel solid? I mean, there were lads all over the square moving things around. Why were these boxes special? How did the boss know it was gear inside rather than rice or veg?

It was like Slasher read my mind as he looked back at me. 'Trust the intel and the boss.' He smiled. 'And hope it is the drugs. It's the only way this patrol will end before midnight.'

With Tommo at the rear, we joined up with Giffer's crew and the boss, all ten of us grouped in the shadows. I ignored the temptation to wipe the sweat off my face, and tried to match the others' intensity, even though inside I was pure dust.

The boss spoke quickly to each of us, searching our faces to check we were up for it. Desperate to please him, we gave him everything, even Tommo.

'Listen up. They've been in and out twice now, each time with boxes. They've appeared at seven-minute intervals, meaning they're possibly going up to the top to collect. There are stairwells at each end of the building. Giff, your boys take the southern stairs and cover odd floors. Slasher, yours to the north on even. Keep comms to a minimum, but clear. If these lads are the ones, we can't afford to lose 'em now.'

I waited for one of the boss's sayings, a joke to put us all at ease, but it didn't come. His face said it all. This was it. Big game time.

SONNY

There had to be a way out of this, but it was hard to focus when the only thing separating me from the ground were the hairy, clenched fists of a Cuda crew member.

The wind pulled at my jumper, reminding me how many floors up we were. Twelve.

My new hair colour might have fooled the police, but not these two.

My head was swearing at me for climbing the stairs when I saw them coming. How stupid was that? At least if you keep your feet on the ground you don't have far to fall. I was well into broken neck territory here, no way was I walking away if this gorilla was in a *really* foul mood.

As it turned out, he wasn't the talkative type. Maybe he didn't have the gene pool to string a sentence together, because when a voice came, it came from behind him.

'You must think we're stupid or something, bruv. That right?'

The accent was pure Ghost, drawling and slow, like some low-rent Bond villain. I expected him to appear stroking a flea-ridden cat.

What he did have, when he leaned over the balcony and

into my face, was the foulest breath imaginable. If his pal hadn't been the only thing preventing my first and last skydive, I would've told him so. Instead I winced and said I had no idea what he was on about, adding 'bruv' on the end, just so he could hear how ridiculous it sounded.

'Come on, Sonny. Everyone knows what went on with that van from the cash and carry. Word gets round, and know what? We was impressed, till you started dishing out the goods to our customers. Don't reflect well on us when someone else muscles in, you hear me?'

I didn't bother denying it. There was no point. Maybe coming clean might see me pulled the right side of the railing.

But it didn't. Instead the chimp with the missing link lowered me backwards, daring to loosen his grip on my hoodie. I thrust my hands around his, desperate for some kind of leverage.

'How much did you get for it?' His voice was battling the wind in my ears.

'What?'

'The vodka and smokes. How much did you make?'

'Forty quid. Something like that . . .'

'Be more specific.'

They leaned me out further.

'Fifty! Fifty quid. That's all. I'm telling you.'

'Then you owe us five hundred. And we'll leave it at that, long as you deliver within five days.'

Ridiculous as the interest was, I wasn't exactly in a strong position to barter, and as I toppled even further back, grappling with the air around me, I knew I had no option.

'Five days. Five hundred. Got it.'

'Right decision, bruv,' and he hoisted me back on to the balcony, the ground spinning beneath my feet.

I wanted to front up but could do nothing but fall on to my knees and try not to spew.

'So we'll see you back here then on Tuesday, six o'clock, yeah? And no coins neither. No raiding your piggy bank.'

I was relieved enough to feel the fight seeping back into me. 'Tens or twenties?'

'We in't fussy, long as it folds.' They made to walk off, then stopped and looked back. 'One thing,' added the mouthy one. 'You must have been desperate, to trade on our patch. What you need the money so quickly for?'

'Flowers.' The word came out before I could stop myself. It sounded so lame I wondered if I'd have been better to let them toss me over the balcony and avoid the embarrassment.

It took a second for the word to register with them, but when it did, they lost it, nearly ending up on the floor with me. They leaned on each other and howled, pulling out their phones as they told me to repeat myself.

'Flowers *and* that haircut? People will start talking. The boys have got to hear this.'

I told him where to go. The meathead took a step forwards.

'Say it again.'

I refused.

His trainer slammed into my ribs, knocking me on to my side, a thousand thunderbolts lighting up my chest. My fingers flew to my ribs, expecting to find his laces embedded in them. He must have cracked one. I hoped he hadn't punctured anything.

'You get that?' asked the gorilla, still filming.

'Yep. That'll do. He won't be too chatty for a while anyhow.' He leaned over me, hoicked up a mouthful of spit and let it fall on to my face. 'Five days. Five hundred quid. Six o'clock.'

They gripped palms in celebration, moved into some elaborate handshake, then left me to make sense of where on earth I was going to get the money from.

It wasn't an easy conversation to have with the lads, not days after shearing them like sheep. And besides, they thought the only people after us were the coppers, they had no idea I'd been treading on Cuda toes too.

I wanted to drop it in casually, without any big deal or fuss, but with the time deadline *and* the agony coursing through my chest, it wasn't really an option.

Wiggs had found me on the way home from my 'meeting' with the crew, slumped over a bench, thinking I was about to cough up a lung. He freaked out big time, got straight on the blower to Cam, who rang Den, who wanted to find those responsible and give them a sorting.

Nice sentiment, but with me no use and Hitch predictably not answering his phone, we talked him down, sort of.

'What is it with Hitch?' he raged. 'What's the point of having a phone if he never has it on?'

'When did we last even see him?' asked Wiggs.

None of us were quite sure. Could've been the scam, but that seemed too long ago to sit comfortably. Still it gave me something else to worry about apart from battered ribs and a painful death in five days' time.

By the time Dennis carried me home and Cam had strapped two carrier bags of ice to my chest, I was fit for nothing. Unfortunately the others wanted answers.

'So what's going on then?' demanded Wiggy, cig burning in the corner of his mouth as ever. The directness of the question put me on the back foot.

'About what?'

He looked at me like I'd had a lobotomy.

'Er . . . this?' he pointed at me.

I tried to play dumb and shrugged, which started him prowling around the lounge, lighting another smoke before his first was even finished.

'Don't try and play it down, Sonny. Look at you. Look at the state of your ribs.'

'What went on, fella?' asked Dennis with a wry smile. 'Who've you been upsetting this time? Been picking a fight with a pit bull again?'

'Don't bring that dog up. I did nothing to provoke it, you know that.'

'Well it gave you nothing but a kiss compared to the state of you now. What happened?'

'Got into a dumb argument with some Cuda lads. That's all.'

Wiggy snorted, a plume of smoke billowing from his nose. 'What are you doing getting into a ruck with them? Don't you know anything?'

'Wasn't my fault, Wiggs . . . '

But he wasn't having it. 'Come off it, mate. Them lads shouldn't even know you exist. You must have done something to be on their radar.'

51

I blew hard from my mouth, about to come clean, when the door opened and Hitch walked in, looking rougher and paler than usual. If his feet hadn't been touching the ground, I'd have sworn he was a ghost.

'What's occurring? Not picking a fight with that dog again, were you?'

The other two idiots laughed their bits off, but not Hitch. His jaw was clenched hard, like he thought they were laughing at him. Cam clocked it too, taking his arm as she explained. It did little for his mood, so I moved the conversation on, painful as it was.

'I had a bit of a chat with two of the Cuda lads. Turns out I might have sold some of that vodka we lifted on their patch.'

The laughter stopped as all four of them shot me a look that told me I was mental.

'What?' I asked. 'I was in a rush. Needed some quick cash.'

It was Hitch who laid into me hardest, anger forcing some colour into his cheeks as he paced about, agitated. 'Well, that was dumb, wasn't it? What did you need money for in such a hurry?'

'You trying to impress some bird?' asked Wiggy. 'Not that lass from Holtby House? I thought you'd kicked her into touch. She was rank. Looked like a shark, she did. More teeth than a Great White.'

'Yeah, yeah, all right,' I blushed, risking a glance at Cam, who fortunately was laughing too. She was used to the banter. 'I haven't seen her in months.'

'Dump you, did she?' Wiggy found himself way too funny.

'All right, wind it in.' Hitch was raging again. He didn't look himself; sweat lined his face no matter how often he rubbed it away. 'What did you need the money for if it wasn't this *Jaws* bird?'

I puffed my cheeks out, couldn't say they were for flowers for the parade. All right, they might have understood, but somehow I couldn't find the words to tell them. Turns out I didn't need to worry, as Cam dug me out.

'I asked him for the money.' She said it with such conviction that she even had me believing her.

'But you look nothing like that bird from Holtby,' Wiggy deadpanned. 'You couldn't bite my leg off like her, could you?' He paused a second. 'Could you?'

'Keep talking like that and I'll take your *head* clean off,' Cam replied, before turning to the others. 'I needed the cash. Dad's been drinking more than he can pay for. I had a visit from a *friend* of his, had to sort it out before he took it out on Mum, or me. Sonny said he'd help me out.'

'And it's sorted, is it?' Hitch was bristling.

'Completely. And Dad'll be face down in a bottle for a good while.' She said it without hesitation. She was some player. Braver than me, too.

'So is there anything you can do to help, lads?' I felt bad even asking, but I didn't fancy bungee-jumping without a cord.

'If you mean have we got any cash left, forget it.' Den sighed. 'Mine's dust already.'

'Smoked mine,' added Wiggs, flicking his cig upwards between his lips.

Hitch looked shifty and rammed some gum into his mouth. A man of few words as ever.

'Don't worry about it,' interrupted Cam, still playing the guilty party. 'Me and Sonny can sort it out.'

I could've kissed her. It took all my determination to stay at the other end of the settee.

'No need for that,' growled Den, slapping my shoulder way too hard, the tremors jangling every rib in my chest. 'Between us we can get it together. How much?'

'Five hundred,' I replied, waiting for the backlash.

'Keys to the bank come through, then? What are you, some kind of moron?' asked Wiggy.

'You got any ideas?' Hitch asked him irritably. 'For once?'

Wiggs opened his mouth but nothing came out. Hitch waved his hand at him, goading him to even try and continue.

'No, thought not. So shut it, will you?'

Den stepped in between them, backing Wiggs away. Just as well. The mood Hitch was in he could've crushed him with one hand.

Maybe having Den there took the pressure off, as Wiggy suddenly piped back up.

'We could pull a scam again. Turn another van over.'

Den didn't like it.

'You reckon? It's not even two weeks since last time and we've been lucky they haven't picked us up for that.'

Wiggy deflated in front of us as he rubbed at his shaved head and remembered what our first attempt had cost him.

I liked it though. It had balls about it.

'Think about it. It's the last thing they're going to expect.'

'You reckon?' Den was no coward, but he definitely wasn't up for a second go. 'For all we know they could've started carrying baseball bats in the van just in case.'

'So we just let Sonny take a kicking, do we?' spat Hitch. 'Nice.'

'What is it with you?' asked Den. 'I'm not saying that . . .'

'Well, what are you saying?'

The gap between them shrank.

'I'm saying you should back off. Don't barge in here when we haven't seen you in weeks and start telling us how things are. Where were you before all this went down?'

But we never found out, despite all wanting to know who'd carried out Hitch's personality transplant. I didn't like this new one with all the bile and aggro.

As they began to circle each other, stepping over a line none of us had crossed before, the door blew open and there was Mum, wearing a scowl as big as theirs.

'Everything all right?'

Fists dropped instantly, though Hitch's entire body remained riddled with menace. Sensing she'd cut the tension, Mum turned her attention to Wiggs, who tried to look all coy and innocent.

'Last time I caught you smoking in here, you promised me a new settee. So where is it? Delivery men better be humping it up the stairs right this second.'

'Out of stock.' He blushed. Mum was the only person I knew who could leave him practically mute. 'Next week, I promise, Mrs M.' He headed to the kitchen to dot out his smoke.

Happy that the first trouble-causer was back in his box, she winked at Dennis, stroked the back of Cam's head and smiled reservedly at Hitch. I don't think she'd ever worked him out either.

It was only when she clocked the state of my chest that her expression changed.

'Sonny?' she yelped, like I'd lost a leg or something. 'I think it's time you lads went.'

And they did, filing out without a whimper, Wiggy daring to plant a kiss on her cheek. 'Later, Auntie Shell.'

Cam didn't shift at first, only leaving after blowing me a sly kiss when Mum shooed her out.

After the front door closed the room was silent. For once, you couldn't even hear the neighbours having a beery row.

I braced myself. Wasn't in the mood for the sort of fuss I knew was coming.

'You're going to need more ice. And painkillers. So don't think about moving until I get back.' Mum grabbed her purse and headed for the door, blowing through it quicker than a tornado.

She wouldn't be long. Not at that pace. I closed my eyes and made a pathetic attempt to sleep, my ribs making me anything but drowsy.

Mind you, it wouldn't be a patch on the pain in my ears once Mum got back. She'd make sure of that. Over the years I'd given her plenty of practice.

 SONNY

Mum knew me. Or thought she did. She didn't have a clue who'd busted my ribs up, but there was no doubt in her head that she would find out.

What surprised me was that she waited so long before asking.

After strapping an iceberg to my chest and funnelling half the chemist's down my throat, she eased me into bed, adding, 'Don't be expecting miracles. It'll feel worse in the morning.'

I didn't know if she was on about my ribs, or the interrogation that lay ahead. I had a feeling that bruising was the last thing I should be worrying about.

My night's sleep was littered with dreams. Predictably, I was always falling, but it was never me who hit the ground. When they rolled the body over it was always Jammy, dressed in full combat kit, helmet in pieces.

It gave me the fear. Where was he right now? Was he sleeping, or patrolling god knows where? The bombs on the news flashed unhelpfully into my head. Was he even still alive or was this some kind of mad premonition? It wasn't like I believed in that stuff, but with the pain and the stupid hour, I couldn't dismiss it like I normally would.

It's not often I don't have an answer. It's my greatest asset as well as the thing that gets me in trouble. But right then, I had nothing. No answer to Jamm's whereabouts, Mum's mood or how to drum up the money to pay for my mistake. It scared me. Scared and shocked me so much that I felt a tear slide from my eye, barely stopping before the second, third and fourth caught it up.

Tears don't come often; they can't when you're constantly moving from one moment to the next, sniffing out the next opportunity. I remember Mum's expression as we waved goodbye to Jamm, the look of shock in my direction as I toughed it out, stony-faced. She hadn't spoken to me for the rest of the day, though I knew there were a hundred things she wanted to say.

It was a look I couldn't forget. It branded me more permanently than any tattoo ever could.

If I could've moved without screaming, I'd have gone into Mum's room right then, to show her I wasn't made of stone like she thought I was.

I didn't, of course. Instead I lay there, shoulders shaking, fighting every demon that strode into my head, whether they'd travelled from Afghanistan or closer to home.

I won't lie and tell you I didn't sleep. Somewhere between my darkest nightmare and dawn I finally went under, a handful of hours that hugged and rocked me. The next hands to make contact weren't quite as mellow. I'd know Mum's fingers anywhere, every inch was covered in rough skin, evidence of all her waking hours spent scouring, scrubbing or sorting.

When I was younger, I used to look at her and wonder

why none of the men who occasionally appeared ever stuck around. The other lads reckoned she was a looker and, although I couldn't compute that, I had to accept it as truth. Like the naive kid that I was, I put her singledom down to the state of her fingers. All I could think was, *Why would anyone choose to hold hands when hers are so rough?* Stupid I know, but I was a kid.

I wasn't disappointed she was single. None of the blokes I met awkwardly over their bowls of Frosties – they always took the last from the packet before I had chance – had anything going for them, just an empty wallet, a taste for sugary cereal and a love of booze. I'd seen enough of that at Cam's house to not want it for us too.

There was no sign of sympathy for my difficult night as Mum pulled me from my bed, frog-marched me to the shower, then waited outside the door for me to come out. She really did know me. That would've been my moment to sneak out.

After a breakfast of no substance but surprisingly little nagging, Mum strapped more ice to my chest and practically held me by the ear until we reached the front door.

'Leave my side and I will hunt you down,' she said without a trace of sarcasm. She meant it, which meant I was glued to her.

We waited a lifetime for the lift as usual, but once inside, instead of taking us to the ground, she sent us trundling into the clouds.

It wasn't until we reached the top floor and stepped out into the light that I realized just how early it was. The sun was only just showing itself above Pickard House.

'What time is it?' I asked, lifting Dad's watch to my face,

ignoring Mum's grimace at the sight of it. 'Five o'clock? Are you mental?'

In one second she'd reduced my already short sleep to a blink.

'Just because you haven't seen this time in your life, doesn't mean it doesn't exist.'

If she was trying to be deep it didn't suit her. Didn't soften the blow either.

'This your breakfast spot, is it? 360-degree views of the Ghost? Nice.'

She didn't look cross, or frustrated at my comment. I'd imagine it was exactly the answer she expected. It summed up where our relationship was, and had been for as long as I could remember.

'I don't know.' She sighed. 'It's not all bad.'

'It'd look a lot better if they blew it up.'

I suppose I was provoking her, wanted her to get to the point and put me out of my misery.

'Knowing you, you'd end up at the bottom of all the rubble. I mean, look at the state of you!'

'Take more than a stick of dynamite to stop me.'

'Of course it would. That's why you're in such good shape now. Honestly, Sonny, how many times is this going to happen? How long till I find you in hospital instead of laid out on the settee?'

'Don't over-react, Mum. It's not so bad. I've had worse.'

'Oh, I know you have. Like the time you had a fight with that daft dog.'

'It was a pit bull! Thing should've been muzzled, never mind on a lead. And it wasn't like I started it.'

'That's just it. You never start anything, do you? According to you, there's not been one incident when you weren't standing up for yourself or doing the right thing.' She sighed and straightened a grip in her hair. 'The thing is, son, it's getting worse all this, not better. Ever since Jamm's not here to keep an eye, all you do is wade further and further out of your depth.'

'I can look after myself.' Irritation fizzed in my head. Everything came down to Jamm with her. Like he was the boss of me, like he had Superman's cape hidden beneath his clothes. 'And anyway, why do you have to bring him up every time you give me a lecture?'

'Who?'

'You know who! Jammy.'

'Your brother's got nothing to do with this.'

'He's got everything to do with it and you know it. It's always been about him. You've never given me a chance to get close to his standards. Well, maybe you should think about that. It might explain why we're stood here after all.'

'No one expects you to be the same, Sonny. Certainly not me. The only one imagining any kind of competition is you. All I want is for you both to be happy. And safe.'

'But *he* isn't, is he? Either of those things. So why is he over there? Why risk everything when all the bombs and the fighting has got nothing to do with him?'

'He did what he thought was right. The army offered him a wage when nobody else would and we needed it. We can't go on like this forever.'

I should've backed off when I saw the pain on her face.

She had nothing to feel guilty about. She'd fed me every day for the last sixteen years.

But, as usual, all I could see was the gulf between me and Jamm widening.

'If money's that tight then you need to tell me. I can do my bit too, you know, I'm not completely useless.'

'No one's saying you are.'

'So I'll get a job. I'll talk to the factory. Get some shifts.'

'But what about long-term, Sonny? I was hoping you might go back to school. Give it another go?'

The conversation was going the wrong way and I couldn't hide how I felt about it. 'Forget it, that's not going to happen.'

'Why not? You're so bright, but you need your exa . . . '

'What, so some guy can look at a string of Cs in useless subjects? Who's going to give me a job in an office? One look at my address and that's it. Game over.'

'You think people can't see past where you live? They don't care about that. They care about what you can give them.'

I tried to walk away, waving my arms in frustration.

'This is pointless. You only ever see it your way, so why are we even doing this?'

She took me by the arm and led me to the edge of the roof. 'Because I want you to see the same as me for once. To realize that there's something out there apart from this estate.'

Her argument was as tired as I was, but it didn't put her off.

'Your head is so full of scams to get by every day, that you can't see it doesn't have to be like this.' She grabbed my face, which was doing its best full-on sulk. 'Look out there, Sonny. LOOK! There's so much more. For you *and* Jammy. You don't have to stay here like the rest of them, or like me, so think about that. Think about what you're worth!'

All right, there were buildings beyond the boundaries of the Ghost. Loads of them, most of them more attractive, better kept. But they didn't mean anything to me. I'd seen some of them up close once on a field trip, but had been sent home early for nicking packed lunches off the other kids. And off the driver. So what? I was hungry.

But this is what Mum didn't get. What was out there for us, really? Me or Jamm? We didn't know their rules, but here we did. I told her as much.

'You know what? That's the only difference between you and your brother. He'd see out there as a challenge. If he got it into his head that he wanted to leave, he wouldn't stop until he filled up a van with everything he owned. And if it scared him? Then even better. He'd take it on, and he'd take us with him.'

I swore. Turned the air blue with how lucky we were to have Jamm in our lives. But I didn't mean it, not really. I was just stinging at how far short I kept coming up, and strangely Mum looked just as raw as me. Lines creased her eyes as they filled up with tears.

'You can do it if you want to.' I heard the words clearly despite the emotion in her voice.

'I can't be like him, Mum. I can't do it.'

'I don't want you to.' She took my cheeks in her cracked hands. 'All I want is for you to look out there and think about it. You can do that, can't you?'

'I'll think about it,' I murmured, the words sounding emptier than I meant them to.

'Make sure you do.' She sighed, taking one last look at the view. 'Because the next time you're in a hole, we might not be able to dig you out quickly enough. Me or your brother.'

She picked up her bag and walked off, looking a decade older than her thirty-six years.

I turned back to her view, trying to see what she did. If there was hope out there, then I had to find it quickly. I had four days to make five hundred quid, so unless the trees beyond the estate had twenty-pound notes growing on them, I was going to have to look a lot closer to home. It wouldn't please Mum, but she didn't have to know. Not this time, this *last final* time.

JAMMY

I was standing on the edge of something. Glory or a stretcher: it could go either way and there was nothing I could do to influence it. We weren't on the PlayStation any more, couldn't hit pause when we wanted to draw breath. We just had to trust the boss and look out for each other as well as ourselves.

The other group peeled away. I kept Tommo in front of me where I could see him. He was sweating heavily but his pace was fine. We hit the stairs in a cluster, gun barrels fanning out to cover every wall, every inch that opened up as we climbed.

I listened for updates but nothing came. All I could hear was the blood pumping in my ears, keeping me on hyper-alert. I felt strangely invincible: nothing could touch me, bullets would crumple and hit the floor instead of entering my body. The four of us were some mad new cross-breed put together in a lab. As long as we stuck together, we'd find the drugs. There was no other outcome possible.

We hit the second floor as Giffer's boys cleared the first. Nothing to report. I felt torn, wanted to do well, to be the ones to find the stash, but wanted to walk out at the end of it too. Find the drugs and we'd find bullets. That had to be how it worked.

Slasher scanned the corridor in front of us. 'Twelve doors,' he whispered in his broadest Scouse. 'Jamm, Tomm, take the left side. We'll do the right.'

We nodded our agreement, Tommo relieved to be paired with me. Without hesitation we tucked guns against chins and spun into the first room, to find nothing but an ancient mattress. By the smell of it, it had doubled up as a toilet too. Grimacing, Tommo waved me forward to search it, which I did, flipping it with my foot.

Nothing underneath or stuffed inside.

Room clear. Move on.

Our confidence didn't grow with each cleared room, but the routine did, and within minutes the four of us were back on the stairwell, climbing higher, up to the fourth.

But when none of us found anything on either level, the fear ratcheted up a notch. We'd only two floors left, twenty-four rooms, and in one of them there had to be a shed-load of gear and even more weapons guarding it.

I was buzzing so hard now it was like being plugged into a socket. I could hear every rustle of my uniform, feel every millimetre of my lungs expanding as I breathed deeply.

'This is it, Tommo,' I whispered, but got no response. I hoped it was because he was bang in the zone.

Top floor. Identical layout, same number of rooms. Rooms one, two and three were trashed but empty of anything important. As we spun into the fourth, nothing appeared any different. Except it was hotter and smaller. A good third smaller than any of the others so far. The skin on my face shrivelled at the heat.

Tommo swore. 'What's going on!' He aimed a kick at the

wall, showering us with yet more dust. 'There's nothing up here. It must be on Giff's floor.'

Through the doorway I could see Slasher and Guido pulling another room apart. It gave me a second to yank Tommo back into line.

'What is wrong with you?' I asked, checking my comms weren't live.

'Isn't it obvious?' He looked around, like the answer was painted on the walls. 'It's this place. The heat. The locals. None of them want us here. These drugs we're after, how do we even know they exist? The intel could be nonsense for all we know.'

I could hear the panic in his words, see he was on the point of freaking out. Right when I – we – needed him calm. I closed the gap between us but he took a step back, eyeing me suspiciously.

'What?' he asked. 'What are you doing?'

'Keep your voice down, will you?' I spread my arms in front of me as I reached for his drinking tube, to make him hydrate, but before I knew it, he'd deflected me, grabbing at my armour instead, spinning me straight into the wall.

I should've been shocked. Fifteen years and he'd never so much as raised a finger in my direction. A white flash of anger lit up my head, only to be replaced by something strange, a thought that something was wrong.

It was the wall. Instead of crumbling like the others, it had bent as Tommo flung me on to it. Not massively, but enough.

I raised my finger to my lips and stepped away from the wall before pushing it a second time. Again, I felt it give. It was wood, not stone.

'What are you doing?' Tommo was angry still, that or fearful that the slap he deserved was yet to come. But I didn't answer.

My head was racing with the possibilities. Why was this one room smaller than every other one we'd searched? Hotter too? Shoving my fingers into my mouth, I pulled the gloves off and felt the wall. Warm.

I mouthed at Tommo to do the same, but he didn't get me, was still foaming like a lunatic. Without hesitation, I grabbed him by the straps of his pack and dragged him to the door, spitting in his ear as we went.

'Calm down and *listen*! There's something going on in there. It's a false wall. I think we've found them.'

His anger was replaced by a whimpering panic. 'Well, what do we do?'

Guido and Slasher approached, eyes quizzing us, so I let go of Tommo and tried to act normal. Quickly and quietly, I passed on what I knew. Told them to cover me as I went back to the wall. My first instinct was to unload into it. Pump every bullet I had deep into its surface in the hope of stopping anything else coming back. But I didn't. Didn't have a clue what was on the other side. What if it was an IED, a chance for them to blow us sky high?

Instead I took my gun, and turned it quietly in my hands before pummelling the wall with the butt. Instantly it gave, my momentum shooting me forward as the weapon went clean through. At the same time, there was a crash from the corridor, a volley of bullets and a blur as two figures raced towards the stairwell. Slasher tore from the room and, with a shout, let rounds fly in their direction.

There was a cry, the most piercing noise I'd ever heard, more bullets, more pain, two thuds. Silence.

I was jammed, arms half in, half out of the wall panel, heart assaulting my ribcage. Using my gun like a crowbar I ripped at the wood, feeling a huge chunk come away, exposing a hidden room behind, packed full of tubing, buckets, vats. Cellophane parcels lined the floor, awaiting the men's return. They'd be waiting a long time.

After kicking at the last of the panelling, and bundling as much heroin into my arms as I could, I made for the door, waiting for the boss and the others to arrive.

What I found in the corridor drained me of any triumph I was daring to feel.

Two bodies. No movement except for the blood pulsing from them. It ran past Slasher, who was frozen to the spot, gun still cocked in the direction of the corpses. Guido patted his shoulder before easing the rifle to his side. 'They aren't going to fire back, pal.' Slash said nothing, couldn't take his eyes anywhere else.

The blood collected at my feet, staining my boots, but I didn't move either. All I could think was, thank god it was Slash and not me. Would I have even had the balls to pull the trigger?

Tommo was still in the room behind me, shaking from the clatter of bullets. I was pleased he was there. The mess in the corridor could've been the thing that pushed him to the edge, if not over it.

My headset crackled into life as the boss strode on to the corridor, Giffer and his crew behind him. 'Look what you found!' he yelled.

I held the packages up like I was showing off a newborn, forgetting about all the death around me. I told myself not to feel guilty, that I'd done my job, found the gear and was still breathing at the end of it.

'Top work,' grinned the boss, slapping my helmet roughly. My whole body shook. 'Is there more?'

I motioned behind me, pleased to see Tommo holding the rest of the parcels. Looking like he'd done his bit.

'Proper pair of sniffer dogs. You need to be careful. Keep this up and you'll end up with a good reputation.'

'Not much to do with me,' I gabbled, the words out of my mouth before I even thought about them. 'Was Tommo that found the wall. I just smashed it down.'

The boss extended his arm to Tommo, who almost dropped the stash in surprise.

Come on! I thought. *I've given you this on a plate. Don't mess it up now.*

Pulling himself together, Tommo took the praise before shooting me a confused look. I shook my head subtly: *I'll tell you later.*

We didn't have time now, the room was overcrowded with high fives, relief so overwhelming you could smell it.

The job was done, patrol was over, we simply had to make it back to base in one piece.

I just hoped we hadn't lucked out already.

 JAMMY

The base hummed with the news of our find, carrying us back through the gates like all-conquering heroes rather than a couple of scallies who'd got lucky.

They wanted the story first-hand, in full Technicolor, and we were still so pumped up we were happy to oblige. I led the way, Tommo listening intently at first, getting the details straight before going off and re-telling it to anyone and everyone in sight. I wasn't shy of bigging him up, reckoned that if I gave him all the glory it might make the COs blind to any mistakes that followed. If today was anything to go by, I reckoned there were plenty on the way.

After half an hour he'd adapted to his full-blown hero status, riffing further on things he hadn't done, the bravery he'd failed to show. I made a note to give him a slap about that later. But not now, all I could think about was getting my body armour off before it pulled me to the ground. If I didn't get into the shower quickly, they'd find me sleeping in it the next morning.

The spray of water was more a trickle than a jet, but at least it was cold, teasing my skin slowly back to life. I watched the dust slowly dissolve, dirt sliding reluctantly to the floor, sticking to my feet then the plughole. I don't know if it was tiredness or what, but after a while it seemed to turn from brown to red, until I was back in the corridor, watching the Afghan pair bleed out in front of me. I felt dizzy: deafened by the sound of my heart, the cubicle began to spin, every noise amplified. My arms shot forward instinctively, grappling at the wall to hold me up.

Not now. Not when I've survived a first patrol. No glory in flaking out in the shower.

I pushed a breath out, then another, again, more, until the carousel slowed and stopped. The water ran clear. I was clean, but empty.

Back in control, I slid to the floor and let the water hug me for another minute, until I was ready to get dusty again and face the others.

The walk from showers to barracks dried me quicker than any towel could, although I had to fight to keep mine tied around my waist as spirits were still high. There was no sign of Tommo, though, which bugged me. I'd hoped he'd still be telling stories when I came out, didn't like the thought of him on his own, chewing stuff over. I quickened the pace, despite my legs complaining, and didn't slow down till I'd slung our door open to find him asleep on his cot, fully clothed.

He'd managed to take his helmet off but nothing else, body armour, boots, fatigues all still in place. Slumping on to my bed next to him, I tried to work out what to do. Leave him or try and get him sorted?

I didn't have to chew it over long.

'I'd let him sleep if I were you,' said Giffer, reclined on

his cot, drawing heavily on a cigarette. 'He won't thank you for waking him.'

I nodded, relieved someone else had made the call. Though Giff instantly had me back on edge.

'There's plenty of things he *should* be thanking you for, though, I reckon. Don't you?'

He was staring at me, but not in an accusing way. One thing I knew already about Giffer was that he didn't roll that way. He wasn't stirring, just observing.

He was spot-on too, not that I wanted him to know.

'What are you on about?'

Sitting forward, he ground his butt out on the floor and smiled again.

'You're close. I get that. Nothing wrong with it. I've seen plenty of mates join up, can be a big help when the real stuff hits. You know who to trust.'

'Well, I certainly trusted him today,' I bluffed. 'He spotted the wall for starters.'

Giff's eyebrows almost disappeared under his hairline. 'Come on now, Jamm.' He grinned. 'Never kid a kidder. I've watched your boy there from the minute we arrived and he's been touching cloth ever since.'

I tried to protest but he wouldn't let me.

'It's not a problem. I'm not the CO. And besides, aren't we all terrified right now?'

Was he winding me up? If he was bricking it, then he was a cracking actor.

'Not you though, Giff,' I said. 'Nothing new for you, all this. And anyway, you've done all right, haven't you?' I made a point of visibly counting his arms and legs.

He managed to smile and look serious in the space of a second.

'Nothing but luck, my friend. Don't be thinking it makes me braver than the rest of you, because it don't. I've seen better, more courageous lads come back with bits missing, if they come back at all. All I'm saying to you is, I get what you're doing with your boy there. I'd put a month's wages down that our success today had nothing to do with him. I saw him, saw his eyes going in every direction in that market. He couldn't focus long enough to know where he was, never mind spot and break down a false wall.'

I said nothing, which told him everything.

'I'm not judging. Him or you. All I'm saying is that we're all as scared as him. He just has to learn to bury it, before it buries one of us. You understand me, don't you?'

I nodded, but hadn't a clue what to do about it.

'I promised people,' I said in a rush, before Giff moved on. 'When we left. That I wouldn't dare show my face back on the estate without him next to me.' I thought of Cam and how I'd meant every word.

'We've all made those promises,' Giff sighed. 'Always meant them too. Especially when they've got sisters we'd like to impress.'

He had a knack of getting to the truth that was both quick and terrifying. And a laugh as loud as a bomb-blast.

'He has got a sister, then?' he boomed. 'Knew it, I did. Fit, is she?'

I didn't answer, didn't need to.

'Looks like she's made a mark on you, though, eh? You didn't join up just to impress her, I hope. Because I'll bet

74

she'll have moved on by the time you get back, all bronzed and desperate.' There was a tone in his voice that said he was speaking from experience.

'There's nothing going on between me and his Cam,' I sighed. 'There's a group of us that knock about back on the estate. We're all tight, so we made this stupid pact when we were eleven or something, you know, before the lust had kicked in, that we'd leave each other's sisters alone. Kept it simple that way. No reason for any of us to want to kill each other.'

'Sounds like a schoolboy error to me,' laughed Giff.

'Been regretting it for about two years. Still, I promised her I'd keep him whole, so thought today was a good idea. Keep any heat off him for as long as I can.'

'You're a good man, Jamm. Good soldier too, for what it's worth. Best chance we have of flying out of here minus the bodybags is that we all act the same. I know they feed you this line in basic training, but it's true. The boss, me, Slasher, Guido, even that idiot Caffeine, they're the only family that counts while you're out here. No one back home's going to keep you alive, only us. Scary thought, like, but true.'

He flicked my arm with his towel as he moved for the showers, leaving me with plenty to think about, my head torn between my two families, thousands of miles apart. It didn't feel like there was space for everyone, but there had to be. Sonny still needed me as much as Tommo did. And as for Cam? Well, she wasn't going to disappear no matter how hard I tried to forget. And to be honest, that suited me fine.

JAMMY

The glory of our find didn't last long. The heat soon sapped the buzz out of us, forcing us back into the shadows. We'd been warned that we might not be sat around for long.

'Expect a response, lads. You don't lose as much as they did and not see a kickback.'

Patrols were doubled. The officers were worried that the Taliban would take our heist out on the locals, reckoning one of them had given the drugs up in return for protection. We needed to be visible as a result, do our jobs, keep things normal. As normal as you can with a machine gun in your hands.

We felt the tension on every patrol; the number of locals on the street was down, even with the market in full swing, our arrival in the square greeted with greater doubt than ever. No one wanted to be seen too close, which suited Tommo, gave him time to find some confidence.

Every patrol made the streets more familiar and we scanned them greedily for vulnerable points: windows tailor-made for snipers, roof-tops wide enough to launch a mortar attack from. I saw Tommo scope them, then check to see how each of us were doing. He looked like a soldier, like the hero I'd told the others he was. All I could do was hope this new varnish wouldn't blister in the heat.

The temperature didn't seem to bother the kids who lived in the village, nor did our presence. They carried none of the adults' suspicion or doubt, saw us instead as walking sweet shops. From the minute we appeared in the square they'd surround us, dirty fingers rifling our pockets for whatever bounty we were carrying.

You had to be firm with them, set rules, despite feeling appreciated for once. Sweets were always the ultimate rewards, more popular than the pens and pencils we had, but they came with a risk. Everything had risk attached to it round here, even a boiled sweet.

'Have the wrappers back off them if you can,' we'd been told by the boss. 'Encourage them to eat them there and then, or have the terps tell them to bury the wrappers.'

We'd looked at him baffled.

'You worried about litter?' I asked with a smirk.

'Couldn't give a toss,' he'd snapped back. 'But unless you want that same kid having his hands burned with cigarettes, then you'd better think about it seriously.'

'What do you mean?'

'It might only be a sweet to you, but there's kids tortured for accepting them.'

'What?'

'All it takes is a Taliban fighter to find one wrapper in a pocket. Says to them that the kids, their families, are all sympathizers. There's been plenty of nine-year-olds walking around with only three or four fingers as a result. So give 'em out responsibly, with as much caution as every step you take on patrol.'

We'd nodded, sobered by yet another thing to remember, as well as just trying to keep each other alive.

There was one bunch of kids, though, who weren't bothered about our booty. They only had room for one thing in their lives and that was football.

I'd clocked them about two weeks back, amazed by the length of their games. The sun didn't seem to touch them: instead they sprinted for hours, only stopping when the sun gave up, knackered.

They played typical football for ten-year-olds, swarming after the ball like bees, shouts of a single word again and again that I guessed was 'pass'. There was one lad, though, who went about things differently. He wasn't about the big boot. Instead he kept the ball tied to his foot, flicking it past the others whenever they dared to stand on his shadow.

He was fast too, despite being a good half-metre smaller than the bigger lads. The thing I liked about him was that he had some spirit. There were dozens of times when the others were so frustrated by his skill that they hacked at him, leaving him hugging the dust. But he never moaned about it, or rolled fifteen times clutching at his leg. He just looked for the ball, jumped to his feet and ran until the game was back under his control. It never took him long.

'You seen this?' I laughed to Tommo. 'Mini Messi, this kid.'

Tommo let the gun drop to his side, face softening as he watched.

'How old do you reckon he is?'

'Dunno, can't be much older than nine, ten.'

'He's got it, though. Reminds me a bit of myself back in the day.'

I laughed. Great to hear the Tommo humour returning, even if it was complete nonsense.

'Back in the day? You're eighteen, not forty-eight.'

'Yeah, but before I spotted women I had the same hunger he's got.'

'Hunger, yes; skills . . . not so much.'

'What are you on about? I had that scout come over, tapping me up for a trial.'

'Oh yeah, the mythical trial. Funny how no one saw a thing except for you.'

I heard him huff and tried not to laugh. We knew all about the scout and weren't surprised either. Tommo was skilful and pacy. Had enough about him to get on a club's books.

What he couldn't do, though, was get it past his old man, who said he hadn't the time to drive him all the way to Leeds just to be told he wasn't good enough.

'Who's going to pay for the petrol?' he'd moaned. 'And anyway, I'd have to miss a shift. No shift means no food to eat, you selfish little . . . '

Tommo had bitten back, something about all the money going on beers not food, which led to the mother of all fights and an end to his dream. The trial was a week later and the bruises were only ripening by then.

He seemed to lose interest after that. Football didn't seem as important as the next girl that he promised he'd marry – and there were plenty of them.

It was great to see him now though, completely fixated by the kids' game, almost itching to get among it. We didn't have long to wait either, as the ball ended up booted at my feet. Without wanting to make an idiot of myself I flicked the ball up on to my knee, but it was so flat it fell, pudding-like, to the floor.

'Feel how soft this is,' I laughed, side-footing it to Tommo. 'Shows how good the little kid is, if he can control that.'

Tommo squeezed it into a rugby ball shape. 'Fair play to him. We should smuggle him back with us, be his agents. Twenty per cent of what he's worth would see us sitting pretty.' He dropped the ball then flicked it effortlessly into the air, bouncing it off his knee, before dipping forward and catching it on the back of his neck. It nestled between his backpack and helmet, sitting tight, even when he stood upright. The kids whooped and shouted, surrounding him in a second, begging him (I guessed) to teach them the trick.

It was hilarious to watch him. The ball was still stuck, so he made out like he'd never even seen it. Every time a kid jumped to dislodge it, he'd spin out of range, making out he had no idea what they wanted. The grin stretched across his cheeks, threatening to disappear into his ears, and there was a cockiness to him, a swagger I hadn't seen since we'd arrived. It was the Tommo I knew, so I smiled stupidly at him.

If I'd known all it would take to make him feel at home was a footie, I'd have kicked one at him weeks ago.

SONNY

Four days had passed. Four days, twenty-three hours and thirty-two minutes to be exact, and I was still three hundred and eleven quid short.

I'd raided everything I owned, taking anything of worth down to Cash Converters. I walked out only sixty quid richer but a hundred times more depressed. If that was what my life added up to, then I reckoned I should give in and take the kicking that was coming to me.

The others did their bit, Wiggs threatening to pawn his silver-plated Zippo lighter (complete with engraved Playboy logo), Den boycotting the essentials for three whole days. It was the longest he'd gone without a beer in years. As I said, they did what they could.

Cam did oceans better, pressing a wad of creased tenners into my hand on day two.

'Savings,' she shrugged. 'Sorry it isn't more.'

'It's loads. But how am I going to pay you back?'

She leaned into me, her whisper sending a glow through my terrified body. 'You already are.'

The other thirty-nine pounds came from a variety of places. Six fifty-pence coins from behind the settee cushions, plus a handful of twenties from the ashtray in Wiggy's mum's car, which gave us the idea of washing motors at a fiver a go.

We didn't get far, there were too many cars sat on bricks for people to take pride in how shiny they looked.

Which left me well short. I thought about coming clean to Mum, but couldn't bear to see more disappointment on her face at my expense.

All I had left was my motor mouth. I'd have to front it out with the crew and hope I could negotiate another few days. It was my worst idea yet, one that would probably lead me to a whacking great fall, but at least I'd have Den and Wiggy with me before I flew. There was no way they were letting me go on my own.

'I promised Jamm I'd keep an eye on you,' Den argued as we stood in the lift at Pickard House.

'And there's nothing on the box tonight anyway,' grinned Wiggs.

It was selfish of me – after all, this was my mess – but I couldn't help but curse Hitch as the lift creaked upwards. He'd gone underground again, but not before a cryptic text, arriving not long after Cam's donation, had offered a bit of hope.

Won't let u down

But since then? Nothing, nada. Not a text or a call or even a book token came my way, making me think that his message wasn't even meant for me in the first place.

It wasn't just me that noticed his absence. Den was still smarting from Hitch's last aggressive appearance.

'Something's going on with that boy,' he said as we trundled past the fifth floor. 'Something weird.'

'Weirder than normal?' puffed Wiggs, filling the whole lift with smoke. 'He's hardly sane at the best of times.'

'Yeah, but I didn't like the way he was the other day. All creased up like that. And to be honest, he stank.'

'I thought that was you.'

'Do you want to eat that cig? It can be arranged.'

Wiggy said nothing else and neither did I. I hadn't mentioned Hitch's offer of help to anyone. Just as well, it would only have made matters worse, especially as neither he nor his cash were anywhere to be seen.

The lift arrived as the last of my bravery departed. The doors slid open to half a dozen meatheads, all dressed in regulation high-tops, hoodies and caps, the brims unbent and sporting the shop tags. I didn't know if that was a fashion statement or whether they'd come straight from a spot of ram-raiding, but it didn't seem the right time to ask, especially as they weren't impressed to see my reinforcements.

'You was told to come on your own.'

'Eh? What about you, then? I might have been concussed but I could swear there was only two of you kicking me before.'

'Security, bruv. Reckoned we'd need back up to carry all the coins you were bound to turn up with. So? Where is it?'

I pulled a thin roll of notes from my pocket, managing to scatter a load of coins on to the walkway in the process. Not the best start when you want to stay in control. The leader ignored the shrapnel and ripped the notes from my hand, sucking his teeth in disgust when he finished counting.

'It's not what we agreed.'

I tried to get him on a technicality. 'What you *demanded*, you mean.'

'What's the difference? You take business from us then you have to pay it back.'

'And I will. I just need a few more days.'

He said nothing. Just stared hard into my eyes before turning to his pals and nodding, as if agreeing to my request.

It had been too easy, of course, but a small part of me celebrated anyway as he stepped forward, head still bobbing and teeth bared in a dumb grin.

It was only when he was right up in my face that his expression changed, jaw clenching as his forearm slammed across my neck, pinning me to the lift door.

I heard a scuffle beside me as Den reacted, ploughing towards the other crew members, who all pulled knives from their pockets. He was bigger than all of them, stronger too, but was packing nothing but his fists, and within seconds found himself backed up next to me and Wiggy.

'You must think we're mugs, turning up like this. You really think we'd accept this as payment? Or give you more time?'

I had comebacks queuing up in my head but none of them were right, not unless we actually wanted to get shanked. Instead I imagined what Jammy would do if he was stood here, but came up with nothing. Because he was too smart, too savvy to ever find himself in this mess. Unlike me, who'd walked slap-bang right into it.

The pressure on my neck increased as a second hand came into view, waving a switchblade with a rusty sharpened tip.

I knew it was dirty as it rested a millimetre from my left eye, teasing my pupil with its filth.

My whole body tensed, my neck threatening to dent the lift door as I tried to lever myself away. Den made one last attempt, but got a blade to his throat for the trouble. Wiggy said nothing, but I heard his chest rattle; craving a smoke more than ever before.

They had us in a place there was no way back from. Or so I thought. As my eye began to water at the full horror of the blade, the lift doors opened behind me and I crashed to the floor, falling at someone's feet.

He must have cursed his luck, walking into the middle of our ruck. My first instinct was to pity him, couldn't see how he could back away and claim to have seen nothing. But instead of running for the stairwell, the feet stepped over me and backed the crew leader up a step or two.

'I'm late, aren't I?' he said, his voice familiar but in my panic impossible to place. At first I thought some weird time-slip thing had happened and Jamm was back. But then I saw the scabby clothes and unwashed hair, heard the nasal whine of his voice and knew it was Hitch, later than he'd ever been. Late and unprepared.

Except he wasn't. He seemed to know exactly what to do and wasted no time in doing it.

'How much?' he asked as I scampered beside him. He was wearing that look again, a whirlwind of agitation, working a ball of gum around his tight jaw with a ferocity that was making me dizzy. Although he had no weapon in his hand, no knife to match that of any of the Cuda crew, they eyed him with a look that screamed 'danger'.

I'd seen the expression on Hitch's face before, on other lads as they stalked the Ghost. It was a look you'd cross the road to avoid, one you didn't ever want focused in your direction.

And from what I could see, the crew knew it as well as I did.

'Who are *you*, then?' my tormentor asked, unsure if he really wanted the answer.

'Never mind that,' Hitch answered. 'I asked how much?'

'How much what?'

Hitch took another step forward, so full of aggression that I swore he was on the edge of exploding, taking not only the crew, but us and the whole balcony down with him.

'How short is my mate here?'

'Call it three hundred,' the guy answered, confused by how he'd lost control in thirty seconds flat.

'And that's what you need to disappear?'

'Always was.' He tried to look brave but failed miserably.

I watched Hitch ram his left hand into his rear jeans pocket, all eyes going with him, not knowing what he was going to pull out. His movements were so twitchy and taut that I had no idea what game he was playing, if any at all.

Fourteen years of friendship in that moment meant nothing. It was like none of us knew him.

His hand stayed hidden as he moved forward, past the crew until he reached the balcony edge. Then, casually, he brought a huge wedge of tenners out into the open, but instead of paying them off and getting us out of there, he let his hand drift over the edge of the rail, allowing the tops of the notes to flutter in the wind.

What was he doing?

He seemed calm, although his eyes continued to bulge out of his head.

'I've got three hundred and fifty here,' he chewed. 'More than you want.'

All six lads took a step towards him, drooling, only to have their tongues rammed down their throats as Hitch threw his arm further into the abyss.

'But from what I saw when I arrived, maybe you'd rather have a ruck instead.' The cash went back into his pocket as he fronted up to the crew, causing Den, Wiggy and me to suck in air; I wanted to scream, 'NO!'

What was he doing? Give it to them! Even if he was wired, he could still see we were outnumbered and out-tooled.

'So which is it?' he asked, and I swear all nine of us stood stunned, no one understanding which way this was going to go.

'For three hundred quid, pal,' their top dog answered, 'it makes no odds to us. It's pocket money.'

My heart sank. This couldn't be happening when we were so close. I wanted to bolt but couldn't; all I could do was brace myself and watch as Hitch moved, his pent-up aggression fizzing as he took two steps forward.

That was all it was.

Two steps: not even a metre, but they were so full of intent, the muscles in his face screwed so tight, that every one of the meatheads took a step back, clueless as to the lengths Hitch would go to.

I didn't know either. He could've had an iron bar down the back of his jeans for all I knew, and that uncertainty was enough to see the balance shift.

'You're mental,' the leader spat. 'You know that?'

Hitch shrugged, keeping up the mystery.

'And you do it well. But you know what? I'm going to take your money anyway, fruit loop.' He paused, in control again. 'Despite you needing to spend it on a shed-load of deodorant.'

He held his hand out, waiting for the cash. But Hitch didn't move, apart from the grinding of his jaw.

'Give him the money,' I begged, not caring how desperate I sounded.

Nothing.

'Just do it, will you?' Den was feeling it as badly as me, but was Hitch?

He turned to the three of us and smiled, every inch of him buzzing. Slowly, his hand disappeared, pausing at his back pocket before a mad flourish had me cowering again.

But there was the cash, changing hands not a second too soon for my nerves or theirs.

'Didn't have to be so painful, did it?' I swear after he pocketed the cash, the Cuda's front guy checked his hand to see what lurgy Hitch had left behind. 'But you know what, pal? It's been a buzz. We'll be keeping an eye out for you.'

Really? I couldn't imagine any of them would relish another run-in with Hitch in this mood.

With a last warning in my direction, they skulked to the stairwell. Taking the lift meant more time in Hitch's presence. And right then? I'm not sure any of us wanted that.

SONNY

Fear does strange things to you.

Right then, I felt like the crew had pummelled me anyway, whereas Wiggy acted like he'd won the lottery, bouncing round the balcony, threatening to hug Hitch until the smell of him hit again.

Den wasn't feeling the love, though, far from it. The only thing he wanted was answers.

'Where've you been?' he yelled, fingers crunching into fists.

Hitch stared at him, bemused and no less riled than before. 'You what?'

'I said, where've you been? And while you're at it, what was *that* all about?'

Hitch spun on his heels, like Den was speaking to someone behind him.

'Don't be smart, I'm talking to you.'

'What's your problem?'

'My problem?' Den couldn't believe what he was hearing. 'My problem is the fact you almost had us stabbed. What were you doing playing god like that?'

'Like what? They were never going to hurt us once they knew I had the cash.'

'You reckon? What would've stopped them from shanking us all then taking it anyway? It wasn't like we could fight back.'

Hitch wasn't having a bit of it, still pumped up and strutting. 'Course we could. We've been in worse spots than that, haven't we, Sonny?'

Talk about a loaded gun. I had no idea how to answer without hacking one of them off. Den was right but Hitch had just paid me out of a mighty fall. It wasn't easy to round on him after that, despite how psychotic he'd acted.

'What we're saying is that it's not like you, mate.' I stepped towards Hitch, then thought again when I saw him scowl. 'To go in hardcore like that, especially when we didn't know you were coming at all.'

Den took over again, not as softly. 'Wouldn't have killed you to tell us you had the cash.'

'I told Sonny I'd sort him out.'

Den's eyes were on me now, demanding to know why I hadn't told him.

'But that was days ago, mate, and when I heard nothing else I thought it had fallen through.'

This was crazy, we should've been celebrating, not pulling each other apart.

I saw Hitch bristle at Den and stepped nearer to try to calm him, failing to ignore the unbearable smell as I got in close. Whatever Hitch had been taking, it was stealing what we knew of him. I could see every muscle in his body was tense, almost to the point of shaking. Made me wonder if he was as high as a kite or craving a hit. Either way, he wasn't interested in what we thought, even when Den asked him outright what he'd been taking.

'Why do I have to be on something just because I sorted this out? It's not just you or Jamm who can get things done round here. And you needed my money, didn't you?'

'Maybe we did,' Den was standing firm. 'But that doesn't mean I have to like where it came from. So what is it, then? You dealing for someone, taking a bit for yourself at the same time?'

Hitch twitched as he straightened his shirt, not realizing just how rank he looked.

'Bit rich coming from you, isn't it? How much beer have you put away this week?'

'Not enough to stop me changing my clothes and having a wash. I mean, Hitch, have a word with yourself. You look like a bum.'

What followed was unforgettable, burned itself on to the inside of my eyelids, haunting me for nights to come. It defeated everything about us, what we'd managed to avoid all our lives: in a heartbeat, the gap between the two of them disappeared, Hitch ramming Den against the balcony, a knife of his own wedged hard below Den's ear.

I couldn't believe it; if he was carrying, why not show it to the crew. Why save it for someone you were tight with?

Maybe I should've held my ground but I couldn't; even if Hitch turned the knife on me I didn't care. This wasn't what we did.

'Get off him!' I yelled, hanging off Hitch's arm, which refused to move. 'Den's right. This isn't you. So whatever's eating you, let us help.'

'I don't need your help,' he spat, the words only just recognizable through his gritted teeth. 'What I want is some respect for once. For one of you to be grateful for what I did.'

'I am. They'd be scraping me off the pavement if it wasn't for you. But I didn't want it at the expense of all this, of you in this state, threatening us. Come on, Hitch, put the blade down, we can help.'

The knife held firm, but in the seconds that he stopped to listen, Den snatched the initiative, jamming his knee hard into Hitch's groin, skittling him, the knife spinning across the walkway.

Den was on it in a flash, holding it at an angle from the floor before stamping hard on the blade, snapping it in two. Hitch yelped again like it had caused him more pain.

'That's it,' Den roared. 'No more. Now you've two choices, Hitch. We can forget this, all of it, and whatever's eating you up, we can sort it out. Or . . . ' and Den paused, offering him both pieces of the weapon. 'You can take this and go.'

Hitch was hurting, but from the laughter that left him as he crouched, he seemed to be buzzing off it too.

'You're hilarious, you know that? The fact that it's so simple for you, that you can sort this out for me, just like that? Well, *MATE* –' and there was such venom in that word that I already knew which way he was going to jump – 'looks like you've made my mind up for me.'

Hitch stood slowly, not bothering to dust himself down. His clothes were well beyond that. Instead he gave us all a look that could bend steel and twitched his way to the stairwell, not caring if he found the Cudas there waiting.

I tried to follow him, but was yanked back by Wiggs. 'Not now. He'll calm down.'

He lit a cig and pulled hard on it, tension leaving him as he exhaled.

I felt envious, would kill for that release, but knew I wouldn't get it from a smoke.

Instead I let myself slide down the wall and cupped my head in my hands, looking for something, anything, that would stop my brain from exploding.

SONNY

One problem replaced another, which wasn't alien to me. I just wasn't used to problems being quite so big.

It should've been a relief to get the Cudas off my back, but instead I spent all my time either worrying about Hitch or looking for him.

I did it on my own too; no way Den was going to join me, while Wiggs was too scared of the big man to go behind his back.

The hunt started in the obvious place, his flat. But the only thing I found as I pushed the letterbox open was a toppling pile of pizza menus and an overpowering smell that took me straight back to the face-off on the walkway.

It smelt like someone was rotting in there, too much for either my nose or one of his neighbours, who had a pop as I staggered away.

'You a friend of his?' he yelled. 'Tell him I'm calling the council. Always people coming and going, making a racket.'

I didn't bother asking if he'd seen him, didn't reckon he was the Samaritan type, so instead I scoured every inch of the Ghost, even the darker spots we normally avoided.

I didn't have much to go on other than the involvement

of drugs. You couldn't grow up on the Ghost and not guess that it had something to do with gear. Drugs made the estate go round. All right, the colour might vary from brown to white depending on whatever music had some heat, but there wasn't a minute in the day when a wrap wasn't passing from one palm to another. Everyone saw it and knew about it, even the coppers. I just presumed that most of them were taking a cut too. Why stop it when there was a slice in it for them?

There'd been other lads, other Originals over the years, that had made the choice that we'd walked away from, but that didn't make us smarter or better, it just defined us as Originals. The odd toot on a smoke was one thing; smack, crack and pills were another.

Out of all of us, I'd come closest to caving in, not that that will surprise you. I was thirteen when Jamm found a pill in my pocket. Wasn't a full one, just a yellow half-crescent that I pathetically tried to pass off as a hayfever tablet.

I thought he was going to rip the hair out of my head as he marched me up every flight of stairs in Pickard House. He didn't stop till I'd seen every toothless skaghead on every landing.

I didn't tell him that it got to me, but I dreamed of nothing else for the next month, which was why I was nervous going back there now, in case I found Hitch slumped among them.

Not a great deal seemed to have changed: stairwells were still littered with charred foil, bent spoons and, where the stuff was strongest, blissed-out bodies. The girls still looked twenty years older than they really were, cheekbones jutting through taut skin, crumbling teeth accompanying every offer that came out of their mouths.

What I actually needed from them was a heads-up on Hitch, but no one seemed to know of him. So I trawled every inch of the Ghost, my blond hair still shining like a pelican crossing. If the police were staring at me, it was in shock not because I matched who they were looking for.

The endless scouring mashed my head. It was agony, searching the same spots every day, seeing the same faces slowly rotting away. I couldn't help imagining Hitch going the same way, wondered how long it would take before I didn't recognize him either. The thoughts clung to me as I dragged them home, and only dissolved with Cam's help. She was amazing: calm when I was stressed, tough when I was unravelling. And she managed it all despite her old man crawling out of his latest whisky bottle in a predictably violent mood.

I tried to offer a shoulder for her when every inch of me was desperate to give him the same pasting back. Not that Cam let her raw nerves get in the way of seeing things clearly. She made me feel calm in a way I'd never experienced before. And I loved her for that. Completely.

She also had a playful side that was hard to resist. I was never at my sharpest first thing, took me a good hour to string a sentence together, so when Jamm decided to call before eight in the morning, I was completely blindsided. Especially as Cam was lying next to me.

The conversation started with the normal banter, but I tensed up when he realized I was distracted.

'You all right, pal?'

What did I say to that?

'Yeah, fine, just tired, you know.'

'Tell me about it. Too hot to sleep over here.'

I wasn't helped by Cam either, who'd woken up in a mischievous mood. 'Stop it, will you?' I whispered, hand over the receiver. 'Just for a minute. It's Jammy.'

'Is that Mum in the background? Stick her on if you like.'

Cam heard what he'd said and started pulling one of Mum's faces. Then a grin stretched the width of her face, and although the last thing she wanted was either of our brothers finding out about us, she giggled, ready to test my powers of concentration.

It was too much, way too much, and as much as it killed me, I had to jump out of bed and leave her. She gave me a look of mock disappointment.

'She's just leaving for the factory. Can't be late for a shift, you know how it is.'

I thought for a second I heard disappointment in his voice. 'OK. So, how's the lads? All good?'

It felt like every question was loaded with a bomb. Didn't want to go anywhere near any of them in case they went off.

'Everyone's fine. Busy, you know.'

'Doing what?'

'The normal stuff. Trying to earn some cash.'

'You're not telling me you've all found jobs, are you? Honestly, I can't leave you lot for a minute.'

I spelled the word out slowly. 'J.O.B. I'm sure I know what that is. Can't say any of us have got one, though. Not spotted very often round here, those things.'

It was the normal Jammy call, the same old banter, but I knew he was ringing to check on me. Make sure I hadn't burned the place down. So I got frustrated like I always did as the questions built up, then flat-out sarcastic when he asked about Cam.

'Have I seen her? Yeah, course I have. She's around, you know. I see more of her some days than others.'

At that very moment she was circling me, pulling me back towards the bed, and there was no way I could handle two things at once. So I did the stupid, selfish thing and chose the one who was stood right in front of me.

'Look, Jamm, I'm going to have to go. Mum read me the riot act about the flat. Says I have to get it spotless by tonight. You know how she is.'

'Right. Yeah, well go do what she says for once. And tell her I'll phone back, will you?'

'Course. Go steady.'

I ended the call way too quickly, pushing the guilt to the bottom of my gut as we hit the bed.

It wasn't till later, when Cam had gone home, that it surfaced and smacked me across the face. That might have been it: the last time we'd speak.

I buried my head in the pillow and let out a muffled scream. It never failed to amaze me, how many times I could manage to get everything so wrong.

SONNY

Home offered no sanctuary. Mum went into overdrive as Jammy's homecoming drew nearer. With a week to go, there wasn't a surface, cupboard or picture rail that wasn't scrubbed within an inch of its life. I think if she'd had her way, she'd have done the same to me.

'What exactly *was* the plan with the hair colour?' she asked. Not really a question I could answer honestly.

'It's called being on trend,' I said, not having a clue whether I was right. 'You should try it.' It sounded harsher than I meant, but once it was out there I couldn't take it back.

'Yeah, well, that costs, doesn't it? And strangely, by the time I've filled the fridge for you and the other animals, there's not a lot left for hair dye.'

It didn't bug her really, the lads making themselves at home and feeding their faces. With Jamm away, their presence was one of the things that put a smile on her face.

Ironically, it wasn't them who'd been doing the damage to the fridge, it was Cam. The girl could eat, and with her dad in residency with the strongest twelve-pack he could steal, she was spending most of her time with us. Keeping me calm about Hitch, offering distractions.

'Road trip!' she yelled one morning, ignoring my typically grumpy response. I had no idea what she was going on about. Didn't have a clue how we could have a road trip when we had no car, was even less impressed when I found myself at the bus stop an hour later, clutching a round of sandwiches made from slightly mouldy crusts. It didn't exactly have the makings of a classic day.

'So where are we heading?'

'Does it matter?'

'Er . . . yeah?'

She didn't let my miserable mug put her off, just shrugged and told me we were taking two buses to the end of their routes, see where that led us.

'But that could be anywhere.'

She punched me on the arm and smiled. 'That's the whole point, numbnut. Does it matter where we are, as long as it isn't here? Anyway, it'll do you good to spend a few hours not looking for Hitch. He will turn up, you know.'

I smiled and nodded, hoping it wasn't in a bodybag.

The bus came after an age, the driver getting the hump when I paid the fare with the last of the shrapnel I'd found in my room. I didn't have enough to pay for a second bus, never mind for Cam too, and the realization cemented the wall of fog that filled my head.

'You know what I love about you?' she asked, as we sat in silence. 'It's the constant banter. Shut up, will you? You're making my ears bleed.'

I gave her a gentle dig, the strange sensation of a smile lifting my spirits as she went off on another tangent.

'What do you think they'll want to do when they get home?'

'Who?'

'Who do you think? Tommo. Jammy.'

I hadn't a clue. Wasn't like there was more to do here than in Afghanistan. Nearly as many weapons, though.

'Do you think we should have a party?' she asked. 'Nothing special, just a few drinks, tunes, you know? Reckon your mum would be up for it?'

I knew she would. She'd cover anything that didn't move in streamers if it made her big boy happy.

'Will you even have any time for me when they're back? Fit me in among buttering bread and blowing up balloons?' I was only half-joking.

'If you're lucky you might get five minutes.'

'Enough time to tell everyone about us, then.' I didn't like the thought of disappointing Jamm yet again, but we had to come clean at some point. At least I hoped we did. The thought of her cooling off gave me the fear.

'You do still want to, don't you, Cam? You know, carry on?'

'You know, for someone so sharp, you're also the dumbest person I know. Where have I been for the last seven nights? Who have I spoken to? Who knows every secret I've got in my head?'

I hated it when she did that, put me so completely at ease in seconds.

'What, you've been seeing Wiggy too? Unbelievable.' It was lame, the only defence I had left, and she stuck me in a headlock for my trouble.

'What do you want, Sonny McGann? Matching tattoos?'

I fought back, flipping her on to the bus seat, ignoring a tut from a granny in front.

'Now you're talking. My initials on your neck. You know, something classy, like the lasses from Pickard House.'

'I'll need a baby if you want me to nail that look . . .'

'It can be arranged.'

'Not with me, it can't. Unless you want to feed it at four in the morning?'

The wise-cracking went on. All the way to the end of the line, the driver eyeing us suspiciously as he kicked us off. Idiot! It wasn't like there was anything we would nick from his scabby bus.

We destroyed our sandwiches on the next ride, despite it being way off lunchtime.

I'd got past the problem of no cash by sneaking on through the back doors as an old fella creaked his way off.

'I could've paid for you,' Cam smiled as I slid in next to her.

'I have my principles.'

She laughed hard. 'Really? Morals of an alley cat, you.'

'And that's why you can't get enough of me.'

Her hand rested on my knee and stayed there for the next hour as the bus stuttered its way beyond town and on to narrower roads.

It might have been the vibrations of the bus hypnotizing us, but we didn't say much for a while. Instead I sat and watched the landscape roll by.

It was strange, all a bit chocolate-box and smug. Nothing needed painting, all the cars gleamed as the sun bounced off them and I found myself craning to see through the windows of the houses. I'm not sure what I expected to see there, but my interest was pricked by just how alien it was.

Cam didn't seem quite as interested and was on the verge of sleep when the bus finally stopped and the lights flashed on and off.

We were the last people on board; I could see the driver trying to remember where I'd got on in the first place.

We'd ended up in a village, if you could call it that. How many houses make up a village? It didn't matter. We were faced with twenty or so bungalows, a poky shop, a pub and the biggest sky I'd ever seen.

Seriously, it was *huge* and filled every corner with a light that I wasn't used to. On the Ghost you were always stood in a shadow from one of the towers. But here? Nothing but undiluted sunlight.

It was a strange feeling, had me feeling relaxed and tense at the same time and made me aware of how scruffy I looked. The fraying mess at the bottom of my jeans seemed to be growing by the second; I had to fight the temptation to tuck my t-shirt in. It was ridiculous but I couldn't help it.

'What are we going to do, then?' I asked.

'Eat!' shouted Cam as she pulled me towards the pub, only to find it shut, which baffled us. Pubs on the Ghost opened at nine a.m. Regulars were often seen with a full English and a pint of lager. Whoever owned this place was missing a trick.

So we turned to the shop instead, Cam insisting I let her pay instead of me filling my own pockets. Chances of nicking anything were minimal anyway: the old girl in there followed us round until we left. Even opened the door for us on the way out. That's how desperate she was for us to leave.

If I hadn't been so hungry I'd have kicked up. Plus Cam

thought she was sweet, in a mothball and blue rinse kind of way.

We exhausted the rest of the place in about ten minutes flat, and I could feel myself starting to twitch at the quietness when Cam spotted the village green beyond the pub. Kids' playground all made out of wood, cricket pitch and pavilion. It looked like the sort of place Miss Marple hung out before busting a vicar for some vicious murder. I thought spots like this only existed for afternoon TV repeats. Turns out I was wrong.

We started in the playground, passing a bag of crisps to each other as we crossed on the swings. Didn't drop a single crumb either.

'Made for each other, we are,' I laughed through a full mouth. She didn't disagree, which sent me swinging higher.

'How long do you reckon this playground's been here?' she asked.

'Dunno. Few years?'

'Imagine how long it'd last at home.'

'Week, maybe? They couldn't make it out of wood like this. Someone'd torch it.'

'Wiggy probably, burn it down with one of his cigs.'

'Wouldn't be the first time,' I laughed.

We swung on for a while, passing each other at the bottom as we flew in different directions. Not once did we fall out of time.

'You think you could live here?'

'Are you having a laugh? I can't afford a bag of crisps here!'

'You know what I mean.'

'Mum could. She'd drag me and Jamm here in a second.'

I must have had a sour look on my face because Cam piped up to defend her.

'She's all right, your mum, you know?'

'If you're Jammy she is.'

'Come off it. She loves you like she does him. You just don't want to see it cos you'd rather be the tough guy. But it doesn't suit you, you know.'

'It's not like I have a lot of option, is it?'

She didn't understand.

'There's no point me trying to be like Jamm. Ask anyone and they'll tell you they broke the mould with him.'

She could see it bugged me, but wasn't the type to pander to it. Instead she stifled a mock yawn and moved on. 'It'll be amazing to have them home though, won't it?'

I had to agree. Couldn't imagine the relief to see them in front of us, safe.

Be even better if they arrived to find everything in one piece and Hitch not AWOL. Make me feel like I'd kept my part of the bargain.

We chatted on, had the headspace to, there were no car alarms or dodgy deals going on to disturb us. I told her about me and Mum on the roof, about escaping the Ghost, how Mum believed we were capable of doing it.

'So why couldn't you?' she asked.

'What?'

'Escape. Why not fill up a van and get out? Doesn't mean you have to do it overnight. Think about it. Buy a scabby old Transit, get it running and hire it out. Do the whole white-van-man thing. You've enough charm between the two of you to get plenty of work.'

'And that's going to be enough to set us up somewhere else?'

'Depends how much you want it. Because from what I've seen, if you really want something . . . ? It tends to happen one way or another.'

'And you reckon Jammy would want to do that, with me, I mean?'

'Are you kidding me? He'd love it. He could keep an eye on you that way.'

She laughed, a joyful noise that almost made the swings shake.

I chased her from the playground, feeling the first drops of rain as I tackled her to the ground. Perfect timing.

'Reckon that pavilion's open?' she asked.

It wasn't like we had the luxury of a brolly.

'Soon will be.'

I pulled her towards it as the drops pricked our scalps.

It didn't take me long to get inside with the minimum of force. A small, unhooked window was all I needed to drag myself in, though I'm not sure whether I looked so impressive opening the door to her in cricket pads and a helmet. I wasn't exactly the country squire type, but we were dry, and once I found a kettle and some coffee we were sorted again, stretching beside each other on a couple of benches, talking when we had to, silent when it suited. It felt so comfy I almost forgot I was a long way from home, well, relatively. Two-buses-worth felt like a million miles to us.

We left an hour later, after rinsing the cups and latching the back window properly. The buses arrived quickly, bouncing us home as we bantered and daydreamed.

I hadn't thought about Hitch for hours, and although he came to mind as soon as Pickard House loomed into view, I didn't let it puncture the day. I wouldn't let it. I had to do what I could to level the decks before our brothers came home. Then we could do the important thing and celebrate.

The bus doors closed behind us as the last of the sun hid behind the towers. A breeze nipped at my neck but I left my collar turned down. I'd soon heat up as I climbed the stairs again, looking for Hitch.

JAMMY

One patrol followed another. Twelve-hour gaps between the sun baking us, hardening our skins. Shame it couldn't do the same to what was going on inside. I was running on pure nervous energy.

Sonny's phone had rung out each time I'd tried it that morning and I left no messages. What was there to say? Wish you were here?

Besides, if this was the last time he heard from me, I wanted him to be able to talk back. He'd always liked the final word, it was the thing that defined him.

Reluctantly I pushed home out of my head and focused on the village. We were back gathering intel: what did people know about our drugs raid? Was there more for us to find?

Someone here knew everything, and we were pumped on sniffing it out.

The terps were working overtime, coaxing everyone we met. I knew they were stripping the aggression out of our questions, trying not to offend the elders they were questioning, but two hours later and tempers were frayed, patience in tatters.

I drew hard on my drinking tube, but the water was

warm, like the weakest tea I'd ever tasted. I needed something else to fill my mind, something simple, and felt a terrific burst of energy when a footie rolled past me. Instinct had me follow it, and tap it foot to foot.

But then it was gone. Nicked from my boot as someone flashed past me. The young kid, the skilful one from the last match. He stopped a metre or two away and started keep-ups of his own. Left to right foot, up to the knee for a few, then he lifted it skywards, trying to copy Tommo's trick. But he didn't quite have it mastered and the ball bounced off his back and towards me again.

I grinned, remembering how flat the ball was. The inner must have been shredded – seemed a shame when all the kid wanted to do was practise. The lads back home were skint, but there was always enough money to fund a decent footie.

I rolled the ball back to him, but instead of trying again, he spoke to me. A jumble of words I couldn't understand.

'Yumanu?'

Cupping a hand to my ear, I told him to say it again.

'YUMANU?' Same jumbled words, more volume. No use.

I shrugged, and kicked the ball at his feet. If I couldn't understand him, we could have a game instead, but he was too quick for me, back-heeling the ball out of my reach.

Outskilled by a ten-year-old.

He wanted an answer, so the question came again.

'YUMANU?' He was getting proper hacked off with me now, like I was thick or something.

A terp would help, but none were free, they were still grilling the elders.

'Listen, mate. I haven't a clue what you're on about.'

He growled. I thought for a second he was going to kick my shins, but instead he flicked the ball into his hands and held it right in my face.

'Yu. Man U?' I heard a question for the first time as he waved the ball at me. 'MAN. U. Roonee, Giggsie. GOAL!' With that he chucked the ball in the air and pulled his tatty shirt over his head, waving it in a circle.

I got it. Finally. 'Manchester United?' I asked, saying the words slowly. 'R-o-o-n-ey?' Did I like Man Utd?

He slapped his head with relief. Finally!

'Man U. Best team. Chelsea?' He went to stick his fingers down his throat, before telling me in one impressive English swear word exactly what he thought of them.

I laughed. It was impossible not to. Here we were, trying to find out who was responsible for a massive stash of heroin, and the only sense I was getting was from a ten-year-old about the Premier League.

He was right about Chelsea if nothing else. I called Tommo over. He had to hear this.

Our little friend, however, didn't want to wait any longer for an answer and gave me a whack to the shin.

Tommo thought it was hilarious, until he almost got a boot of his own.

'Steady on, big lad,' I laughed. 'You'd fit right in at Chelsea playing like that.' He cocked his head, still wanting an answer: who did I support?

'Tigers,' I said finally, trying to say it clearly.

He looked confused, so I said it slowly.

No use either.

Instead, I pulled my hands into claws in front of me and roared.

He laughed. So did Tommo and the rest of the lads who'd started listening in.

'Cat?' the kid asked, then shrugged. He'd never heard of us. No wonder.

'Campest tiger I ever saw,' grinned Tommo.

'You try! His English is nearly as bad as yours.'

The kid had lost interest in who supported who now. All he wanted us to do was show him some tricks. Anything to improve his skills. It was a challenge we grabbed hold of quickly – hearts and minds and all that.

What followed were ten of the best minutes I could remember; despite the heat melting us and the weight on our backs, we could've been anywhere, instead of a crummy dustbowl village. We even got a little crowd going, saw a few smiles, rows of rotten teeth from the elders.

It made a change from shaking heads and frowning faces, and we owed it all to our mate, Little Wayne. It was the perfect name for him. He had the same thick neck and silky skills, the identical spirit to the real Rooney. And after what he'd shown us back there, I reckoned I owed him. Knew I had to pay him back.

I grinned all the way back to the base that evening, as a plan mushroomed in my head. Nothing could wipe the smile off my face. If this was what being a soldier meant, then maybe I could hack it after all.

JAMMY

A roar went up. An Old Trafford-sized racket that pulled everyone's eyes to the middle of the square.

I didn't kick the new ball that high, but I swear by the time it landed, there were forty ecstatic kids underneath it, fighting for possession. And in the middle, of course, was Little Wayne.

Funny how a nickname sticks so quickly when it's spot on.

I hadn't told anyone about the plan. Didn't reckon I needed to. It fitted right in with gaining the locals' trust, didn't it? Think of the number of hearts we'd win with one simple present. The kids would give up their own granny for a brand new footie.

And anyway, there were loads more balls back at camp, more than we'd ever need.

The game that kicked off was ferocious, like a cup-tie, end-to-end with not much skill apart from our little friend. Wayne had scored a hat-trick within ten minutes, but didn't stop charging around for a second, bossing his team-mates about every time they failed to pass to him. I'd have loved to know what he was saying.

A crowd built up. Elders leaned on their sticks, one guy

approached me and Tomm with a bottle of lemonade each, which we necked with a grin.

It was working, the whole thing. I felt a charge run through me, which zapped away the months of no sleep. I wanted to join in, show them how it was done. Reckon I would've done too if Little Wayne wasn't playing. He'd have had the ball off me in seconds and that was a defeat I couldn't face in front of the lads.

Conversations were happening all over the square, the terps were properly busy. I just hoped they weren't talking about Chelsea's chances of winning the League: there was bigger stuff than that that needed sorting.

The only person not wearing a smile was Giffer. He stood in the shade, arms still cradling his gun, eyes flicking at windows, doors, cars, anywhere a bullet might fly from. Born to fight, that one, and I found myself resenting him for a second, wishing he'd let his guard down long enough to see the joy we'd briefly brought those kids.

I pulled my gun into a pose to match his, and strode over.

'All calm, Giff?'

'Oh aye,' his eyes never stopped scanning. 'For now. But you never know, do you?'

'I dunno. Can't see anything kicking off when the mood's like this.'

'You reckon?'

I gently pulled his gun to waist level and demanded his attention.

'What's up, Giff? It's not the kids, is it?'

His eyes drilled into me. No anger . . . If anything, I saw a flash of something like fear.

'Not as such. Fills me up to see them acting like they should be. It's them who misses out in all this mess.'

'What is it, then?'

He thought hard, like he was searching for the right words. And at first I reckoned he was going to say nothing. I was wrong.

'I rate you, Jamm. You know that. Not just as a soldier, but as a bloke. What you did for Tommo before? There aren't many who'd give up glory like that. I wouldn't.'

He paused again, like the words to follow were causing him pain.

'But I don't think the ball was a good idea . . . '

I laughed, surprised really.

'What do you mean? Have a look, Giff. Look at 'em.'

'Oh, don't get me wrong, the kids love it. And they'll love you as a result.'

'And isn't that the point, mate? Aren't we supposed to be winning them over? Showing them they can trust us?'

'We are. But we're also here to keep them safe. To keep them away from the idiots who would happily blow them and us sky high.'

'I don't get you.'

'Look, don't take this the wrong way. But giving them the ball like that, in full view of anyone watching, was a mistake. Now you, or rather they, might get away with it. But all it takes is one pair of eyes to notice, and it could all get messy.'

'You're over-reacting, Giff. It's a ball. That's it.'

But he wasn't having a word of it. 'To you it is, and to the kids as well. But to them whose heroin we took, it's like a red rag. They won't like it, Jamm, I'm telling you. It's stuff like this that fires them up. They'll hurt these people if they see them being disloyal.'

For the first time he got under my skin. Could he not relax just once and see we were finally making a difference? It was a risk worth taking.

Was it because it wasn't his idea? I should've asked him but couldn't be bothered. I knew he'd just bat it back to me.

Well, knackers to that. I wasn't going to let him drag us down today, when we'd finally found one bit of sanity in this whole madhouse. Instead, I turned and wheeled away, arms flexed, weapon ready. I wasn't going to give him anything else to criticize.

I went back to the game and tried to push Giff out of my thoughts, but couldn't quite do it. Every time I tried to focus on the football my eyes found their way back to the broken windows above, hoping to god I wasn't going to see a rifle barrel poking through one of them. I felt torn: I wanted to enjoy what I'd managed to pull off, but heard only the boss's demands for the locals' safety first.

As the game moved on, the only danger I could see was to the dignity of Wayne's opposition. Their team had doubled in number, dragging in as many bigger lads as possible to try and get close to him. Not that it made much difference, he had such skill that by the time they swung their legs in his direction he'd already skipped past.

It was fantastic to watch. Like something out of a film. We couldn't work out if he was getting more joy out of his own skills or from the irritation of the lads chasing him, but we loved both and started cheering him on, yelling, 'OLE!'

every time he knocked the ball past or over them. It spread round the old men watching too; none of us dared take our eyes off him for a second.

Unfortunately, his skills ended up costing him, as after fifteen minutes of embarrassment, the older lads decided if they couldn't kick the ball, then *he* would have to do instead. It took them a while to knock him to the ground, but when they finally managed it, Wayne went down hard. And initially, he didn't move.

This brought uproar from the crowd and saw us parting them to get to him. His knee was in a right state. Grit had torn the skin, and immediately I saw something else jagging from the middle of the gash, a shard of green glass.

He yelled in pain when we tried to hold his leg still, spitting a sweary insult we knew wasn't thanks. I wanted to grin: another sign the boy was a born footballer.

It was in that moment, when his eyes were most fierce, that I knew why I warmed to him. When I looked at him, I saw Sonny. Had seen that mixture of steel and cheek every day for the last sixteen years. Never on a football pitch, but in the flat, on the stairwell, any place you wanted to name. Instantly, I wanted to be on the Ghost with him.

Giffer broke my concentration.

'We should get him home. Let his family sort him out.'

But I wasn't having it.

'I'm not moving him until his leg's clean.'

'Well, you won't achieve that here.'

'I can't imagine his house is much better. Plus he's in pain. So let me get on with it.'

He leaned over me, his voice still gentle, concerned, but

ultimately annoying. 'Remember what I said, Jammy. How this would look.'

I couldn't believe this, had to fight the temptation to get to my feet and into his face. 'Doesn't it look better than leaving him to get gangrene? There's enough kids with stumps round here as it is.'

He had no answer to that, just smiled sadly and backed away through the crowd, leaving me and Tomm to get to work on Little Wayne's leg. We might not be able to solve much, but there was no way I was backing away from this kid now. He needed me. That was all I needed to know.

JAMMY

Giff's words stayed with me, flying round my head as we waited endlessly for patrols. Was he right? Should I have left well alone, let the locals sort Wayne out? I didn't have any answers. They didn't seem to exist in this place. Only operations that would succeed or fail. Success meant we all kept breathing. And failure? Well, none of us dwelled on that for too long. We all knew what that meant.

Time merged and meant nothing. We waited, we patrolled, we sweated.

We gave up guessing the temperature: it was irrelevant. We were sweating like pigs, didn't need a thermometer to tell us that.

It wasn't just us feeling the frustration either. The boss was simmering too.

'We're at a difficult point now, fellas,' he growled, every inch of him tense. 'Almost three months in, first tour for many of you, and we've not established the stability we'd hoped for.'

We didn't need telling: we'd seen the number of explosions triple in the last week, been shocked at the deviousness of the traps set, the number of their own people they were prepared to hurt in the process.

'But remember, you're here to work. No point dreaming about your own bed and Mum's cooking. You'll only be tasting blood if you don't concentrate on the job at hand.' He dropped his voice and leaned in to us, like he had a cunning plan to speed us home. 'So while you're out here, remember who your family is. I'm the only mother you need right now. Remember that.'

My eyes slid to Tommo, nodding in the right places, eyes front and centre, unblinking. He was learning. Quickly becoming a better solider than me. Whatever that actually meant.

I didn't find him next to me as often any more, hiding in my shadow, and although he still spent most of his downtime in the yard kicking a ball to himself, it was working for him, switching his head off from the rest of the chaos.

I envied him, had to stop myself from pinching him awake at night as he snored in the cot beside me. I was watching the sun rise every morning, snatching just handfuls of sleep when my head finally cleared itself of daisy-chain bombs and snipers.

But the less sleep I got, the messier my head became, incapable of sifting through suspicious thoughts about every local I met. Even the toothless old women who pushed vegetables at us in the market were holding bombs as far as I knew.

It could've been me, but the town felt different. You could feel the tension, smell the resentment that came with each patrol. As our notebooks came out, backs turned and doors closed. We were losing them, their faith in us dying. And if they turned instead to those we were looking for? Then we were all in danger.

Patrols had changed for me. As soon as we stepped on to the square my head turned to Little Wayne. After his fall I'd seen nothing of him. A week had ticked by since his accident, which gave me the fear about his leg. What if I hadn't cleaned it properly? Infection could kick in easily if I'd done a shabby job.

Fearful, I started questioning the lads who still kicked his ball around the square, but they either didn't know, or didn't want to help. Their game was always more important.

'Do you think the terps could ask them where he lives?' I said to Tommo, feeling increasingly paranoid.

'I reckon you should let it go, mate. If the kid was hurt, they'd have been battering our doors down to sort it out. The nearest clinic's fifty miles away.'

'But still, it's not like him to not be out here playing.'

Tommo took a stride towards me, arms on my shoulders, eyes boring into mine. 'You've got to move on, because from the look of it, him and his folks already have. Anyway, he's just a kid. There's hundreds more of them out there. Pick one of them instead.'

He didn't get it. And to be honest I didn't have it straight in my own head.

Nothing we were doing made any sense, or even the slightest difference to the locals. The only thing I knew was that the sight of that kid with a ball at his feet had kept my head straight, stopped it from flipping out at the thought of what I was still doing here. That ball I gave him had made a difference, to me as well as him.

Clocking him became the focus of every patrol I made. All right, I put a gloss on it, made sure the boss saw me doing my job, but every corner we turned, every door we knocked on in the name of intel, I was looking for the same face.

I had to wait another week before I finally laid eyes on him. And at first it was only the ball I saw. It sat in the middle of the market square, as if waiting for kick-off. Scanning each corner of the space, I looked for Little Wayne, still surprised not to see him attached to it.

It was early, but the town was waking, expecting a busy trading day. Boxes were being stacked outside houses, the tang of spices cutting through the dust. It would only be minutes until the ball was surrounded by stalls, so with Wayne in mind, I walked towards it to keep it safe.

I'd only managed a handful of steps when he skidded into view. Limping slightly, but not enough to keep him from running, eyes fixed on his prize.

I forgot who and what I was, a greeting booming from my lips before I could stop myself. The early traders broke their step and looked my way, as did Little Wayne, a cocky grin snaking from ear to ear. My arm lifted into the air, then pointed at the ball. He saw what I wanted and half ran, half hobbled towards it.

In that moment, I was the happiest I'd been since arriving.

It made sense, all of it; even the heat and the suspicion didn't matter. With a quick movement, I shook my pack to the floor then unclipped my helmet, waiting for the pass.

But it never arrived. As Little Wayne planted his right leg by the ball and swung with his left, the world did a strange and sinister thing. It twisted and bucked, kicking a storm of debris into the air with a boom that lifted me clean off my feet. The ground surrounded me, flew with me, then landed on top of me.

And in that instant, with a simple kick of the ball, the world ended. Everything changed.

#

I panicked. The new world didn't make sense. Buildings lay in weird shapes, jutting from the ground where the stalls should've stood. There were craters, cavernous holes straight from a lunar landscape. But most of all, there was dust. A thick thunderous cloud that had fought the sun and won: it clung to every strand of clothing, swirled in every particle of air.

I tried to stand but couldn't, not until I heaved a chunk of rubble off my stomach, which felt battered and grazed.

There wasn't time to worry about myself, though. I had to find Little Wayne, check he was all right; hope that somehow he might have avoided whatever had just gone off.

Groping blindly in front of me, I searched for my helmet and pack but found nothing but my rifle, which I leaned on to push me up.

I felt more dust rain down, sticking to my forehead, which was already wet to the touch. Dabbing my scalp, I held my hand in front of my face but saw nothing. It wasn't until my fingers were practically touching my eyeballs that I could see the blood coating them.

Stumbling over rocks that littered my path, my ears

stopped ringing enough to tune in to the noises of the square: bricks being thrown, walls still tumbling, words screamed into the darkness, pleading, then desperate.

I didn't get it, could only think it was our mistake, that a fighter plane had got its co-ordinates wrong and missed its mark, but as I tripped over another hunk of masonry, still yelling Wayne's name, I heard the truth.

'IED in the square. MAN DOWN. MAN DOWN.'

What? It didn't make sense. Improvised devices here? Set 'em outside our camp or in the ditches, like they had the whole time we'd been here, but in the middle of their own people?

My stomach twisted and my breakfast left me, the acid threatening to burn a hole in the dust. I retched until empty, only stopping when I felt an arm lift me to my feet, heard a familiar voice.

'You all right, Jamm?' asked Tommo, his breath rasping.

'What's going on? Where's the bomb?'

I felt him grip my shoulders, bracing me as the words tumbled out.

'You didn't see? The kid. Little Wayne. They must have rigged it . . . ' The pause lasted too long, he wanted me to fill in the gaps. 'It must have been set with a pressure switch. Soon as he kicked the ball, it all . . . '

I didn't hear anything else apart from the sound of Tommo hitting the ground as I pushed him away. My head was bursting, full of my own screams and gunfire as I waded forward, unloading rounds into the mist. They were out there, they had to be watching, and I was going to take them down for it.

The rifle's nozzle spat left and right, arcing wildly until spent, the crack of bullets being replaced by the boss, screaming in my ears.

'HOLD FIRE! HOLD FIRE!'

It made me want to laugh. Was he crazy? They'd just blown the world sky high and he wanted us to stop? Was he going to have us with our notebooks out again, gathering gossip? That moment had passed. No more.

I looked for ammo in a pack that wasn't there. Searched my pockets instead for anything I could launch, a boiled sweet if I had to, but instead found myself wrestled to the floor, rifle knocked from my fists, Giff's voice in my ear.

'JAMMY! Calm yourself! The lads are in there. You'll take them out.'

It was too much, all of it. My brain was rolling around my head, knocked senseless by the blast, but I had to sort this out, track the boy down. So I shook Giffer off, not bothering to pick up my rifle. He was welcome to it.

'Where are you going? Boss says hold your line. You could be walking into anything!'

I ignored him and paced forward, tripping on my first step. He chose to pick me up, I chose to push him off and move on again.

'I have to find him.'

'Find who? Tommo's behind us. Taking orders. Like you should be.'

'Not him!' I was in his face now, washing him with my spit. 'He doesn't need me. It's the kid. He was walking straight into it before it went off.'

The world twisted again, but there was no second blast.

Instead I was pinned to the floor by Giffer, straddling me, right hand clenching my cheeks.

'LISTEN! LISTEN TO ME! You won't find him, Jamm. He's gone. He triggered it. When he kicked the ball, that's when it blew. They set it, pal, but probably hoped you'd be the one to kick it.'

I heard his words, and felt something break. It started in my chest then sped to every muscle, every joint, every cell in my body. It was like they'd plugged me into the socket then set me loose.

Giff was way bigger than me, with a neck almost as thick as my waist, but his head still rocked back when my fist made contact. He fell, and as my chest filled with air I leapt to my feet and into the abyss.

I had no idea what I was looking for, could do nothing but waft stupidly at the dust, flooding my eyes with the stuff. Every third step brought another tumble, another knock to the legs and head. But I wouldn't stop, not till I had to, not till I found him and got him safe.

There was noise, but none of it meant anything. It was all static. White noise. My only thoughts were of him.

Figures stumbled past caked in dirt and blood. War-torn zombies, walking dead. I grabbed each one as they reached me, only pushing them on when I was convinced they weren't him.

Not everybody I saw was as mobile. The square had been filling up and the blast had been so shocking that many had been sucked into the middle of it. Arms waved from under piles of rocks, which I pulled at furiously, exposing whoever lay beneath. Bile brewed and spat in me angrily. On I went.

I finally caught sight of him, half-buried in a mountain of bricks. I put a dozen unbroken steps together, only falling as I reached him, my fingers jammed to his neck. Pulse. Pulse. Pulse?

I shouted for medics. At least I think I did. My hands scooped and pulled at the wreckage. If I could get him flat and pump his chest, then we had a chance. The medics could do it. They had to, they wouldn't stop, wouldn't dare.

The rubble piled up around me. I was winning; I'd have him out in time. It would all be fine.

But then the bricks kept coming, and his body . . . stopped. I'd reached his waist, expected to dig around his thighs, but there was nothing there. Instead, there was only blood and dust.

It was wrong, a mistake.

I clawed furiously at the brick and plaster, all stained the deepest red.

There was nothing more to free.

A noise left me, louder than the roar that had filled his last seconds.

I wanted to bring every single wall down.

And I didn't care where they fell, as long as they covered me too.

SONNY

When the call came I was ready. Terrified but ready.

Cam sounded broken, like he'd beaten fifteen years out of her, and she was three years old again.

'Sonny, I need you.' I could hear how difficult it was for her to even spit out four words.

'What's wrong?' I shouted. 'What's he done?'

'Please come. Come now.' And she was gone, leaving me to tear towards the door. As I reached it, I considered turning round for something – a knife, rolling pin, anything that would help me give Larry back everything he'd dished out. But that meant time, and she needed me *now*. I didn't bother with the lift; instead I took the stairs as quickly as I could while punching in Den's number. He answered on the third ring. I ignored the small talk.

'Can you get over to Cam's?'

'What's the rush?'

'I think it's all kicked off again. I might need you.'

'I'll be there before you. Want me to call Wiggs too?'

Wiggs wasn't much of a scrapper, quicker with his mouth than his fists. But he was another body to put in front of Larry if he'd really lost it.

'Yeah, please. See you in two. Quick as you can.'

For the following minute my head spat out every scenario imaginable. Cam was badly bruised; he'd beaten her unconscious since she called; even that she was leaning over him with a knife, fingers wrapped around the handle, blade buried in his chest. I shivered as I ran. It was possible, everyone had a limit.

It was hard to keep calm when I was so out of breath, and as I approached their ominously open front door there was a split second where I thought about turning round and running the other way. But it was Mum who stopped me, cos she didn't think I had this in me. And even if she couldn't see me front it out, I'd know. And that was a start.

It was deathly quiet inside, but that wasn't a surprise. If Larry had got tasty, he wouldn't have stuck around to fetch ice packs and plasters. The surprise came when *he* was the first thing I saw; sat on the hearth, head in hands, shoulders shaking violently. Instantly I looked for Cam, seeing instead a huge wet patch on the wall opposite the fire, a whisky glass shattered on the floor below.

Something had gone on, but it wasn't as clear-cut as I'd expected, especially when the next person I saw was Dennis, who paced into the room and straight into me, arms snaking round my shoulders, holding me way too hard.

'What's going on? I asked, but there was no time for him to reply, as in stumbled Cam and her mum, Gill.

In that second I knew. There wasn't a bruise or cut on either of them, yet every inch of their bodies screamed in pain. It was scratched deep into Cam's eyes, causing tears to snake down both cheeks, so many that she hadn't the energy to wipe them away. With difficulty I removed myself from Den, feeling his tears on my t-shirt before catching Cam as she collapsed.

'Two soldiers,' she wept between violent shudders. Every sentence was punctuated by a wail. 'Came. With news. There was a firefight. Jamm and Tommo. They were caught at the front. On their own.'

I listened hard. Harder than I'd ever listened to anyone in my life, but my heart was pounding with such violence that I could barely hear her. Who was hurt? Not Jamm. Please don't let it be Jamm.

'It's OK,' I whispered, kissing her tears, not caring who saw. 'You can tell me. I've got you.'

'They found guns on a patrol. Explosives. And followed them into this village. Tommo and Jammy were trying to get to them and make it safe. But there was a stand-off. They were isolated and jumped on. And Tomm . . . Tomm . . .'

'It's OK. It's OK.'

'It's not OK!' she screamed, her heart splitting in two right before me. 'They shot him. He's gone. He's gone.'

I thought I'd have an answer for what I'd find here, even if it simply lay in my fists, but this floored me. Even in her devastated state, Cam was the only thing separating me from the floor. We clung to each other, bodies shaking in tandem, my head craving details that it didn't really want to hear.

'They found him with Jammy. He'd tried to keep him alive.'

I wanted, *needed* to know that Jamm was OK, but how? How did I ask that question of her when Tommo was gone?

'I can see him. See him bleeding. And the only thing that

makes it bearable is the thought of Jamm being with him, being the last thing he saw.'

'Jamm loved him. Tomm was his brother as much as me.'

'Jammy killed the guy who got Tommo. Shot him. I know that shouldn't help, but it does. He's a hero. They both were.' She choked on the words and shoved her head deep into my chest, the responsibility terrifying me.

All I wanted to do was take the pain for her, but knew I couldn't. Would I have swapped my own brother for hers? Never. How could I even think about it without tearing myself in two? Every sentence I could offer her, every line that came into my head wasn't either enough or even vaguely true.

It'll be all right.

I know how you feel.

We can get through this.

I had nothing, so offered nothing, apart from every ounce of strength I had, knowing it was nowhere near enough.

There was movement around us, Gill stooping to collect the broken glass from the carpet, Den spotting Wiggy in the doorway and leading him into the hallway to explain. The only thing I didn't hear was Larry moving up behind us. It wasn't until he spoke that I smelt the waves of alcohol pouring off him.

'Cam,' he whispered, his right arm trying to wedge us apart. 'Cameron. Cam, Cam!' But she didn't want to move. I felt her arms tense, pulling me closer to her as his efforts increased.

It became a weird dance: Larry's drunken stumblings pushing us round the floor like the last smooch at a long wedding party. I wouldn't let her go, not if it wasn't what she wanted, so I turned my head, and in the most sympathetic voice I could dredge up for him said:

'Give her a minute, Larry, will you? She can hardly stand up here.'

'Then she should be with me.' His breath was indescribable, the grim aftermath of years of getting tanked. It didn't smell of any one drink, just a rotting blend of anything he could get his hands on. It wasn't just his breath: the stink clung to his clothes, his body; every pore leaked its foulness in a way that made it virtually impossible to breathe around him. Hitch flashed into my head. A horrid premonition.

It had obviously reached Cam too as I felt her face press closer to my chest.

'I don't want him.' Her words reached me through my t-shirt, loud enough for him to hear too. He didn't take it well.

'You don't want me? I'm your dad!'

A simple sentence, but enough to flick a switch in Cam's head. She lifted her face, still clinging to me as she spoke.

'You haven't been my dad for years. You haven't a clue what it even means.'

Larry's face creased in pain, but it was a pantomime expression that fooled no one. 'They've killed my boy,' he wailed. 'My boy, your brother, but you'd rather cling to *him*?'

He pushed me, almost sending us flying into Gill. I felt my heart leap and my blood simmer.

'He's shown me more love than you ever have!'

'Oh, I bet he has, but if you want to blame anyone for

Tommo, maybe you should blame *his* family. If it wasn't for his brother signing up, our Tomm would never even have thought about it.'

They were the first of his words to make sense, as there was no doubt Tommo had always looked up to Jammy: wanted nothing more than to step in his big shadow, the shadow I wanted to escape. What sort of *brother* was I compared to Tomm?

The room felt like it was getting smaller, the floor no longer level under my feet. I had the feeling it was now Cam holding *me* up instead, except she wasn't even doing that, as she launched herself at Larry, arms wild, nails glinting.

'Don't you do that!' she screamed. 'Don't you dare blame anyone but yourself. The only reason Tomm signed up, the only reason he was desperate to go somewhere even worse than here was YOU! You drove him to it, you made him leave. You might not have pulled the trigger, but it was you that killed him.' And with a ferocity that terrified me, she drove him to the floor, swarming all over him, pouring back on to him every minute of fear that he'd inflicted on her.

I hoped he was as scared as she'd been her whole life.

It was surreal and terrifying how quickly heartbreak had turned into anger, and as much as I'd dreamed of Larry getting what he deserved, this wasn't the time for it. Gill was trying to get between them, but didn't stand a chance. Even her grief-stricken screams weren't enough, so I yelled for the lads, who, with a monumental effort, pulled Larry away to the settee, his right cheek wearing the marks of Cam's rage.

He gave in quicker than she did. It took the best part of

a minute for my voice to reach Cam's brain, for her to realize she didn't have to fight any more. Tommo was gone, and killing her dad wouldn't re-start her brother's heart, despite how good it might feel.

Her rage finally gave way, replaced again by tears and questions, *why* asked in a dozen different ways. I did what I could, smoothed her hair, kissed her face, yet inside all I had were questions of my own.

How had this happened? They were so close to coming home.

Where was Jamm now? How was he coping?

I thought about Mum and how she would react, and I thought about us all, and how things were never going to be the same again.

SONNY

It didn't make sense on this side of the street. I was only twenty metres from the lamp post where I'd watched the others come home, but I might as well have been in a different town, a different world.

I didn't belong on this side, had no business being here, or that's how my head saw it. The reality was different. I had to be here, wanted to be here for Cam, and for Tommo of course, but a lot of my head wasn't here at all.

It was full of Jamm. We'd had no word from him since the news hit. We'd bombarded him with texts, calls, emails. I'd have sent a carrier pigeon if I thought it would work.

The silence hit Mum ferociously. Her mobile was always in view, on the table, in her palm. I caught her calling it from the landline to make sure it was working. I tried to calm her, remind her he was due home in days, but the only time she looked even vaguely at ease was when she was preparing for the parade, making sure I did it right. In a weird way that helped me too, stopped my head from coming up with the grimmest of reasons for the lack of a call.

She started by demanding I buy a suit. It had to be a suit. There was no way I was welcoming Tommo home in jeans and a t-shirt, and this meant trawling the charity shops until I found something that wasn't a) ancient and b) terrible.

Charity shops weren't new to me; Mum had had us trawling them since we could walk. Our wardrobes were eighty per cent cast-offs, so I should've been used to it. I wasn't, though. No matter how many years passed, it still felt like I was wearing dead man's trousers.

I had a strategy for using charity shops now. Whenever I went in one I always had a full carrier bag with me. That way, if anyone from the estate spotted me, I could say I was here to donate. It's only embarrassing if you're caught spending in one.

The suit was OK, though. Not black . . . the nearest I could find was dark grey. I knew it was the one for me when I tried it on and found a twenty pound note in the pocket. That was the kind of charity I could deal with.

Mum looked almost impressed when I brought it home, standing me on a chair as she pinned the trousers and cuffs. Made me realize how much she probably would've liked a girl, someone to dress up and make fancy. She was never going to get that from me.

By the time I left the flat for the parade I was wobbling. Couldn't look at the statue on the estate for fear of losing it. As I walked, a couple of girls from Pickard House wolf-whistled, and as I caught a glance of myself I didn't feel like me. Didn't look like me either. On any other day Cam might have been impressed. I mean, this was the kind of kit you went to your prom in. That's what kids my age were doing, not burying one of their best mates.

It felt like we'd been stood on the roadside forever. People had been kind. There was one guy, part Hell's Angel, part squaddie, who met us by the town hall and guided us to our spot. He walked with a stick, but never grimaced at the impact of his leg. I had no idea if the damage was war-related. From the look of him, he'd been in a ruck or two, but the way he spoke, the care he showed Cam and Gill, it didn't matter. He had 'GOOD' running right the way through him.

So we stood in front of the whole town. Cam, Gill, Larry, Den, Wiggy, Mum and me. I'd called Hitch, course I had, but got no joy. The phone kicked to answerphone every time. He didn't want to be reached and, wherever he was, I doubted he was reading the paper. It felt like we'd lost two of us when one was bad enough.

The crowd gathered and swelled ten deep. Passions never ran higher than when one of our own was brought home. People talked us down, the residents of the Ghost, but it felt like every one of us was there now, when it mattered.

The only problem was that we were on show, the centre point for everyone else's grief. Once that hearse stopped in front of us, every single pair of eyes would be staring in our direction, and I doubted any of us were ready for that.

I looked at Larry, wavering on the kerb edge, dressed in a suit worse-fitting and older than mine. I could see the shape of the hip flask through his inside pocket, the weight of it pulling his jacket clumsily to the left. His face was clammy; every minute without a drink was torture, and I knew that was all he could think of, not his son. His hands fidgeted at his side, occasionally grappling for a hand to hold. His wife and daughter stood either side of him, yet neither wanted to acknowledge that he was even there.

The bell chimed as it always did, the crowd falling silent, necks craning for a better view. I couldn't look. Closed my eyes and wished harder than I had in my life that this wasn't happening. But once I opened them again, there they were, the hearses, rolling so slowly that the wheels hardly appeared to turn. Cam leaned against me, tears falling, her face scrunched up so tightly in pain that it made me wince too. I had to get her through this, keep her on her feet when all she wanted to do was lie in the gutter and wail.

People threw flowers like they always did, collecting untidily on the roof, others falling under the wheels, petals collecting in the tread of the tyres.

Finally, after what felt like an age, the first hearse pulled up in front of us and stopped, its paintwork gleaming so brightly we could see our tears in it.

It took every ounce of strength I had to look in the window, to see the garlands in his honour.

Tommo

Brother

One in red, one in amber and black to match Tommo's team.

We'd talked about the wreath a lot, wanted one that read *True Original* but couldn't afford it, the florist charged by the letter. 'Brother' still worked, summed up what he was to us as well as to Cam.

It wasn't the wreaths that killed me, though, it was the coffin, wrapped in the Union Jack. Tomm had never been the tallest, but as I stared at the box I couldn't believe it was big enough to hold him and everything he meant to us. There was no space for the laughs, the banter or the scraps he'd fought. To fit all that in they would have needed a bus, not a hearse.

We knew what we had to do once the hearse arrived, but as Cam stepped forward with me to guide her, I felt every muscle in her body tremble. She stumbled into the bodywork, forehead pressing against the window as she reached to drop her flowers on to the roof. There were so many things I wanted to scratch from my memory about this day, but none of them got close to the noise she made as she stepped back. Neither a sob or a wail: I'd never heard pain like it, could only hope I never would again.

In turn we stepped forward, and paid our respects. It wasn't until I placed my own flowers that I saw the blood on my palm, a thorn dug deep into the skin where I'd pressed without even knowing. I felt guilty for noticing: it was hardly going to kill me.

Finally, with each of us back on the kerb, I heard the hum of the hearse again, another wave of emotion crashing over me.

It could have been tiredness, relief or guilt, but whatever it was, something weird happened as I took one final look at the coffin. For a split second, through the windows of the hearse, I saw Jammy.

He was dressed in his kit, beret sat proudly, face set like stone. There was no mistaking it was him. I stood transfixed as the car edged by, not daring to blink until I clocked him properly. But as the last of the coffin disappeared, so did he. He wasn't there, just another veteran, decked out in his medals, a maroon beret slicked across his head.

It was like one of those comedy moments when you want

to rub your eyes and look again, but there was no point. It wasn't real, but my tears were. They fell so hard I didn't think they would ever stop. There was no faking this kind of pain.

SONNY

I wasn't sure which was worse, grieving in private or in public, but by the time Tommo's funeral was over, some six hours after the parade, I knew I was done in.

Any emotion that we'd hidden from the rest of the town flowed once we were in the crematorium. There weren't many of us invited to watch Tomm's body slide behind the curtains, but I could guarantee none of us would ever forget it.

Mum sat next to me, not a crease on her, but I knew inside she was in absolute chaos, not believing her own son was still alive until she laid eyes on him herself. For both of our sakes I hoped that was soon.

We headed back to Cam's afterwards, to swap stories and eat dry, curling sandwiches. Well, I say 'we', but predictably Larry went missing between the ceremony and the flat, and although we all knew that he'd disappeared to one of his watering holes, none of us commented on it. Let him stay there for as long as he wanted. No one would miss him.

It was dark by the time I left Cam's, my head swimming with the memories of Tommo that we'd dredged up over the afternoon. I was the last to leave. Wiggs had struggled all day, not knowing where to put himself when there were no jokes to be made, so him and Den had disappeared about six-ish. Mum had gone earlier, couldn't afford to miss two shifts in a day. She engulfed me with a hug as she left, like she thought she might never see me again, and as the door closed behind her I felt an overwhelming wave of guilt. It was a day for big emotions.

There was nothing complicated about Cam's day, though, just the most overpowering grief. The tears stopped occasionally, replaced by the briefest of smiles at the thought of Tommo, but they were never far away, so it was no surprise that by eight o'clock she looked like death. Her mum spotted it too, palming one of her sleeping pills with a demand that Cam took it. She didn't need any persuading.

I sat with her when she'd got into bed, stroking her forehead until she dropped off, sleep taking back every line on her face. I'd never felt so relieved to see anyone pass out. I knew I could've stayed, slept on the floor so as not to disturb her, but somehow I needed my own bed. I felt like I should be back when Mum got in from work, in case she needed me. So, as silently as I could, I let myself out and walked across the Ghost, ignoring the usual banter around me as I headed towards the statue.

Flowers had been left for Tommo, notes, even teddies, which seemed a bit weird. The sentiment was right, though: it wasn't like he knew all these people, but maybe they were just grateful for what he'd done, his sacrifice. Either that or they were just relieved it wasn't *their* son who had died.

I stopped and read a few messages, felt myself getting

upset again, got angry, cursed Jamm for not being in touch, then turned for home.

Where was he? It wouldn't take much for him to hammer out a text. It wasn't even like he had to send it to me; Mum would do fine. She just needed to know he was OK. We both did.

All the way home, my head filled with scenarios, the places he could be, each of them disturbing me more and more. By the time I reached our landing I was practically begging him to be OK, promising I'd sort myself out, treat Mum right, whatever it took to have him back and safe, even if it was only for two weeks R&R.

He'd make contact tomorrow, I told myself as I reached for my keys.

I was still telling myself that as I searched my pockets for the fourth time, realizing that I'd left them in Cam's room. With no chance of waking her and no desire to anyway, I was left with three options: sit and wait for Mum, crash at Den's or Wiggy's, or revert to type and use my brains to get in.

It was the easiest decision of the day, made easier when I explained to Old Man Gash next door that I had to borrow his balcony for a minute. The old fool never usually gave me the time of day, but word of what had happened to Tommo had changed things. I was suddenly decent *by association*, so after a quick explanation and a gummy smile from him, he waved me through to the back of his flat.

The gap between balconies was centimetres, so getting between them wasn't a problem. I didn't look down as I scooted over, though, didn't need to be reminded of my run-in with the Cudas. All I hoped was that I'd been the last one through the sliding doors, as I never bothered locking them. What was the point? Anyone with the motivation to climb fifteen storeys of breeze-block and barbed wire deserved a twenty-inch telly. They could have the kettle too. It wasn't like it worked properly.

I felt my heart leap as the door slid open, the first joyful moment of the day. It was warm inside, the central heating from a hundred flats around us toasting ours nicely.

I would've padded straight to bed had I not smelt smoke. I checked the kitchen, but the cooker rings were switched off. Anyway, it wasn't a burning kind of smell; someone was having a cigarette.

I thought of Wiggy instantly. He had a set of keys in case stuff kicked off round his, but he'd been battered by Mum once too often to light up in here.

Next I thought someone must have broken in, but not even the biggest smackhead on the estate would have the balls to smoke while he was on the rob. I felt paranoid; little wonder given the day we'd all had. Picking up the rolling pin from the knife drawer, I tiptoed towards our bedroom, the smell getting stronger. I didn't let my pace drop – if someone was in there, they'd made a massive mistake. With a deep breath I raised my knife arm to shoulder height and piled through the door.

What happened next was a blur. It was dark, but I definitely saw a cig burning. It was attached to a figure that jumped me from behind the door.

I was handy in a scrap, but couldn't get near the speed of this guy. He was so quick I didn't see the arc of his arm as his fist flashed towards me.

I did see one thing, though, before the lights went out. I saw his face, but it wasn't one I was expecting. It didn't belong to a bigger chancer than me, or even to a Ghost estate skaghead.

It belonged to my brother. Jammy was home.

SONNY

I came round to water. Not a reviving cup pressed gently to my lips, but splashes flicked irritably by Jammy's fingers.

A roar of delight left me as I stumbled dizzily to my feet, arms outstretched. But our hug was sad and one-sided; his arms levered me roughly away.

'What were you doing, creeping round in the dark?' he spat. 'I thought you were turning the place over. And what's going on with your hair?'

I ignored the last question, didn't know how to tackle that one.

'I was locked out. Old Man Gash let me in by the balcony, cos I left the sliding door unlocked.' I was rambling, couldn't believe he was here in front of me. 'Anyway, where the hell have *you* been? Mum's been going mental.'

He didn't seem to like the question, let his gaze drop as he wrestled a packet of cigarettes from the pocket of his fatigues, which didn't make a lot of sense: Jammy didn't smoke. Mind you, him smoking seemed like the least of the things I needed answers to.

'Mate, where have you been?' I asked, throwing myself into his arms again and squeezing hard. Not much came back. 'We've been doing our nut about everything. Thought you might be back for today, what with Tomm being . . . well, you know.'

My head flicked back to what I thought I'd seen through the hearse window. I couldn't let it pass. 'You weren't at the parade today . . . were you?'

His eyes told me one thing and his mouth another. 'Course not. I was meant to be, but they let me down. Didn't get me here till an hour ago.'

'So why didn't you ring us? You must have a hundred missed calls.'

'Phone's broke. Just as well by the sounds of it. Not sure I could cope with all the questions.' He tried a smile, but it didn't settle. He just looked sad, among other things.

In fact, he didn't look like Jamm at all. He looked tired, properly wasted, but that wasn't a surprise if he'd been travelling. Add on everything with Tomm and you could forgive him the creases on his face. But he just didn't look right. Didn't have his own uniform on for starters; it looked like he'd picked a bigger one off the peg by mistake. I remembered what basic training had done to him, leaving his arms almost bursting through the seams. But now it sagged at the shoulders, like someone had pricked him with a pin. His punching ability was unaffected, though; it felt like I'd been whacked with an iron bar.

'You're bleeding.' He pointed at my mouth. No offer of a tissue or anything approaching sympathy.

'Well, you didn't exactly give me time to defend myself, did you?'

It was the first time he'd ever laid a hand on me like that.

All right, there'd been scraps, handbags at dawn, but never this. And if I'm honest, it rocked me, my mouth running off stupidly.

'Can't be the first blood you've seen lately either.'

He took a long draw on his cigarette, his hand shaking as it fell.

God, what a stupid thing to say.

'Ignore me,' I cringed. 'That was dumb. I'm just a bit freaked out. We've been . . . well, it's been . . . difficult. You know what I mean, don't you?'

He nodded, didn't need me to go on; I saw a pain that outstretched mine by a mile. Whatever was playing out in his head, I wasn't sure I could cope with knowing about it. Not today.

'How's everyone? Cam OK?' He looked at the clock on the wall and frowned. 'Maybe I should go see her.'

'She's sleeping,' I stumbled, realizing that might sound a bit weird. I should've left it at *she's tired*, or *she's with her mum*. How would I know that kind of detail unless I'd seen it? Would he guess something was going on?

Man, I was tired. My paranoia levels were going mental. I was almost glad when the front door slammed to interrupt us, although the clatter put Jamm back on edge. He'd heard that noise all his life: the door was so warped with age you had to give it a whack to get it shut. But tonight it was enough to have him twitching and stalking towards the hall.

'Relax. It'll only be M– '

But words weren't necessary as Mum appeared in the doorway, her legs buckling like Cam's at the parade when she caught sight of Jammy.

She spoke, her words mangled so badly by tears that I hadn't a clue what she said. She stumbled into him, eyes wide like he was an apparition, arms clinging to his uniform as she wept on his shoulder, repeating again and again 'you're home'.

I was relieved for her, for Jamm, for us all, but the gnarly bit of my head couldn't resist twisting it, shouting that I mattered even less now. Now he was a war hero.

I pushed the resentment away, hating myself for even thinking it.

'Do you have any idea how much I've thought about this?' she asked him, hands cupping his face, eyes scanning him for injuries. You'd have thought he was a kid who'd fallen off his bike, not a squaddie home from war.

'Me too, Mum.' He always did say the right thing.

'And are you all right? You've lost weight. Are you hurt? Do we need to change dressings or anything?'

'Do I look injured?'

Worry flashed across her face but she was hardly going to tell him he looked like death. She'd put him straight by feeding him within an inch of his life. He'd be in elasticated trousers within a week.

'You look tired. When did you last sleep? Or eat?'

'I've not stopped eating since we hit the UK. The chocolate over there is rubbish.'

She grabbed him by the hand and pretended to scold him, slapping at his palm as she walked him towards the kitchen.

'Well, that's no good, is it? Let me make you something. We should have a drink. I would've had more in if we'd known . . . we should have been sorted . . . organized a party, or something.'

Jamm's face fell. A shadow covering all of it.

'And who would we invite?' he asked, words emotionless. 'Cam and her folks?'

Mum covered her mouth with her hands like she was trying to cram the idea back in. 'I'm sorry, love, I didn't think.'

But then Jamm did something I'd never seen before. Something I never thought he'd ever do. He laid into her. 'No, really, it's a great idea,' he spat, reaching for the phone. 'Let's give them a buzz and get them over. Larry's bound to have a bottle of something cheap. We can all have a glass while I tell them how I killed their son.'

Silence. Just the sound of Jamm's breath from the exertion. Mum flushed bright red, then stepped towards him, arms held out.

'I'm sorry. I didn't mean it like it sounded. I'm just so relieved.' Her eyes filled up but it didn't help. 'We didn't know what had happened. I thought they weren't telling us something, maybe something had happened to you too.'

'Do I look injured?' he yelled.

I told him to calm down and for a moment thought there was a second fist coming my way. But instead he kept his focus on Mum and carried on his rant.

'I'm fine, aren't I? And know why? Because bullets slide off me. I'm invincible. That's why they got Tomm instead. Because of me.'

Maybe it was his aggression, but that comment ignited Mum's fire too.

'Hey, that's enough of that! Everyone knows what you did for Tommo. How you shot back, how you tried to keep him alive. It's not just us that knows it either. It's Cam and her folks, everyone on the estate knows what a hero you . . . '

'Don't you dare call me that!' he roared, voice catching in the back of his throat. 'Not to me or anyone else. Because that's not who I am. You hear me?'

It's not often I find myself silent. More often than not *I'm* the one spewing that kind of bile, waiting for a carpeting from Jamm for my efforts. But there was no way I was going to tell him to calm down. My mouth was still stinging from ten minutes ago.

Instead I stood, slack-jawed, as he turned and ran past me in the direction of our room. A gust of wind whipped us both as the door swung shut, blowing me to Mum's side, holding her up as she sobbed.

Jammy McGann was home and safe, but it wasn't the glorious homecoming any of us had hoped for.

SONNY

We sat for a while, Mum and me.

But no matter how many times she asked me, I didn't have an answer to the question that troubled her most.

Do you think he's OK?

My head was too mashed to know what my own name was, never mind anything else. So I sat there and listened, filling Mum's cup when it was empty, nodding at what I hoped were the right bits. In the end, though, I could feel my nose edging closer to the table and she insisted I took myself off to bed.

But as I headed to our room, Jamm was coming the other way, towards Mum. I stopped, wondered if I should follow him, but after a pat on my shoulder (it beat another right hook) and a 'Sorry, pal' I decided to keep on walking. The walls were thin enough to listen in if I wanted to anyway.

I didn't spend the next half-hour with a cup to the wall, but the conversation seemed to take a far less shouty route. It wasn't without emotion: Mum's sobbing filled the whole flat, but it was Jammy's responses that brought the relief. No yelling or explosions, just the even tone that we were all used to. It allowed me to lie on my bed, rather than pace the floor, and think about what it meant to have him home.

I suppose most sixteen-year-olds would be hacked off to lose the privacy of their own room, but sharing a room with Jamm had never bothered me. The council weren't in the habit of dishing out three-bedroom gaffs with en-suites, so this was how it had always been. In fact, I'd slept way worse while Jamm had been away. There was no humming from the bunk above to hypnotize me and after sixteen years I missed it. I reckon if I hadn't replaced that with Cam's breath whistling in my ear, I wouldn't have had a decent night in the whole time he'd been gone.

I had got a bit weird about Jamm's bunk while he was away. I don't know if it was superstition, but I hadn't let anyone sleep or lie on it. Wiggs had crashed over a few times and looked at me like I was a loon when I told him he had to sleep on the floor. He was even unhappier when I stopped him using Jammy's duvet, instead giving him a scratchy blanket that looked like it had been knitted from barbed wire.

Even when Cam stayed and we had the option of creating a double mattress on the floor, I chose not to. Not because of the 'no sisters' pact; it just didn't feel right. As long as Jamm's bunk stayed intact and where it was, then somehow he was going to be all right.

Staring at the underside of his mattress, hearing his muffled voice from underneath the door, was enough to rock me gently and force my brain to finally switch off.

That should've been it. Eight hours of unbroken bliss. But it wasn't, because just as the night was at its darkest, I was rocketed awake by a scream from above.

I sat bolt upright, grazing my skull on the slats of Jamm's

bunk. There wasn't time to think about the pain, though, as the noise above me filled my head.

What made it worse was that the racket came with movement: a rocking that sent the bunks swaying like a rowing boat in the middle of the Atlantic. Fearing we were about to topple over, I staggered to the floor and peered at Jamm's bunk. I couldn't make much out, but I could see his outline, duvet tangled around him, squeezing him like a snake as he writhed and bucked. I had no idea what he was dreaming about; wasn't sure I wanted to know either.

It's hard to think clearly in the middle of the night when your head's screaming for sleep, but I couldn't ignore him. I could've pulled my duvet through to the lounge, but there was no way I could leave him. There was too much violence in his movements. So, climbing the ladder, I tried to separate him from his sheets.

The duvet clung to him like ivy, and my clumsy fingers seemed to only tie him up tighter. The only option was to roll him and hope he unravelled that way, but as my fingers made contact with his burning-hot shoulders, it broke him from his dream, eyes flying open, pupils glowing in the dark.

I'm sure someone told me once that it's dangerous to wake people when they're dreaming, that it can mess with their head. Well, in that second, I wished I'd listened, as without warning Jamm's arms shot towards me, his hands wrapping around my throat as we tumbled from the bunk to the carpet below. The impact winded me, but there wasn't time to whine or whinge. If I didn't get him off me quickly, I wouldn't have the breath to make any noise at all.

I tried to tell him it was me, but got nowhere. My gasping

didn't reach him. So I had no option but to fight back, ramming my hands under his chin and trying to force his head back to break his grasp. At first I thought it might work, his hands weakening enough to let a shot of air down my throat. But with a vicious shake of his head, he broke free, leaning right into my face as his hands tightened again.

'You killed him,' he spat. 'You killed him.'

Fear flooded me: I hadn't a clue who this was I was fighting. Jamm's dog-tags were dangling on my face as he squeezed, but this wasn't my brother.

'Jamm. Let go. Let go!'

His cheeks bulged with exertion as his knuckles strained harder.

'I should've done this weeks ago,' he was hissing. 'For killing him. For killing Wayne.'

Who? There were plenty of kids knocking about on the Ghost called that, but none we'd had any issue with.

'It's me, Jamm. It's me. It's Sonny. Look!'

I saw his eyes widen, adding to the madness, before narrowing again. There was no sign of life or love anywhere in them. It was like he was on autopilot, doing what he had to do, what I guessed the army had trained him to do. Kill.

I just couldn't understand why it had to be me.

It was getting desperate, his thumbs pressing harder on to my Adam's apple. I felt the room darken. I had one last chance to get him off me. It wasn't the kind of move I wanted to pull, but he left me with no choice. So with every single ounce of strength I had, I swung my right arm, slamming it hard into his kidneys.

The effect was instant. With a howl, he rolled to the side,

and I gave him another shove before wriggling away, to the other side of the room.

As I crouched against the radiator, lungs heaving and sweating furiously, I watched him roll around, words spewing from his mouth. At times I heard that name again. Wayne. Or thought I did. It was so mixed up in other mutterings that I might have got it all wrong.

A minute passed, then two, his body straightening, becoming still. Part of me wanted to rush over, check he was OK, but the survivor in me said *no way*, I didn't fancy feeling that power again.

Instead I waited until his only movements were the slow, constant risings of his chest, hard evidence that he was asleep. Then, and only then, I tiptoed over, draping his duvet over him before returning for my own. Wrapping it around me to squash my shaking, I headed for the door. There was no way I was sleeping in there tonight. Not until I had a clue what was going on.

Instead I walked past Mum's door, fighting the urge to wake her and tell her what had just happened.

Would she believe me?

Think I'd provoked him?

Probably.

It was the only answer I needed to keep me walking straight past her room into the lounge, jamming a chair behind the door.

It had been the longest and worst day of my life. No way was I making it worse by allowing my brother, or whoever that was in there, to finish me off properly.

SONNY

I woke to three things:

1. An unfamiliar bed (well, a settee)
2. A cricked neck (caused by number 1)
3. A raging hunger (caused by the most ridiculously over-powering smell of food from the kitchen).

Numbers one and two were sort of forgotten thanks to number three. I presumed the smell of food had been made by Mum, backed up by her face half hidden behind a pile of bacon sandwiches.

'You never cooked like this when it was just you and me,' I grunted, then felt bad, remembering her tears.

'Wasn't me this morning either,' she answered. 'You can thank your brother.'

The mention of Jamm shook the remains of sleep off me.

Instinctively, my hands went to my neck. Was it sore, bruised? It'd explain how stupidly stiff it felt.

'Slept funny?'

There was a lot I could've told her then, but settled for a nod and a little bit of the truth. 'Kipped on the settee.'

'Why did you do that?'

I shrugged, building up the lie in my head. 'Couldn't sleep.' Unlikely after yesterday, but it was all I had. 'Didn't want to keep Jamm awake, so I got my head down in the lounge.'

She stared at me with a look I wasn't used to. I couldn't be sure, but I think she might have been impressed. 'You big softie,' she laughed, reaching for a sandwich. 'You want to be careful behaving like this. People might start thinking you like them.'

'I'm not a complete horror show, you know.'

She laughed at me. 'Obviously. But I reckon you've got Cam to thank for that.'

I said nothing. Why was it I wanted everyone to know about us (I'd tie a gigantic banner between the high rises so I didn't have to sneak around any more), but as soon as my own mother made reference to it I wanted to hide behind a mountain of bread and pig? I made a note to have a word with myself later on, when I'd finally stopped blushing.

'You know, you're going to have to mention it to Jamm at some point, about you and Cameron.'

'What about us?'

How lame did that sound?

'Oh, give over, Sonny. I know all about the pact you boys have about sisters.'

'Do you?'

'You think I sit here and cover my ears when you talk all your rubbish? I could humiliate you all for the rest of your lives, the stuff I've heard over the years.'

My head scrambled, thinking about the other gems she could've picked up. She could probably have filled a book with them. Still, if she had heard, then she might be able to help me this time.

'And how do you reckon Jamm'll react? You know, when we tell him?'

She thought about it for a good couple of mouthfuls, only answering when she'd washed them down with a glug of tea. 'He's just spent three months in the worst place on earth. He's seen things that we clearly haven't a clue about, and to make it worse, he's had his best mate die in his arms. I'd have thought you snogging Tommo's sister will barely scratch the surface, to be honest.'

It wasn't often she put me at ease, but she'd managed it this time, letting me return to Jammy as the topic of conversation. I wanted to know if he'd freaked *her* out last night too.

But, surprisingly enough, he hadn't. After his first outburst, he'd come back and apologized, sat long enough with a cup of tea for Mum to put his outburst down to a long journey and a mountain of stress.

Looked like he'd saved up the big amounts of crazy for me in the middle of the night. God knows what was in store from him next.

'So do you think he's all right, then?'

'I would imagine he's feeling pretty awful, especially to miss Tommo's ceremonies like he did. I just don't think we should push him, or ask too much about what happened. If he wants to tell us, he will. Let's give him time to get his feet under the table, realize he's home instead of there.'

I know I should've told her about the stuff that went on later. If ever there was a time, that was probably it. But to see her with it all so straight in her head, and knowing that it was only two weeks before he was off again? Well, I wasn't that heartless, despite what you might think of me. I had to chalk it up to over-tiredness or grief or whatever.

'Where is he anyway? He not eating?'

'Said he already had. Then he nipped out for a walk.'

'A walk? Has he forgotten where he lives? It's hardly the Dales, is it?'

'Listen, we've no idea what it's been like for him. By the look on his face this morning, your brother's clearly missed it here. Maybe he wanted to catch up with the others, or Cam, I don't know. He probably has a lot to talk to them about.'

My stomach tightened at the thought of him seeing Cam without me. She wouldn't come clean on her own – would she? I could imagine the grief I'd get from Jamm if he reckoned I was hiding behind her.

I grabbed a wedge of sandwiches and slurped some tea that my throat wasn't ready for. 'I should go and find him,' I gasped. 'See you in a bit.'

'Don't be disappearing for the rest of the day. I'll be cooking for us all later.'

'All of us? Den and Wiggy might already have plans.'

Her lips tightened. 'Don't be bringing those clowns round here tonight. They might think they live here, but your brother needs some time while he's home to relax. Tonight's about the three of us.'

I nodded and smiled. Balancing the sarnies in one hand and my trainers in the other, I left her to her plans of a cosy family reunion.

The Ghost buzzed as I walked and ate. Stuff passed from palm to palm. The place was the same as always, unlike the brother who'd come back to it. Easing my neck around in small circles, I was desperate to talk to him about it, check he was all right, but then I had Mum's voice in my ear, telling me not to overload him with questions. And anyway, if he was *that* stressed, what was he capable of doing when he was awake instead of asleep?

It was stupid, I know, he was my brother, but after the funeral I was feeling properly ragged. So much so that I craved some company. I felt myself reaching for my phone and texting the lads.

JAMM'S HOME

No exclamation or smiley faces, just a demand to meet me by the statue as soon as possible. Both came back to me in seconds. It wasn't like I had to pull them out of board meetings. Their diaries were generally as empty as a skaghead's wallet.

They arrived together, eyeing my sandwich enviously.

'When did he get back?' Wiggy asked, blowing celebratory smoke rings.

'Last night.'

'And you didn't call us?' moaned Den.

'It was late . . . and he was, er, tired, you know.'

How did you word it, when you didn't understand it yourself?

Questions followed, loads of them. Most of which I had no answers to.

How was he? Was he back for good? Did he mention Tomm and what had happened?

By the time their mouths closed, my head was spinning.

'Look, I don't know all this, do I? He was knackered when he got in and a bit . . . lairy.'

'Lairy? What do you mean?' asked Wiggy.

'I don't know, do I? It probably had a bit to do with his best mate dying on him. Tends to weigh on your mind, that sort of stuff.'

Den could see I was stressed out and pulled Wiggs into line with a cuff to the back of his head.

'He'll be all right, Sonny. Just give him time. You didn't mention Hitch, did you?'

Hitch. I hadn't even thought to mention what had gone on there. Couldn't imagine how Jamm might react, apart from blaming me for it.

I felt like screaming. There was too much going on. I didn't have a clue if I could juggle it all without going completely mad myself.

 SONNY

We wandered for ages. Looked in all the obvious places: the shops, caff, statue, but there was no sign of him. We even tried Cam's flat, despite the chance of interrupting the most difficult conversation imaginable.

How would Larry react to seeing Jamm in the flesh?

How would Jamm react if Cam let slip about us?

I knew he'd see it as a betrayal, but I needed to be there myself. At least then I could tell him the truth.

Anyway, all the wondering was pointless: the door was locked and the flat silent. Cam's mobile went to answerphone and she didn't call back.

My head threw up stupid thoughts, remembering her face when I came in with my bleached hair, the comment about looking just like Jamm. I hoped the sight of him in person didn't make her realize she'd picked the wrong brother.

The thought got to me, making me irritable, especially by late afternoon, when people started coming up to me, congratulating me about Jamm. It was weird. With some it was just a nod; others wanted to shake my hand, tell me that I must be proud, how much I had to live up to.

I hadn't a clue how to react. Course I was proud of him – what he'd done was amazing, typical of everything he was – but I was torn too.

Spending sixteen years being 'not as good as Jammy' was bad enough, but usually I was only having those conversations with myself. Now it was happening with the majority of the estate.

What would tomorrow bring? A billboard with our faces on it, a red cross through mine and a tick next to his?

All right, I was being paranoid. But why were *so* many people wanting a piece of him all of a sudden?

The answer came when we looped back to Mr De Mel's shop and saw the newsboard for the paper outside. The headline told it all.

WAR HEROES COME HOME

Word was out there. People knew what had happened.

The article was the usual local rag stuff. How proud they were about the town's involvement in the war and the turnout at the repatriation, but they hadn't bothered speaking to anyone who really mattered. They went on about Tommo growing up on the Ghost, but there was no comment from his mum or Cam. If they'd've asked Larry, he'd have demanded beer money, so maybe it was just as well.

They led with two grainy headshots that must have come from army records. They didn't even bother to put their names underneath, just a brief caption per soldier. Under Tommo's it read: KILLED IN ACTION. Could you believe that? Did they have to be so cold? Did Cam need that line to really up her grieving? Unbelievable.

For Jammy it was different: HERO was stamped beneath his photo. It matched the intensity on his face, a look that said no Afghan terrorist was going to get past him.

The report made sure there was no doubt about Jammy's actions. Went into depth about the ferocity of the firefight, the courage they showed despite the lives being lost. Thirty insurgents against two soldiers.

If there was one thing to be grateful for, it was the lack of information about Tomm's shooting. They praised his intelligence in tracking down the heart of the terrorist cell, but offered no details of the sniper attack that wounded him. Instead they focused on Jammy's bravery under fire.

'Our local hero not only managed to repel the rebels, killing one in the process, but also tried valiantly to resuscitate his best friend. He did not leave Private Thompson's side until other members of his unit reached them, too late to offer medical assistance.'

The paper called for both of the men to be honoured by the town, stating the paper was planning a campaign of its own to further the cause.

My heart sank. Not because it wasn't what Jammy deserved. If the details were right, they should fly a flag with his face on from the top of the highest block. What worried me was what he would do when he saw it. A mention from his own mother about being a hero had sent him off on one. I didn't know what he'd do when a whole town started to congratulate him instead.

I didn't have to wait long to find out. By the time we'd all read and re-read the article, wiping at rogue bits of dust that were making our eyes water, we spotted him walking across the estate, hands thrust into his pockets.

There were probably two hundred metres between us and him, but after five minutes he was only about thirty paces closer. With every step he was greeted by a new face, another handshake, someone desperate to tell him they'd read his story in the paper.

The only time his pace changed was when he approached the statue of the soldiers; with a brief gap between locals he pushed his chin into the front of his hoodie and powered on. His eyes never left the ground from that moment until the statue was behind him. It was a small thing to notice, and I doubt the others even saw it, but it was significant to me, especially when he straightened up once out of its shadow.

The banter began: Wiggy dashing towards him demanding his autograph, Den struggling to match his pace. My pulse quickened, worrying how he'd react to them, but to my relief I saw Jamm's face fall into a wide smile, squeezing Wiggs affectionately as they embraced. Den didn't even bother letting Wiggy move out of the way, sandwiching him as he hugged Jammy too. There was deafening laughter and so much relief that I wanted a piece of it. With a running jump I launched myself on top of them: Tomm and Hitch might have been missing, but we had to celebrate however we could.

It didn't take long before my weight sent everyone to the ground, Wiggs whimpering from the middle of the pile. After a lot of wailing everyone rolled away and let him fill up with air, the look of delight returning to his face when he saw Jamm again.

'Gave us a shock, you did,' Wiggs gasped.

'How do you think it was for me?' Jamm was clearly saving his best mood for the lads.

'We're just glad you're home,' blushed Den, never usually one for emotional outbursts. 'Missed, you were. Both of you.'

The vague mention of Tommo drove smiles off faces and left us all gasping for what to say next. Fortunately another Jammy fan-boy saved us the bother.

'I saw what you did in the paper,' the guy said with a swagger. He was probably late thirties, tattoos crowding every inch of skin. 'You should be proud.'

I turned to Jamm, who managed a smile between clenched teeth.

'Want a smoke?' the man offered, obviously wanting to get into conversation. Jamm accepted reluctantly, before Wiggs decided to have some fun.

'Er, hang on there. You can't go around offering the talent your cigarettes. I'm his representative. Twenty per cent of everything comes my way. You want a piece of him, you talk to me first.' He'd tacked on what I guessed was a New York accent, like he was some big-shot dealmaker.

The guy looked at him like he was mental, then turned again to Jammy.

'Anyway. Take care, son. People round here won't forget what you did.' And as he walked away he motioned to the statue, which brought a wince to Jammy's face.

'Let's get inside, shall we?' he said. 'Somewhere I don't have to listen to idiots like that.'

'I've some cans back at mine,' chipped in Den, which had

me cringing. No way Jamm would be up for getting smashed. There was nothing to celebrate.

But I was wrong again.

'Perfect.' And with a turn straight from his drills we were marching back to Den's. We all had a thirst on, but from Jammy's pace, we were in no doubt whose throat was the driest.

SONNY

Jamm swallowed a burp before letting his can join the others on the floor.

It took effort to lean forward and grab another one, but it didn't stop him draining half of it in one go. I thought about moving the box of beers closer to him, or maybe just setting up a drip into his arm. Anything to make the process easier.

'A few beers' had turned into a session, with Den dispatched to fetch more when the first case ran out. And now, four hours in, we were close to running dry again. Well, we were if the alcohol-coma didn't grab us first.

For once, though, the thought of getting legless didn't float my boat. Not like it did my brother's.

Jammy was no angel, it wasn't like he didn't let go or blow off steam like the rest of us, but late-afternoon benders weren't usually his thing. He preferred to drink over a card game, reckoned it gave him the edge when it came to clearing us out of whatever cash we had.

It wasn't like this session was filling him with the joys of spring either. There was banter – how could there not be with Wiggy in the room? – but there was also an uneasy feeling among us. We all had questions we wanted to ask, but nobody really had the balls to put them out there. Wiggs had asked the normal ridiculous stuff at first: *How many bodies did you see? Did you go in a tank, or parachute anywhere?*

Jamm fobbed him off with answers that gave nothing away.

'Parachute? No, but I did bungee jump behind enemy lines. Gives you the real element of surprise, that does.'

Wiggs howled, not knowing after four cans of cheap, strong lager whether he was hearing the truth or not. Nothing really mattered to him as long as he was laughing.

Den was at the other end of the spectrum. Tomm's death had ripped at him harder than I'd thought, so every question he fired linked into that.

He wanted to know if the medics had tried to revive him, and how long for. How did they move his body with all the fighting around him? It was like he had to know the details to move on; to his credit, Jamm answered every one. I watched him fidget and squirm as he spoke, breaking up each answer with a long pull from his can. I wondered if the words would've come at all without the help of the beer.

And as for me? Well, the questions were stacking up so high in my head that they'd already fallen over twice, leaving me to shuffle and re-sort them into order. But there was one that always found its way back to the top.

'You been to see Cam yet?' I tried to sound casual.

He nodded as he drank. 'Went this morning.'

'And?'

'And what?'

'How did it go?'

'Do we have to talk about this now?'

'Why not?'

He put his can down on the arm of the chair and leaned clumsily forwards, looking confused.

'Why is it so important that you know?'

'Isn't it obvious?' I said, although my reasons were actually purely selfish. 'Because she's our friend and Tomm was her brother. And because we had to stand there on the roadside next to her as they drove him past in a coffin.'

I saw Jamm flinch but he didn't back off. 'Yeah, well, we all have to do things we don't want to, don't we?'

I knew what he was getting at. That I'd never pulled my weight like him.

Well, no one asked him to play the big man and sign up, did they?

Normally I would've sucked it up and moved on, but with the beer sloshing around my head I got lazy, pushing myself off the settee and chucking my can at his feet. It was empty, but the message was the same.

'What, like sitting here listening to you?' I didn't mean it, but my head was so mashed I couldn't help it.

'What is your problem, Sonny? I don't get why me seeing Cam is causing you such grief.'

I wanted to tell him about Cam and me, that we were tight, but I just wasn't brave enough. Instead, the barriers went up and I laced into him.

'I don't care who you see. I just want you to talk to me like you do everyone else. I'm not something you've stepped in, you know.'

'You reckon? Cos right now, Sonny, your attitude stinks.'

That was it, all I needed to get into his space.

Within seconds we were chest to chest, arguing like a couple of kids, until Den forced his way between us using his bulk as a barrier.

'What is it with you?' He wasn't finding being the meat in the sandwich easy, so blamed me. 'Your brother's just come home, you idiot. Back off!'

'Oh aye, that's right. It's always me causing the trouble, isn't it? Always me being aggressive. Well, why don't you ask him about last night, then? Ask him to explain what he did.'

'Why, what went on?'

'I lamped him,' interrupted Jamm. 'The idiot lost his keys and broke in, so I decked him, thinking he was a burglar.'

The one person finding all this funny was Wiggs, spluttering from behind his hand. 'You knocked out your own brother?'

'Wasn't a patch on what I'll do in a minute.'

'Or what you did afterwards, eh?' He'd pushed too far, I couldn't help but bring up what happened when the lights had gone off.

He looked confused. 'What are you on about now?'

I should've backed down, waited until we were on our own, but I couldn't stop myself.

'He nearly took my head off in the middle of the night. Was having some kind of weird dream and when I tried to sort him out he nearly strangled me to death.'

Laughter wasn't exactly the response I was after, but it was all I got: from all three of them.

'Priceless,' wailed Den. 'That's just what I'd do after shooting at the Taliban for months. Top of the list when I get home? Strangle my little brother!'

'Go on, take his side. I knew you would. Just remember who's kept you in beers for the last few months.'

Den put me quickly back in my box.

'Sonny, get a hold of yourself, you sound like a whinging kid. Can't you just be pleased Jamm's safe? For once stop trying to compete!' He was backing me off now, away from Jamm. 'And anyway, we can talk about things all you want. Talk about the stuff that didn't quite go to plan as well if you like?'

Jamm drained the last of his can and looked interested. 'Why, what else has been going on?'

'Nothing,' I snapped.

'Plenty,' laughed Wiggs.

'You can shut up as well,' I shot at him. Why was I suddenly the big enemy?

'We got into a few rucks,' started Den.

'What kind of rucks?' Jamm leaned down for another can.

'The tasty kind. And things got a bit messy, with, er, with Hitch.'

Jamm did a comedy look around the room, like he'd only just realized someone was missing. He was leathered.

'Where is Hitch anyway?' he slurred. 'He should be here.'

'That's just it,' offered Wiggs. 'Nobody knows.'

That was it for me. I knew exactly where this was going and where it'd end up. With me in the dock again.

'Do we have to do this now?' I asked. 'Jamm's battered. We'll only have to tell him again tomorrow . . .'

'Tell me now.' His eyes weren't focusing, but his brain wanted details.

'Sonny had this idea, you see . . . ' started Wiggy, a sentence that had me heading to the door.

'Knackers to this. I know what happens so you can get on with it. I'll be downstairs waiting when you've finished. Come and give me a kicking then if you want.'

It was childish, I know, but I'd had enough. All right, it might have been my fault, all of it, but I didn't need reminding. So, stropping like a five-year-old, I grabbed a beer and stormed through the door.

I stood on the walkway for half an hour, sipping a can I didn't want, waiting for grief I didn't fancy much either. But by the time the beer was gone, I was still on my own. So, with curiosity nibbling, I went back inside to find Jamm comatose on the settee, a manky old blanket thrown on top of him.

'All too much for him, was it?' I asked sheepishly.

'Dunno,' shrugged Den. 'He took it all in. Wasn't too happy about it. Wanted to get out there and find him.'

'Only problem was,' butted in Wiggs, 'he was too drunk to stand up. He tried a few times but couldn't manage a step. Two minutes later he was asleep.'

I sighed and rubbed at my head. 'I should try and get him home.'

'Are you mad? Take one of his tanks to lift him up. Leave him here to sleep it off.'

'And what do I tell Mum?'

'Do what you always do.'

'What's that?'

'Spin her a line. Lie.'

I laughed, but it wasn't funny. I could do that. Course I could. Without breaking sweat. But I didn't want to, not this time. It was all beginning to wear a bit thin.

SONNY

It must have been one hell of a hangover, as for the next two days Jammy went AWOL. And you can imagine how well *that* went down with Mum. About as well as a cup of cold sick.

The first morning she was mildly irritated, not that he'd been drinking ('If anyone deserves a blow out it's Jammy'), but by the fact that I hadn't brought him home with me.

'Could you not look after *him* for once?' she'd moaned. 'The lad's slept in barracks for the past three months. He should be resting in his own bed.'

Part of me wanted to tell her he was tucked up safely on Den's settee, but that would only earn me more grief. She always moaned about how dirty his place was.

'He's nearly nineteen. He wanted to keep on drinking. I didn't.'

'You're sixteen. *You* shouldn't have been drinking at all!'

I gave her my finest look and reached for my jacket from the back of the chair.

'Where are you off to?'

'Out.'

'Where to?'

'To find him.'

'Tell him to ring me . . . '

'If I find him I'll push him back in a diamond-encrusted wheelchair. Good enough for you?'

'Just bring him home, will you? He's done the same for you often enough.'

I closed the door behind me, felt the pressure of her words, and headed immediately for Cam's. It'd only been thirty-six hours, but it felt like more.

By the time I crossed the estate it felt like another thirty-six hours had passed.

Jamm's fame had spread beyond the local paper to regional telly. Turns out coming home a live war hero, instead of a dead one, was a real turn-up for the books.

The evening news had run a piece covering both Tommo's parade and Jamm's exploits, and you wouldn't believe the number of people who walked up to me, not just to say they'd seen the piece, but that they knew Jamm had been destined for great things.

I tried to be civil. Wasn't like I wasn't proud too, but by the time the tenth old bloke came up to me, I felt about two feet tall in comparison.

'Taught him everything he knows,' I bragged. 'Those moves he pulled on al-Qaeda? All came from me.' They soon shuffled off once I threw a sequence of intentionally rubbish karate kicks in their direction.

It felt good to have a smile back on my face, but I was soon crashing back down when Cam opened the door, her face as pale as it had been when I saw her last.

She was stripped of make-up, but she'd cried so much it

was like the tears had scarred her face, long tracks stretching from the corner of her eyes until they disappeared at her chin.

'Hello, gorgeous,' I whispered, trying a weak smile and meaning every word. Even at her worst she still took my breath away. I just wished I could say it without sounding like a sleaze.

Taking her hand, which felt like paper, I led her through to the silence of the lounge. Even the clock had stopped ticking, either out of respect, or fear of Larry.

'Your dad in?' I asked, slightly apprehensive.

She shook her head, her voice raspy, like the crying had bruised her throat too.

'Not since you left. Just as well. God knows what he would've done when Jammy was here.'

'He said he'd been round. I'm sorry I wasn't here. I didn't know he was coming, otherwise I would've . . . '

She sat slowly, cutting me off mid-stream. 'It's probably just as well you weren't here really.'

I knew what she meant, or part of me did. The rational part, but that was being sat on by about three tons of irrational stuff, which instantly took over.

'What do you mean by that?'

Cam lifted her eyes from the tissue she'd been wrapping round her fingers. I must have looked massively hacked off.

'Don't be like that, Sonny. You know what I mean.'

'No, I don't know. I'm confused, I thought you could lean on me . . . '

'And I can, but me and Mum needed to see Jamm too. You get that, don't you? He was the last one to see Tomm. We needed to hear things from him . . . '

'Course you did.' I could literally feel the blood simmering as it zipped round my body, but instead of recognizing that and backing off, I ploughed on. 'And what did he say to you?'

I saw a new emotion spark in her eyes as she pushed herself upwards, wrestling for my hands, which I wouldn't give her.

'Sonny, you're being ridiculous. There was nothing that you're imagining. He told us what it was like to see his mate, my brother, die in front of him. Now that might not mean much to you, but it did to me and Mum. Brave, it was.'

'Oh yeah, that sums him up perfectly. Everyone's favourite hero, is Jammy.'

Any attempt from her to touch me stopped.

'I can't believe you're being like this.'

'Like what?'

'Jealous, Sonny. You're acting like a kid. This is your brother we're talking about. The one who's always stood up for you, for all of us.'

'I'm sorry,' I tried, not really meaning it. 'I'm not jealous. I'm just freaked out by it all.'

'You're freaked out? It's not your brother who's been killed, is it?' I thought she was going to be sick at saying the word. 'You should think about everything you've still got!'

'That's just it, though, Cam. I'm worried. There's something going on with Jamm.'

'What do you mean?'

'The way he's acting. It's not like him.'

'And that's a surprise? It's only a week since everything happened. Wouldn't you be a bit freaked out?'

'Probably, but it's more than that. How many times have you seen Jamm use his fists in his life? How many times has he *really* lost his rag?'

'I don't know.'

'Well, think about it.'

'I don't know, Sonny. Not many. Five or six?'

'First night back he went for me *twice*.'

'The way you've hacked me off today I don't blame him.'

I jumped on her. 'Come on, Cam, *please*, listen to me. It's not what Jammy does, is it? Despite everything that goes on round here, it's *never* been his way. That's why it's weird. First he lamps me because he thinks I'm a burglar. All right, I get that. But second time, *in the middle of the night*, and completely unprovoked, he tries to strangle me.'

'What do you mean, strangle you?'

'Exactly that. He was having a dream. Rolling around and moaning about Tomm and some bloke called Wayne.'

'So he was having a nightmare. It happens.'

'But that's just it. In the end, he wasn't sleeping. He was looking straight at me. He might not have known where he was, but he knew he was strangling someone. You can't tell me that's normal?'

'Course it's not, but he must have had a reason. What did he say about it?'

'Well, nothing. I haven't spoken to him about it.'

She was losing patience with me quickly. It looked like she could barely keep her eyes open either.

'So, something happens that *really* freaks you out. Your brother tries to throttle you and you don't mention it to him? Yeah, that makes sense.'

'No, it doesn't. None of it does. All I know is that my brother's back, and everyone wants to either kiss his back-end or protect it. It's like I can't say anything that might upset him, even though I can see things aren't right. Why won't anyone believe me?'

Cam let out a long, slow breath, sagging as the air fell from her. 'I can't do this now, Sonny. But to me it sounds like Jamm's not the only one who's confused. If you're worried about him, do something about it. Talk to him, talk to your mum.'

'Yeah, that'll help.'

'Sonny, get over yourself!' she snapped. 'The only one seeing these problems is you, and you won't do anything about it but sulk. Well, that won't help me, and I need help. I need you, and I need Jammy. So sort it out.'

I couldn't believe what I was hearing. 'What do you mean you need him? You've got me.'

'But sometimes, Sonny, that's just not enough. Maybe Jamm understands some things that you don't.'

'Sounds to me like you've made up your mind.'

'About what?'

'About which brother really matters to you.'

She threw her arms in the air with such force that I thought she was about to take off.

'Sonny, I'm not doing this. Not now. This is *your* issue, not mine. Don't you think I've got enough to deal with?'

She turned for the door, and in that second I realized I was about three steps away from wrecking everything.

'Cam, I'm sorry,' I babbled, stopping the door before she could open it. She didn't bother turning to face me. 'I'm an idiot.'

'That's just it, though, Sonny, you're not. You just behave like one. You really think I'd be with you if I thought otherwise?'

'Then I'll sort it out. I promise.'

'There's nothing to sort except your own head. If you think there's a problem with Jammy then deal with it. I can't do it for you.'

'No, you're right. I will, and I'll tell him about us too. Soon as he surfaces.'

The look she gave me wasn't the one I expected. 'You really think that's the priority right now?' She reached for the door again. 'Look, I need to sleep.'

'Then let me stay. Just till you drop off.'

'No. I think you should go.' Finally she turned, the smile on her face weak. 'For now. Don't you?'

I should've told her it was fine, that she was right, shown some sense for once. But I didn't. Instead I defaulted to idiot Sonny, scowling at her before heading for the front door.

And do you know what I thought as it slammed behind me?

I bet Jammy's already in her room. That's why she wants me out.

That's how wrong I got it. That's what an idiot I really was.

SONNY

Cam's words looped in my head for the next day and a half.

Sort it out.

Talk to Jammy.

Sound advice if he was around, but he wasn't. So instead of talking to him about what had gone on, I was left to try and calm Mum down. If people thought I was losing the plot, they should have taken a look in her direction.

She was still going to work, but would turn up back at the flat between shifts, just in case he was back. And when he wasn't? Her paranoia got worse.

'Where has he got to? Have you tried his mobile again?'

'It's off, Mum. Same as before.'

Round in a circle we went, every conversation we had making our fears worse and worse, until finally, when he did show up, we didn't know whether to kiss his face or hit it.

In fact, scratch that, as from the state of him there was no way I was putting my lips anywhere near him. It's hard to sum up just how lousy he looked, but I couldn't help but see him in my head when he left for Afghanistan, every inch of him pressed and slick.

The only slick thing about him now was the grease that clung to his hair. The rest of him needed sealing in concrete and dumping in the North Sea. His clothes hung limply off him and stains littered his shirt, some of which looked like blood, though it could've easily been chilli sauce.

'Jammy!' Mum cried, almost tipping the kitchen table on top of me, tea and all. 'Are you all right?'

He obviously realized how rank he looked as he held his hands in front of him, warding her off. 'I'm fine, Mum, honest. I . . . er . . . lost track of time.' His grin was cheeky: he knew exactly what he was doing and how easily he could win her over.

'Are you hungry? I can rustle up some tea if you like.'

'Or he could just lick his t-shirt. Looks like there's half a kebab still on it.' It was my lame attempt at a joke to smooth things over, but I doubted it sounded that way.

'I'm not hungry, honest. Listen, sorry for disappearing. Wasn't like I intended to. I just needed to blow off some steam and when I ran into some old mates things got a bit out of hand.'

He said it so easily it was hard not to believe him, but then again I had no idea who the 'old mates' were. Den and Wiggs had seen nothing of him. So unless he'd bumped into Hitch I knew he was being selective with the truth.

Mum didn't bother dissecting his story, though, she was too relieved to see him in one piece. She set about running a bath, filling the flat with some awful smelling soaps. Which left us two on our own in silence.

'You calmed down yet?' he asked finally, after necking a pint of water.

'I have. You?'

'Yeah, I'm sorry I lost it with you. I'd forgotten how annoying you can be.' He was trying to joke with me like he had with Mum.

'I know I'm annoying, Jamm, but I'm not a liar.'

'What do you mean?'

'What I said in front of the others. About you going for me in the night. It happened, you know.' It was risky, going into it again, but I was trying to do the right thing, like I'd promised Cam.

He turned from me to fill up his glass again. 'Why are you saying all this? Where's it coming from?'

'Can't you remember?'

'Remember what?'

He was so convincing, I was beginning to doubt myself.

'Strangling me. I've only just tweezered out the last fingernail from where you left it.' I pointed at my neck, annoyed that there were no bruises for him to see.

There was a pause again as he drank, but no sign of recognition once he stopped. Instead he looked at me and spoke, voice slow and clear.

'Sonny, I've no idea what you're going on about.'

'You must have.'

He shook his head. 'Is this something to do with Tomm? That you'd rather he'd come home instead of me? Well, no one wishes that more than me. You know you can blame me for him being dead, but *don't* blame me for any of this other stuff. You hear me?'

There was a steel to his words, an iciness in his bloodshot eyes that stopped me from coming straight back at him.

How could I do anything about the situation when he refused point blank to admit that anything was even wrong?

The only option I had was the one I feared most. Telling Mum. But how did I do that without alienating her too?

'Your bath's ready.' She'd appeared, towel in hand. 'And leave your clothes by the door, I'll get them soaking.' She saw our faces, full of tension. 'Everything OK?'

'Fine,' he answered, best smile caked on.

'Right. Good.' I could tell she wanted to question me too. 'By the way, Jammy, not something to worry about now, but there's been a journalist calling for you.'

I saw his face switch to terrified in seconds. 'What does he want?'

'I don't know, love. To talk to you? There's a lot of people very proud of what you did.'

'Well, I don't want to talk to him. You tell him that if he calls back.' He'd gone again, his mood flipping quicker than a coin. 'I don't want you speaking to him either.'

Mum's mouth fell open.

'I mean it. We don't speak to him. Any of us.' He was aiming that at me. But Mum wasn't finished.

'Hey. I don't know what it is that bothers you about this, but you have nothing to be ashamed of. Do you hear me?'

'You've spoken to him already, haven't you? What did you tell him?'

'The truth. That I'm proud of you; how much Tommo meant to you. It's nothing that anyone doesn't already know.'

I could see the anger in him, the thought processes running across his face.

'Do you think I want to see myself in the paper? Be reminded of what's gone on? There's nothing to be proud of. *Nothing*. So if he calls again you can tell him that. Do you understand?'

Mum nodded, too shocked to do anything else, leaving Jamm to look the tiniest bit awkward. 'I'll get in the bath, then. Thanks.'

'You're welcome.'

'And I'll probably turn in after that, before . . . well, you know.'

What? Before you go for her like you did me?

'All right, son, it's fine. Sleep well.'

And off he went, leaving me with an opportunity.

'We need to talk, Mum.' My words sounded urgent, but so did her response.

'Not now, Sonny.'

'But it's import–'

'Not now. I can't do this now. I'm sorry.'

And with a feeble excuse about an early shift, she shuffled off to bed, leaving me at the table, with more questions than my head could process, including where was it safe to sleep that night.

I woke suddenly to Jamm shaking me by the shoulders. But as panic gripped me I noticed two things. Firstly, the sun creeping around his shoulders, and secondly, he was dressed. I might have been groggy, but I doubted he'd have pulled on a jacket before throttling me in his sleep.

'Wake up, will you? We're meeting the lads in twenty minutes.'

I swore at him. Nine a.m.! Nine a.m. and he'd already spoken to the others? I imagined he'd got the same response from them as me. Mind you, they'd probably had more sleep.

The good news overnight was that Jammy had stayed on his bunk, his arms going nowhere near my neck. The bad news was that he'd still managed to moan, wail and tilt the bunk in every direction possible as dreams invaded his sleep. I would've been irritated had it not seemed so genuinely terrifying. A lot of it was unintelligible noise like before, but the same names were obviously haunting him: Tommo and Wayne, whoever he was.

I'd had to fight hard not to step in at various points, or fetch Mum. I couldn't believe he hadn't woken her too. Suppose a lifetime living on the Ghost explains a lot. It's not like the place ever really falls silent.

I looked at him through bleary eyes, no evidence of him feeling any effects of a broken night. Annoyed, I swung my legs on to the floor and, once upright, went straight in with a direct question.

'Who's Wayne?'

'What?' He'd been tying up his trainers, but with those two words I had his full attention.

'Wayne. Who is he?'

'Don't know what you're on about. Now get ready, will you?'

'You keep talking to him. In your sleep. From the way you go on at him he seems to annoy you more than I do.'

'No one could do that. Now get yourself up.'

'So who is he, then? Someone in your regiment?'

'Just shut up, will you?' he spat, pulling so hard on his laces they were in danger of snapping. 'For once, just do what you're told. I don't know what you're going on about, so leave it.'

And that was that. Conversation over. Another perfect start to the day. And I'd learned nothing, well, almost nothing. Whoever Wayne was, he'd got right under Jammy's skin.

SONNY

From the state of the other two idiots, I couldn't imagine we'd achieve anything today. We met at the bottom of our block, Den appearing first, a mess of stubble and stale lagery breath, with Wiggy staggering across ten minutes later, wheezing hard on what was probably his fifth cig of the day. He really was a wreck first thing, could barely speak or stand straight until he'd mainlined three cups of tea and ten Marlboros. The steaming mug in his hand told us he was on the way to sorting himself out, though he'd have to drink and smoke quickly if he wanted to avoid Jammy's wrath.

'Where's the fire?' he moaned.

'You should know,' answered Jamm, stealing a cig from him. 'The fire is Hitch. When was the last time any of you saw him?'

I said nothing. Was too busy biting my lip, regretting not holding things together like I was supposed to in the first place.

'About three weeks, I suppose.' Wiggs was typically vague.

'And there's been nothing? No contact at all?'

'Have you met Hitch?' Wiggs again. 'I don't think he's got a fax machine.'

He crumpled under a look from all three of us. It wasn't the time for jokes. Not when we were talking Hitch.

'So we need to find him,' Jamm said. 'He's always liked to keep a low profile, but if he's tied himself up in something dodgy, then it'll make him ten times as elusive.'

'We have tried, you know.' I couldn't forget most of the sights I'd seen while searching. 'But if he's using like we think he is, he could be anywhere.'

Jamm rubbed at his face. It didn't look like a night's sleep had ironed the kinks out of his head. 'If he's using then it's even more important we find him quickly. He could be in a right state by now.'

He looked in my direction as he spoke, doubling the guilt that I carried on my back.

It wasn't as if I'd bought Hitch a crack-pipe and told him to get stuck in, but the end feeling was the same, believe me.

'So let's start again. Couple of hours and we can cover the Ghost between us.'

You had to give it to Den. He might've had a hangover, but it didn't stop him being up for it. Maybe I needed a dose of what he'd been on last night.

So we split up, arranging to meet at midday. Me and Wiggs had to cover the northern blocks plus the parade, with Jamm and Den scoping out the rest. I didn't mind, couple of hours away from Jamm might clear my head a bit. Shame I had to spend it with Wiggy, though. From the look of him, I'd spend every minute carrying him on my back.

So we tried. Tried hard too. Once we were back on the skagheads' stairwells it focused our heads right in. We *did* have to find Hitch, we just couldn't find anyone either prepared or able to help us. We tried every tactic we had. Said it was an emergency, his mum was sick, dying even, but every gaze remained blank. Lips were cracked and blistered but said nothing. They weren't interested unless we could get them mashed.

After three tower blocks and a load of stairs, we were ready to blow, especially me. All this morning had done was remind me how worried I was about Hitch.

Wiggs tried to help, but moral support wasn't exactly his strength. 'Maybe if we hadn't robbed the van like we did, he wouldn't have had the cash to try whatever he's smoking.'

Brilliant. Cheers for that, mate.

Another half-hour and I wouldn't have been able to let comments like that slide, so it was a relief to get a text from Jamm, telling us to get over to Hitch's flat as soon as we could.

'Take a look in there,' gasped Den, as soon as we arrived.

So I did, but it wasn't the view that bothered me. All right, there was a bigger post mountain than before, more pizza boxes and litter on the floor. But the real problem was the smell. Soon as the letterbox opened it overpowered your senses. It was the same rankness I'd got off Hitch the last time we saw him, but multiplied by ten. I told Jamm so as I backed away and Wiggs had a whiff.

'Do you think he's in there?' he asked.

'I can't believe anything alive is,' answered Den, 'unless it's growing out of a pizza box.'

'I reckon he's inside.' The thought filled me with panic. 'We need to get in there. Do we call the police or what?'

The only answer I got was from Jammy's boot as it crashed against the door, splintering the wood like it was a wafer. As the door crashed back on its hinges, Jamm ploughed forward, tucking his t-shirt over his nose as he went.

The stink was unimaginable. It wasn't sewagey, it wasn't a smell that you could place or put some logic to. This was different. Death clung to it, a rotting odour that invaded every inch of the air around us. The prospect of finding Hitch was suddenly a real one, and terrifying too.

We started in the kitchen, but there were no surfaces to be seen and barely any floor either. Fast-food boxes littered every space.

Jamm moved first, the sights not seeming to bother him. Instead he leaned over the sink, piled high with festering plates and rancid water, and unhooked the window. A breeze wafted in then out, probably appalled by what it found.

'Try the lounge,' Jamm ordered in full-on soldier mode. I didn't argue, probably out of relief that he hadn't sent me to the bathroom. God knows what we'd find in there.

The lounge was in no better state: the same food carnage, but there were also blankets thrown across the floor, making half a dozen makeshift beds. Whatever Hitch had been doing (and I could guess by the burnt spoons on the coffee table what that was), he hadn't been doing it alone. I didn't know whether to be relieved or scared.

I kicked at the blankets, not wanting to touch them. I don't know why I bothered. It wasn't like anyone could possibly be underneath them. So with sickness rising in my throat, I headed for Hitch's room. But as I reached the door

I was called back by Wiggy, clearly freaked out by what he'd found in the second bedroom.

Except, like the kitchen, it wasn't a bedroom, not any more. The bed base was gone and the mattress leaned across the window, blocking out the view of the walkway in front. With all light gone, and only one naked bulb buzzing, it gave the room a seedy edge.

In the middle of the space, running its full length, were three wallpapering tables, every one of them crammed with rolls of clingfilm, baggies and weighing scales. Tiny traces of brown and white powder were scattered across the surface: not enough to get you up and flying, but there was no doubt it was marching powder of some sort.

'What is going on?' asked Wiggy, though he knew the answer. 'Hitch can't be dealing this stuff, can he?'

'Hitch can't manage to wash his own clothes. No way he could get himself as organized as this.'

'Could be someone's taken advantage of him. Promised him enough of whatever he fancies to use the place.' Den looked like he was going to throw up.

Jamm, though, was on the move, mumbling something as he marched towards Hitch's room. With his momentum rolling forward, the bedroom door crashed open, exposing us to a whole new wave of nausea.

Seriously, the smell was so intense it burned our nostrils. I felt like I should put my hands to my face to fend off the swarm of flies that had to be heading our way. But none came, and on Jamm's order, we followed him in.

It was like nothing I'd ever seen. Piles of magazines filled every corner, vying for floor space with mounds of clothing so filthy they were in danger of melding into the carpet. Drawers from the dresser lay upturned, scraps of paper and receipts the only things left inside. I'd never seen a place so desperate or chaotic; after just seconds I could feel it sucking at my spirits. God knows what it had done to Hitch.

'Come on,' I gasped, grabbing at Jammy as he approached the bed. 'He's not here.'

But Jamm didn't hear me, or chose not to. Instead he walked forward, reaching for the corner of the blanket on the mattress. It looked identical to what I'd seen in the lounge. Empty, any sign of life long gone.

That didn't stop Jamm from whipping it away, though, and as the dust sprung into the air, we were left with a sight none of us expected or wanted to see.

A body: the thinnest, palest excuse for a human that I'd ever seen. It belonged in some history book from the Second World War, not here in the middle of our estate. Each limb looked withered, ankles and arms jutting out from clothes several sizes too big for them. It was like someone had dressed a comedy skeleton. But there was nothing funny about it as we recognized the clothes. Hitch didn't have an extensive wardrobe. There was no doubt that the wasted face we were all gawking at was his.

The air turned blue, all thoughts of the smell forgotten. Jamm was first on to his knees, his cheek resting millimetres from Hitch's blistered mouth.

'What are you doing?' I screamed. 'Help him, will you?'

The stillness was agonizing. It took every bit of strength I had to stop myself from pulling Jamm away and taking over.

'He's breathing,' he said. 'Shallow. But there's something there.'

I reached for my phone, hands shaking too much to even take the keylock off.

A second later it lay on the floor, knocked to the ground by Jammy who'd leapt back to his feet.

'What are you doing?' he yelled.

'Calling an ambulance. What do you think I'm doing?'

'No ambulances. Not here.'

I couldn't believe what I was hearing. 'What do you mean, not here?'

'Call an ambulance and they'll bring the police. Soon as they turn up, Hitch is in serious trouble. They'll have him for dealing. We've no idea what else is hidden here, have we?'

That was it for me. I was smack-bang freaking out.

'What are we going to do, then?'

We all looked to Jammy. It was like he'd never been away.

But he didn't answer. There wasn't time, as the front door slammed and the hall filled with strangers' voices. It had to be Hitch's new mates, and by the time they reached his door my fingers were already curled into fists.

SONNY

There were two of them. Not Cuda crew. Older, hairier. They didn't look like the sort to give you five days to pay back what you owed them.

As they appeared in the doorway there were the inevitable questions as to who *we* were. I'm sure they probably asked more bluntly than that, I don't remember. Was running on pure uncut adrenalin by then.

We said nothing, to them anyway. Jamm turned to Wiggs and told him to pick Hitch up, carefully. Wiggy did as he was told, a sharp breath leaving Hitch's lips as he was plucked skywards. Evidence that there was still some fight left in him.

The meatheads in the doorway didn't like it, though.

'What do you think you're doing?'

Jamm stood motionless, oozing a calm I hadn't seen since he came home.

'Listen. We don't care what you're doing in his flat. So don't be thinking we're after your gear. All we want is him. He's our mate.'

'And what if he doesn't want to leave?'

Jamm strode forward, Den and me falling in behind. He

didn't stop until he was inches away from the first guy. 'We've already asked him.' He paused, tipped his head to one side and leaned further in. 'And do you know what he said?'

I saw the guy respond to Jamm's challenge, his own head coming forward until they stood like two rutting stags. 'What's that, then?'

But Jamm said nothing. Instead, with a speed that had my eyes blurring, he slammed a headbutt clean on to the bloke's nose, momentum sending them both stumbling. The crack of cartilage was sickening, but it wasn't enough to put the stranger on the ground. Instead he let rip with a roar and piled his huge frame straight into Jamm's midriff. The pair of them sprawled on to the floor, limbs tangled in Hitch's festering clothes.

That was it, the room exploded. The other gorilla, spotting I was the smallest, went straight for me, but as I dodged his flailing arms, he walked straight into a belly punch from Den that bent him double. I didn't give him time to draw breath. Instead I raised my knee into his forehead and felt eight-foot tall when he crumbled in front of me.

Den wasn't finished. It was clear that they were proper players, so as the guy clutched at his face, Den leaned his knee across his throat and rifled his pockets, only stopping when he found a blade in his jeans pocket. 'You wouldn't use this, would you?' Den hissed, and with the blade still shut in his fist, he lamped the guy one last time, sending him deep into a blissful sleep.

My attention turned to Jamm, still trading blows on the floor. He was holding his own, but as they rolled, neither of them could land anything significant. Skipping round I waited till the meathead veered my way, then swung my foot into his ribs. He didn't flinch at first, his attention still on Jamm. So I tried again, taking a run-up this time.

I felt something give, then saw his face crunch in pain. A gasp left his throat, an octave higher than his speaking voice, and as he writhed, Jamm leapt to his feet and weighed in too.

The only thing was, Jamm didn't stop, even after six kicks and the guy had stopped moving.

'Stop it, Jamm,' I called, my arm grappling with his. He either didn't hear me or didn't want to as another volley thumped home. 'Jamm? Did you hear me? That's enough!'

I tried to get in front of him but he wouldn't have it, his face so clouded with anger that I don't think he even knew I was there. I looked at Den, who stared back, his surprise and fear mirroring mine.

In the end we managed to pull him away, both Den and me straining to keep any kind of grasp on him as he ranted at the bloke, words we could barely work out. I'm not sure I wanted to either.

I looked hard at Jamm's eyes, and the hate flooding from them. I had no idea what he was seeing as he stared at the floor, but I doubted it had anything to do with the stranger who'd disturbed us.

'Calm down!' I yelled, not caring if it deafened him. 'It's us. It's done.'

With a final yell he shook us off, and seemed to come partially to his senses. He dropped to his knees and frisked the guy, pocketing a knife similar to the one Den found.

'See if he's got a phone,' he shouted to Den as he patted

him down, throwing a handset to the ground before stamping hard. The phone shattered quickly. 'That should buy us another minute or two to get clear.'

Having watched Den copy him, Jamm marched over to Wiggy and took Hitch himself. No strain showed on his face; it was like Hitch weighed nothing more than a bag of sugar.

'Let's get out of here.'

Dumbstruck, we followed him outside, eyes narrowing at the sun, Hitch's body straining to cope with his first fresh air in what had to be weeks.

'Now can I call an ambulance?' I asked.

'Quick as you can. We'll meet them by the parade.'

As we ran for the lift, I noticed a bunch of girls gawp in our direction. We must have looked a sight, unusual enough to distract them from their phones.

I didn't think much about them as we piled past, why would I? But as it turns out, I should have. Their presence marked the beginning of the end. The end that pushed Jammy to the brink: the end that took me right along with him.

SONNY

We should've turned a corner right then. All right, the situation wasn't normal, but things never were. That's what it was like on the Ghost.

Finding Hitch in one piece, though, and getting him to the hospital the same way, it had to mean something.

It wasn't just that either. Look at *how* we found him: together, standing beside each other. The only person missing was Tommo, and although we all felt his absence massively, it was as close as we'd been to united since him and Jamm had left.

As the ambulance roared through the square, parting the crowd that had gathered, I felt a pulse of positivity in my gut. The paramedics had hooked Hitch up to a drip, and although his heart could only flutter when we wanted to hear it hammer, I suddenly had faith that he would be OK. Jamm was with him and I couldn't believe after everything he'd seen this last month that he'd let another mate slip away.

The good feeling had fractured by the time we reached the hospital, though.

Firstly, the bus didn't arrive, then it was slow progress

running, with Wiggs constantly wanting a smoke. It might only have been one o'clock in the afternoon, but he'd caned a full pack by the time we hit the hospital doors.

If he was nervous, though, Jammy was in a different league.

A nurse, reluctant to let the three of us anywhere near sick people, finally directed us to a stuffy corridor, where I could see Jamm pacing every inch of it. That might have being normal behaviour, what with the worry and the adrenalin still pumping, but what bothered me was the conversation he was having with himself. I might not have been able to hear him, but I could see he was agitated. He only stopped when he caught sight of us, a tight smile edging across his face.

'No news, but he's still breathing. The doctor says they need to get fluids into him as quickly as they can.'

'Did they say what he's been taking?' Den asked.

'No, but they reckon he's in severe withdrawal. What they're more worried about is his weight. It's possible he hasn't eaten or drunk in over a week.'

'But he'll be all right?' Den looked five years old again. I'd never seen a big man look so fragile.

'They said his organs were shutting down. Kidneys and liver. Long as they can kick-start them again, he's got a chance.' But Jamm's words weren't convincing any of us, or even himself.

All we could do was wait, take it in turns to pace or to join Wiggy outside as he smoked himself stupid. He tried lighting up inside at one point, and nearly got throttled by a nurse for his trouble. He looked more scared of her than he did of the meatheads that had surprised us back at Hitch's. It was a rare moment of humour in an afternoon full of fear.

By the time five o'clock rolled around the tension was eating us alive. We were at a new low, hungry and tired, and no matter how many nurses we asked, none of them were able or prepared to give us the tiniest bit of news. I'd found a vending machine, hoping a bit of sugar might give us a lift, but all the thing could do was eat my money and give me nothing in return. But any disappointment at me returning with empty pockets *and* hands was soon forgotten when a doctor headed over to us.

'You're with Mr Hitchcock?' I searched his face for evidence of what came next, but couldn't read a thing. 'You are family, aren't you?'

Four yes's flew back at him, each of them technically a lie, not that it mattered. We were all he had, and that seemed to be enough for the doctor. Just.

'Well, it's positive news. His body is responding slowly to the treatment we've started, although it's very early days.'

'So his kidneys and that have started again?' Den might not get exactly what was going on, but he desperately wanted to.

'They're responding well at the moment. Had he arrived a couple of hours later, it might have been a different story. He was lucky you found him when you did.'

We shuffled slightly, half proud of our part, only for the doctor to cut us swiftly off at the knees.

'However, he should never have been allowed to approach this kind of state. His malnutrition and dehydration levels were horrific. I've no doubt the drugs he's been using have been cut with some damaging chemicals, but still . . . ' He looked at us pityingly. 'He should never have been exposed to them in the first place.'

He made to walk off but Jamm called after him, asking if we could see Hitch ourselves.

'Perhaps in an hour. He hasn't come round yet and I don't want him stressed when he does.'

'So that's not a no, then?'

'It's a "not yet". And that's all you'll get for now.'

'Then we'll wait, doctor,' chipped in Wiggy with his best plummy accent. 'We don't mind, especially with so many fine nurses to admire.'

I didn't mind laughing if Hitch was fixable. The doctor didn't take Wiggy's impression so well, marching off, jotting on his clipboard a reminder to call Security.

Waiting didn't seem quite so bad now. Wiggs got the bit between his teeth and carried on with his impressions, mimicking every doctor and nurse who walked past. Not many of them saw the funny side, but it worked for me.

Jamm remained distant, though; pacing, lost in his own thoughts.

I watched him and tried to pick up on anything, even the tiniest sign of what was going on in his head. Was he thinking about Hitch, or the kicking he'd dished out to that meathead? I had no doubt that a massive part of him was still in Afghanistan, though what he was doing there, or how I could reach him to help, I had no idea.

Nothing could stop him patrolling the corridor. No offer of food, drink or a smoke was enough. Or so I thought, until the moment Cam appeared. Suddenly he was back with us.

It was hard to see her, especially knowing what an idiot I'd made of myself the last time we spoke. We hadn't caught up since; texts had been brief, distracted, there'd been no talk of us.

She looked amazing, which made me feel worse. There was no sign of make-up and she still had a tired sheen to her face, but she smashed it out of the park regardless. I felt like sitting on my hands. It was the only way I could stop myself from marching over there and showing her how sorry I really was.

'How is he?' she asked, unsure she really wanted to know.

'Better than he was,' I answered quickly, hoping that if the good news came from me it would remind her I was worth caring about. 'Doctor reckons he'll wake up soon if they can keep the fluids going into him.'

A single tear left the corner of her left eye but her face didn't change. She didn't even bother to bat it away. Instead it slid off her face as her lips stretched into a wide smile. It was the best thing I'd seen in days.

'How are you doing?' Jamm asked her, his hand touching her elbow. 'Your mum coping?'

'Not really, but people have been kind. Not that it helps. Well, not until this afternoon.' It was like she'd remembered something, a light coming on in her head as she pulled a newspaper from her back pocket.

'I hope you're not still feeling modest,' she told Jamm as she handed the *Gazette* to him. 'You certainly won't be once you read this.'

Jamm looked confused, then irritated, then on the verge

of freaking out, all in the course of ten seconds. Whatever he was seeing, I needed to see it too, so I pulled at the corner, peering straight into a half-page photo of Jammy with Hitch lying unconscious in his arms. I could see me, Wiggs and Den behind them, our faces blurry next to Jamm's determination. I should've read on, but couldn't get past the headline: a single word that took up nearly as much space as the photo.

HEROIC

The line underneath was just as clear.

WAR VETERAN SAVES TRAGIC FRIEND FROM OVERDOSE

'You're famous, Jamm,' said Den, beaming.

'It's only the *Gazette*,' answered Wiggs, disappointed he'd been reduced to a supporting role.

I said nothing, just followed the article as quickly as I could.

A local soldier, heralded as a hero for his bravery in Afghanistan, today cemented his reputation by saving a man from a near fatal overdose.

James McGann, 18, a resident of the infamous Ghost Estate and currently between tours of duty, was photographed at lunchtime emerging from a flat clutching a man ravaged by heroin addiction.

It is less than a month since Private McGann was praised for his bravery under fire while on a tour of duty in Afghanistan. While there, he was caught in a firefight that claimed the life of his best friend, Robert Thompson, also 18.

Despite the intensity of the firefight, Private McGann showed incredible tenacity in repelling insurgents while

trying to save the life of his friend: an act of bravery
described by his senior officers as 'incredible. Private
James McGann defines the integrity of the modern soldier.'

It was impossible to read it and not be swept up. Mum
would weep for England when she saw it.

> *Today's developments added weight to this paper's call*
> *for the town to honour both Private McGann and Private*
> *Thompson. Local council officials have commented that*
> *an announcement will follow shortly, and that some sort*
> *of ceremony was 'extremely likely'.*
>
> *Gill Thompson, mother of Robert, who was killed in*
> *Afghanistan, welcomed our campaign.*
>
> *'It would mean the world to see our boys honoured by*
> *the town. Jammy is the closest thing we now have to a*
> *son. We will never forget what he did for Robert in his last*
> *moments.'*

I felt my throat close as I looked at Cam and saw what it
meant to her.

'Thank you, Jamm,' she added. 'You've no idea the boost
this will give Mum. She thought Tommo was going to be
forgotten, but not now.'

Jamm's eyes didn't move from the page, but he didn't
seem to be reading. The only thing that did move was his
face: a series of lines creasing his forehead, then his eyes,
until, without warning, his whole face caved and a torrent
of tears fell.

I thought that had to be the moment, the time that he

gave in and let us know what was going on in his head, but as we circled him, trying to give him the comfort we thought he needed, he broke away, a single loud 'NO!' bursting from his lips.

'It's all right.' Cam smiled through her own tears. 'It's OK.'

But it wasn't. It clearly wasn't. One by one, Jamm fixed us with a stare so pained that we all felt it too. He didn't seem able to understand why we were proud, how we could possibly care, and with one last huge roar, he sprinted from the corridor. I started to follow him but Cam stopped me gently.

'Give me a minute,' she said, with a look that told me somehow all of this mess was going to be all right.

I had to trust her, give her the time she wanted. If she needed a minute, then that was fine. I'd just have to keep my jealousy in check.

SONNY

'Er . . . I don't get it.' Wiggs was bemused. 'Seriously. They want to build a statue of him or give him the key to the city, and he freaks out?'

'He's not well,' I answered, feeling like I hadn't slept in months.

'Clearly. If they wanted to put up a statue of me I'd be all over it. Long as it was gold.'

'Didn't you hear me?' I yelled. 'I've been telling you this since he got home but you wouldn't listen. He's not well. And I'm scared. The mad episodes at night, the way he went for that dealer earlier. I thought at one point he was going to kill him. Even when we arrived here, and he was pacing, he was arguing with himself. You can't tell me that's normal, can you?'

Den looked like his head was going to explode. He liked life simpler than this.

'Mate, I'm no doctor. I don't know what to say. Maybe you should talk to your mum.'

'And that's the answer, is it? Mum'll know everything? She's so grateful he's still breathing that she doesn't want to talk about anything else. If he'd brought a wife and four kids home with him, she wouldn't have batted an eyelid.'

'Maybe this ceremony might be good for him, then. Show him how everyone appreciates what he's done.'

He didn't get it. If just one person told him he was a hero, Jamm looked like he wanted to puke. Stick him in front of a few hundred and I had no idea what he'd do. But I'd guess it wouldn't be pretty.

My feet were itchy. 'I'm going to see how they're getting on.'

'Do you think that's a good idea?'

'When's it ever stopped me before?' And I turned for the doors, feeling a waft of cold air as the evening hit me.

It wasn't hard to spot them in the middle of the car park, huddled against the wind. From a distance they looked like a couple; you couldn't have squeezed a credit card between them. When she spoke to Jammy, Cam's arms waved in that way that I loved, the way I never wanted to end when she was talking at me. You could see she was trying to persuade him, and that it seemed to have calmed him down a bit, despite him still rubbing at his hair.

I picked my way along a row of cars to their left, not wanting to listen, but feeling like I needed to.

The conversation seemed to go back and forth and I couldn't help but tense up when their hands rested on each other, even if it was for only a second.

But then the tears started, firstly from Jamm. I saw his shoulders hunch and shake, his hands moving to her shoulders. As he spoke he leaned forward, his forehead almost touching hers, and although I hadn't a clue what he was saying, my head mangled an answer pretty quickly, especially when I saw tears on her face too.

Somehow I held myself back. Every inch of me wanted to burst their moment but I knew I would lose her altogether if I did. But when her hands held each side of his face my legs betrayed me; I practically leapt into their eye-line.

'What's going on?' I demanded, my head cringing as the words left me.

'It's fine, Sonny, just give me a minute.' Her voice was firm.

I didn't move. Just stared at their closeness, their tears.

'Please.' She wasn't begging, she was telling.

My legs still wouldn't budge. Jammy's did, though, breaking away from her and towards me, his blood-red eyes furious.

'What is it with you?' he seethed. 'We need a minute.'

I might have walked had he not asked so aggressively.

No. Who am I kidding? There was no way I was backing down now.

'Then have a minute. You'll just have to have it with me here too.'

Cam was the next to move, darting between the two of us, grabbing my arm as she yanked me backwards.

'Sonny, this isn't the time.' She was half-whispering, half-hissing. 'Whatever it is that's going on in your head, you have to leave it and trust me.'

'I do trust you. But I can see what's happening.'

Before I knew it Jamm was hanging over our shoulders and into the conversation.

'What's going on, Cam?'

'There's nothing going on . . . nothing at a–'

'Nothing going on? Nothing?' I'd gone. Lost it. All the

tension of the last few weeks fizzing out indiscriminately. I didn't care who caught any of it either. 'There's plenty going on. Loads of it, and all between me and Cam. Has been for the last couple of months, so I don't like the way you're touching her.'

He smiled disbelievingly as he flicked looks between us. 'You are kidding me?'

'Why would I be kidding? And why should it be such a surprise? I may not be you, Jamm, might not be as heroic or smart, but that doesn't mean I'm nothing either.' I stepped forward, feeling braver than I ever had in my life. 'Don't mean I don't deserve the same things you clearly want.'

I didn't see his fist. It blurred as it made contact with my cheek, throwing my head to the side as I tumbled over.

No sooner had I hit the gravel than he was in my face, hands gripping my hoodie.

'You haven't got a clue, Sonny. About any of this, about me, about what I am. All of you, you're all clueless. You want me to show you what a hero I am? Want me to show you what I'm capable of?' He paused as he pointed menacingly. 'And as for this? It proves how little anyone else matters to you. Well, I'm done with it, with both of you. I can't do this any more.'

He made to leave, which prompted Cam. 'Jammy, wait. We can talk, sort it out.'

'It's too late for that now.'

'Course it's not. Let me help. Sonny, me, we both want to help.'

He rounded on her with the same ferocious look he'd been firing at me.

'NO! No help. I don't want it. It's too late.' He looked out of breath even though he'd barely moved. 'All of this,' he gasped, 'it didn't have to pan out like this. Remember that.'

He didn't wait for us to answer. Instead he walked calmly away, his movements controlled until he reached the first car in his path.

There, without warning, he pulled back his fist and threw it through the driver's window. The glass shattered instantly, and as he pulled his hand out, we saw blood pouring from the knuckles.

With his face expressionless, he pointed in our direction, before turning and walking again, aiming kicks at every car unlucky enough to be in his way.

Alarm after alarm sang out, not that I needed the warning. I had no idea what was going on, but I knew this was out of control. I knew Jamm had something to prove to us, but I didn't know what it was.

What I did know was that the prospect scared me, and that whatever he did, I'd driven him to it, one hundred per cent.

SONNY

The whack from Jammy wasn't the only one I took. Cam was as hysterical as he was. Not that I blamed her.

All this came down to me, to my complete inability to control my mouth when it mattered. Of course Cam had had it covered when she was talking to him, and if Jammy *had* wanted more? Well, I should've trusted her, shouldn't I?

She told me so in much blunter words as she lamped me around the head. I took the blows; wasn't like I didn't deserve them.

'I'm sorry,' I yelled over the sound of my ears ringing. 'I am. I'm an idiot.'

'There's only so many times you can say it and it still mean something. After a while it just becomes noise.'

I thought about what I might have cost her. What if Jamm *did* go off and cause havoc? Would that change things? The possibility of my brother *or* hers being honoured? How much would that have meant to me if Tomm had come home instead of Jamm? What sort of lifeline would that have offered Mum as well?

And there I was, sending Jammy off in such a state that

none of it even mattered any more. All that mattered now was finding him.

There was way too much of what he'd said, what he'd done, that scared me. I'd never have dreamed that he might ever feel desperate enough to hurt himself. But after what I'd just seen with the car window? With that one punch everything changed. Including things with Cam.

She paced in front of me, no idea how to put things right. How could she, when I'd managed to risk the one good thing that might have come out of Tomm's death?

'It'll be all right, you know.' I sounded way too breezy. 'I can sort this out. I will.'

'You can, can you? You can bring Tomm back? Get rid of the massive hole in his chest and get it beating again? Well if you could hurry up and do that, Sonny, we'd be grateful. Mum's not stopped crying since the knock at the door, Dad's only coming home to take lumps out of us, plus I've got to try and look after your bruised ego, when all I want . . . is my brother back.' There were no tears, but the pain was clear to see. It poured from every part of her, filling the air with static, reminding me of the damage I'd done.

'I wish I could bring him back for you, Cam. I do. I'd swap places with him in a heartbeat. I don't mean to screw things up like I do, it's just . . .'

'You know what, Sonny? This isn't about you. For once, it isn't. This is about Jamm. I don't care what you saw, or what you think you saw. He's your brother and he's the closest I have to one now too. Anything else, me and you, it's irrelevant.'

The wailing of the cars matched the pain in my head. This was unravelling too chaotically for me to keep up.

I wanted to lie down on the gravel until every bit of the storm had blown over. But I couldn't, and fortunately the arrival of Wiggs and Den gave me something else to focus on.

They may only have just heard the alarms shrieking, but I could see the noise was shredding their eardrums already.

'This something to do with you?' Den asked.

I shook my head. 'Jamm.'

'Jamm did this?' Wiggy stuck his nose through the hole in the car window, probably looking for anything worth pinching. 'What did you say to him?'

Cam answered as she yanked Wiggs away from temptation; last thing we needed was to be nabbed for burglary.

'Your mate here decided now was the time to tell Jamm about us.' Her look hit me just above the eyes; it hurt more than the punches did.

'What, you mean . . . you two are . . . a couple? You're kidding!' Sarcasm didn't suit Wiggy. Just as well Den whacked it straight out of him with a slap to the back of the head.

'We should keep walking,' he added. 'Get right away. Security are bound to fancy us for this.'

So we bustled off, filling the other two in on the last few minutes, lingering on the state of Jamm as he left.

'It's not like him. Not just the window, either. The way he spoke. There was something really final about it, like he had something to prove. Something he had to show us.'

'Like what?'

'I don't know, do I?'

'Well, you are his brother.'

I didn't know how to answer that. I mean, I was, but I didn't act like one. What kind of person sees something terrifying in his brother for days and does nothing about it?

Thoughts of what Jammy might do spiralled in my head, looping so badly that I knew I had to find him quickly. Before I had anything else to regret.

'We need to split up. Cover ground. I've no idea where he went, but he'll have to head back to the Ghost eventually. Den – you and Wiggs start at Parkway, then the bypass. Me and Cam'll head to Carr Lane and double back that way. If you see anything, text me.'

I reached for Cam's hand, out of habit rather than hope, but quickly got shot down.

'Why don't I go with Wiggs?' she added, looking me full-on as she said it. 'You go with Den.'

If I needed a sign of where we were, there it was: two sentences that drew a line under everything. But there wasn't time to stand there and plead with her. Why dig my grave any deeper? With a simple nod, Den and I peeled left, the piercing screams of car alarms finally fading as we hit Carr Lane.

'It'll be all right, you know. All this.' I wasn't sure if Den was telling me or reassuring himself.

'You didn't see him.'

'No, but I've known him all my life.'

I smiled at him weakly. I wanted to believe him but couldn't. 'So have I, that's what's scaring me. We have to find him, mate.'

He clapped my back roughly and we strode on, eyes in every direction for any sign of him.

It didn't take long to pick up Jammy's path, and once we did we definitely couldn't lose it. At first the clues were small: a trail of upturned litter bins scattered across the road. Cars veered to avoid them but no one stopped. It only took me a minute to fetch them back on to the kerb. I couldn't have a crash on my conscience too.

Next was more car damage – dented bodies, wing mirrors amputated or hanging off. It was only when we saw a Honda with its front and back screens caved in that we realized it was escalating. Jammy wasn't calming down, he was getting worse.

'What is he going to smash next?'

We didn't have to wait long. A hundred metres later, as the arcade started, so did the devastation. It wasn't like they were posh shops, more a row of beat-up units that specialized in corny names: a hair salon called 'Curl Up and Dye', the 'Town Fryer' chip shop. That wasn't all they had in common, though: all six of them were missing their front windows. Even the chippy that was still open. The owner was prowling around outside wielding a spatula and speaking to a policeman, who looked in fear of his own life. As if you could be killed by a fish slice.

'Did you get a look at him?'

'Only his boot as it went through the glass.'

'Nothing else?'

'What do you want me to say? He looked like they all do. He had a blue hoodie on. Big lad, strong. Not the sort you follow out into the street to confront. That's *your* job.'

The copper looked sheepish. He had practically nothing to go on. But we did. It told us everything we needed to know. The blue hoodie confirmed it. No way it was a coincidence.

We walked down the row, eyeing each of the shops as we passed. Nothing seemed to be missing from the window displays until we reached the decorators' merchant at the very end. Peering through the shattered glass, I could see an elaborate pyramid of paint cans, each one a different vibrant colour, except the top couple of tiers were missing.

It didn't take much for my head to make the leap and I pointed it out to Den.

'What would he want with tins of paint?'

'I don't think he's going to decorate our flat, put it that way.'

Trying to keep my head from racing, I bashed out a text to Cam.

He's getting worse. More wrecked cars, windows smashed
n looted. Get back to ghost ASAP

A reply buzzed back quickly, short on small talk.

WILL DO

Den and I paced on, looking for anything that was newly and badly decorated; at first everything went quiet. A good four hundred metres passed without the sound of a car alarm or the sight of shattered glass. It wasn't until we hit the centre of town that Jamm's trail hit us in the face again.

The local paper, the *Gazette,* was a rag. Everyone knew that. Seemed like it was only kept afloat with ads placed by locals with money to burn. Its offices stood in front of us, a nasty 60s concrete mess that looked like a seedy relative to the towers on the Ghost. And there, smeared across the front windows in bright scarlet paint, was the beginning of Jammy's message to them.

No Her

To anyone else it would've made no sense, but I could see the start of an 'r' before the letters suddenly ended, and I knew instantly what it was going to say: 'No Hero.'

Jammy's response to what they'd called him.

The other thing that was clear to me was that Jamm might not have finished the word, but that wasn't because he'd bottled it. The only thing that would have stopped him was being interrupted.

He'd told us he was going to prove something and I didn't believe this was his end goal. He had other things he wanted to do. Bigger things. And as the possibilities built up in my head, they scared me half to death. We might have been closing in on him, but we weren't doing it quickly enough. Not by a long shot.

SONNY

We should've moved on quickly. I'd been in enough compromising situations over the years to know not to linger when stuff was going down, but tonight seemed to be the night for messing things up royally.

So as we stood and gazed up at Jamm's handiwork, we didn't hear the law creeping up behind us. Not even when they were practically stood on our trainers.

'Doesn't make a lot of sense, does it, lads?' We span round to see two of them, Tweedledumb and Dumber, pleased as punch, reckoning they'd caught us right in the act. Nothing worse than a smug copper, well, apart from a persistent one.

'It doesn't, does it?' No way I was going to kiss up to them. 'Sad reflection on our education system, gents.' I made eyes at Den and we sidled right, only to be pulled straight back.

'Nothing to do with you, then?'

We shoved on our best outraged faces, but managed to look like bigger toe-rags than usual.

'Do we look that thick to you?' Den asked.

'I'm not sure you want us to answer that,' the bigger one

said. He had a cleft in his chin so deep you could park your bike in it. It was the funniest thing about him.

'Look, Sherlock,' I butted in, 'you might think you're some crash-hot super-sleuth. And you *clearly* think you're intellectually superior to us. But –' and I paused for effect, feeling in control for the first time that night – 'you're wrong. The wrongest you've probably ever been. Well, since you decided to join the force anyway.'

I saw them bristle and stick their chests out. I loved messing with coppers. They were so easy to wind up.

'I can prove you're way off the mark.'

Den looked at me, his eyes asking, *You can?*

They laughed, identical barks that must have been standard police issue. 'Go on, then.'

I was well into my stride and took my time, knowing every second I wasted was another second for Jamm to get further away, wherever he was heading.

I beamed. 'First of all, where's the paint? The stuff we haven't used yet?'

They laughed again. 'That's it? That's your defence? There's no paint can here, so it can't be you? Brilliant. Outstanding. You must tell that to the desk sergeant when he books you in for the night.'

I waved my hands and gave them my best fake laugh. 'I'm being silly, aren't I? Come on, then, slap the cuffs on. Just be careful of the paint that's covering our hands, won't you?'

Den looked at his own fingers, grubby but free of paint. He looked ready to explode with confusion.

'What are you on about?' Copper One asked. 'There's no paint on you. Have you two been sniffing a can of deodorant?'

'Nope. I'm just proving, sir, that it isn't us who's responsible for this appalling vandalism. Couldn't have been.'

Copper Two was losing his patience. 'All right, that's enough. You can tell us all this at the station.'

I danced to his left, away from his grasp. 'That's just it, though, we can't. All the evidence is here. Look. Look at the windows.'

They looked but said nothing.

'No, really look. Closely. Look at the letters. What do you reckon they've used to paint them with?'

'A brush, you idiot. Now come with us.'

'But that's just it, they haven't. Look again. Unless you know of a brush that has fingerprints, no way it was done with anything but a hand.'

They looked at each other then peered closely at the glass.

'See it?' I asked, knowing full well there were smeary, smudged handprints mixed in with the paint. There might have been a clean fingerprint or two if they'd looked closely enough, but they'd have to search hard to find them. Longer than either of them would ever be prepared to dedicate. I could see they were losing interest already.

'So if we *were* the guilty parties, then surely, obviously, our hands would be absolutely covered in the stuff, and oh . . . ' I laughed again, 'look, they aren't. Good luck finding them, though. It's a distinctive red, that. "Scarlet Sunset", I think it is. Shouldn't take you long to find it.' And with a wave I pulled a delighted Den away with me, wiggling his fingers in their direction.

Two things could have happened then. Either they'd pull

us anyway, shamed at being made to look such mugs, or they'd let us go, and though at first I heard a shuffle of feet behind us, the noise soon stopped. Only when we were fifty metres on did I dare to look back, to see them both staring at the paintwork like it was the *Mona Lisa*.

'Nice one,' Den grinned. 'I had no idea where you were going with that.'

'I'm not completely thick,' I sighed, my head filling back up with thoughts of Jamm. 'Contrary to popular belief. Just make sure you tell Cam how great I was, will you?'

'Might be a bit late for that.'

He was right too, or maybe not, because as we walked on, my phone rang, Cam's name lighting up the screen.

'You all right?' I asked, trying to keep my voice soft and friendly.

'We're at the bypass.' At least I thought that was what she said. There were sirens and voices fighting to be heard. Another four hundred metres on and we'd be able to hear them too.

'Where abouts?'

'By Walton Street. We were heading back, but there's been a massive crash here. Half a dozen cars stacked up. Both lanes are completely blocked. One of them's gone through the reservation.'

She wasn't ringing with a traffic update. She reckoned it had something to do with Jamm. My head spun; I didn't want to ask the question, but knew I had to.

'Is he there, Cam? He's not, is he? Tell me he's not in one of the cars!'

There was a pause, then she was back, yelling over another siren.

'Not one that's still here, no.'

'Eh? What do you mean?'

'There's police everywhere, Sonny. Taking statements from drivers. Wiggs has been following them round, listening in.'

'And?'

'They're all saying the same thing. That the car came out of nowhere. Started veering between lanes like he was trying to get away from someone. Either that or he'd never driven the car before. They reckon it could be a joyrider.'

'And did they get a look at the driver?'

'Not really. He was driving too quick. The only thing they're all saying is that he was wearing a blue jumper. Hood pulled up over his face. It's Jamm. Has to be.'

I swore angrily, not believing he could do this, break every one of the rules that he set out for us all.

'Sonny, you still there?'

'I'm here.'

'Do you think it's him? Do you reckon it's Jamm?'

'I do, yeah.'

It came to me instantly. Not much of an idea, but it had to do.

'Split up from Wiggs for five minutes and both get in front of as many different coppers as you can, but make sure you tell them the same thing. Tell them you saw the driver, tell them it was a guy in a suit. Flash, well dressed, but clearly battered, that he had a bottle in his hand. Vodka or something. Decide between you and stick to it. Tell as many as you can in ten minutes then leg it back to the Ghost. If it's Jammy in the car he'll be back well before we are. Got it?'

'Got it.'

'And Cam?' The word 'Sorry' formed on my lips but by the time it came out she'd hung up and I had Den in my face.

'What's going on?' he asked, seeing my concern.

'Looks like he's properly lost it,' I gasped, breaking into a run.

'What do you mean?'

'Start running,' I shouted over my shoulder. 'I'll tell you as we go.'

And so we ran, the towers of the Ghost edging quickly into view, but not quickly enough.

SONNY

I'd no idea what Afghanistan looked like. Not really. Apart from what I'd seen on the telly. And I never knew if that was what it was really like, or just what made for the best TV.

All I did know, as we hit the edge of the Ghost, was that Jamm had decided to bring a bit of it back with him. To show us what it was like.

The first thing was the smoke: a dirty black plume of it that managed to stand out against the darkness of the sky.

There must have been a bang before it, a big one if the cloud was anything to go by, but I was glad we hadn't been there for it. Not that sprinting towards it, fearing it had something to do with my brother, was anything of an improvement. Especially once the patrol cars started zipping past us.

Perhaps they were seeing a pattern, realizing the incidents in town were connected, or maybe it was because it was kicking off on *our* estate, but whatever it was, they weren't messing about. By the looks of it they were sending every copper they had on duty, and as a result, the estate was on fire, in every way possible.

As we hit the first of the towers, numbers were out in force, and not just crew members looking for a fight. Others were outside too, ordinary residents who put up with the Ghost because they hadn't the money to walk away. If they weren't brave enough to be in the middle of the parade, they were on the walkways, or filling each others' balconies. It wouldn't have surprised me if they'd pulled their settees outside with them: there was more action down below than on any of their TVs.

As we hit the centre of the estate, with the four towers hanging above us on every side, we saw what was causing the mushroom cloud.

It was a weird sight, one we'd seen in a hundred different action movies, but it didn't belong in our backyard, no matter how rough the Ghost was.

There, in the space where the statue used to be, was the wreckage of a car. The bonnet, from what we could see through the flames, was crumpled like a concertina and wrapped savagely round the statue's plinth. The soldiers themselves were still standing, but at an angle, like they were waiting for one final bullet to knock them to the ground.

The sight of it stopped us dead. The statue was one of the few landmarks anyone on the estate took pride in, the only static thing that wasn't coated in years of graffiti. Too many of our own had paid for it. Not with their cash, but by going out to fight in the first place. So to see it leaning like it was provoked a wide range of reactions, from itching to put the fire out to being ready to kick lumps out of whoever was responsible.

I stood there slack-jawed, looking at the empty driver's

seat, relieved that Jamm had pulled himself from it, hoping that he'd got away before anyone saw him. One sight of anyone leaving that car and they wouldn't be walking for long. Hospital was calling them for a long rest. The type you might not wake up from.

We scurried among the crowd, looking for a sight of a blue hoodie or a bloodied, paint-spattered fist, but there was nothing. Jamm was too good at disappearing, way too good for us, so I told Den to try his mobile again. No way he'd pick up a call from me, but from one of the others? Well, it was worth a go.

Den's face creased as the phone fell away from his ear. 'Answerphone,' he grimaced. No great surprise.

Instead I called Cam, who passed me straight on to Wiggs.

'We're back,' he shouted above the racket. 'Cam's a bit upset. Can you believe all this?'

I told him I could, that I didn't think it was over either. We stayed on the line until we spotted each other.

'We need to split up,' I shouted, 'speed up, cover every inch until we find him. Now he's back here, I don't reckon he's leaving. Whatever he's going to do, he's going to do it here.'

So we parted, updating each other every ten minutes about the fact that we'd found nothing, ticking off every grim landmark that we'd checked out. I even went back to Hitch's flat, slipping back inside, but found it empty. The only thing remaining was the smell. I couldn't believe it was only twelve hours since we'd last been in there.

I rang Cam constantly as I searched, not to try and put everything straight, but because she was the one Jamm would ring if he came to his senses. If he needed a shoulder, he'd go for hers. No way he'd want mine.

So I continued my laps of the Ghost, getting nowhere, finding nothing, watching as the temperature around the place rose by the second. The fire crews had arrived and were setting about the car, the statue still glowing despite the flames being extinguished. Everyone could see the damage the car had done, and there was anger, plenty of it; some genuine, some of it merely to take advantage of the situation.

It wasn't a surprise when I heard the sound of breaking glass again, though I was confident that this time it had nothing to do with Jamm. This would be the crew, the other scrotes on the estates looking to make the most of things. I suppose I should've been grateful to them: they'd take the heat away from Jamm. But that was only some use to me if I could actually find him.

Everything changed a minute later as I stood outside our empty flat, more grateful than I'd ever been that Mum was working a late shift.

From up here, the scene below looked mental. You could see groups gathering in corners, pointing towards the police presence, hatching stupid ideas, and in that moment a wave of tiredness swept over me, almost knocking me off my feet. Leaning on the balcony, I rested my chin against my hands, hoping for the dizziness to pass, only to jump at the sound of a gun firing.

OK, let's not over-react here. Guns were everywhere on the Ghost, whether people were prepared to accept it or not. You didn't have as much smack flowing round a place without people being prepared to protect it.

But you didn't hear them being *used* as much as you might imagine. So when that crack pierced the sky, a flash of light illuminating the top of Pickard House, my senses went mad, as I knew, KNEW, it would lead me to Jamm.

I suppose I shouldn't have immediately leapt to that conclusion. I mean, where would Jamm have got a gun from? No way the army would send him home with one. So when had he bought it? Had he stashed it in our room or tracked one down on impulse? It had been about an hour and a half since we found his graffiti in town, plenty of time to do business on the estate. You could pick up anything if you had the cash, or wanted it badly enough. I looked for panic below, for people running from the sound, or pointing in the noise's direction. But there was nothing. It was like no one had heard it but me.

I couldn't believe my luck. Maybe this was it? The moment when everything changed and I started to put things straight.

A tiny glint of light was all it was, but it was enough. In my head I'd found him. All I had to do now was work out what to do when I got there.

SONNY

I felt torn as I hammered my way across the estate. I'd made this big noise about keeping in contact with the others, but I had no intention of telling them about what I'd seen. If that *was* Jammy up there, I didn't think he'd cope if we turned up mob-handed; and anyway, this was my mess.

But as I took a left by the statue, shuddering at the carnage that Jamm had created, I ran straight past the outstretched arm of Cam. If it had been Den or Wiggs, I'd have pretended not to see them, but her? I had to stop.

'They're piecing it together, Sonny,' she gasped. 'The police. I got close as they were speaking, heard the radio. All the stuff that's gone on, they know it's the same guy. Dark jeans, blue hoodie. We've got to find him now, quick.'

My eyes flicked skywards, waiting for another shot that didn't come. 'We will. He can't have got far. Keep looking.'

She followed my eyeline, forehead creasing. 'Do you know where he is?'

'Not a clue.' The lie came too easy, they always did. 'I'm going to try the stairwells again.'

'You'd tell me if you did know, wouldn't you?'

'Course. I've hunches, loads of them. Just need to check 'em all out.' That felt better as it wasn't a lie. 'It'll be all right, you know. I'll sort it. I promise.'

She tried a smile, but it was so diluted by worry and anger that it barely bothered her face. Instead she turned and pushed through a crowd of lads coming the other way, looking for an excuse to kick off. It was all about to blow, so I had to be on my way before it did.

My head went straight back to Pickard House, legs following as I tore towards the front door, nearly wiping out a bunch of crew members in the process. They'd get over it. I'd done a lot worse in the past and was still breathing.

Instead they spotted a small group of police and decided to get in their faces rather than mine.

I could've kissed them. A diversion was exactly what I needed, time to find Jamm and talk him down before he did anything else. As I piled inside I saw the first punches being thrown, another fifty following in what seemed like seconds.

It sugared the pill of finding the lift was out of order, but didn't stop me kicking the door. The one time I *needed* it to be working and I got this – typical.

Instead I sprinted for the stairs, taking them two at a time, only slowing when I remembered I had another twenty-seven flights to go.

At least the stairwells were clear; one sight of the coppers and the addicts had bolted elsewhere, meaning all I had to avoid were the needles that lined every flight. Standing on one of those was a complication no one needed.

It was agony, my thighs burning after a dozen floors and

screaming by halfway, but at least it gave me time to think. I didn't have a clue what I was going to find on the rooftop, though I was as sure as I could be that Jamm was up there waiting. I remembered the blood gushing from his fist after he'd put it through the car window. Nearly three hours had passed, so what state was he going to be in? I'm sure the army must've taught him first aid, and just as well. It was too long to be losing blood.

By the time the twenty-fifth floor crawled around, my head was no clearer, and as I opened the final door to the roof, a gust of wind blew any remaining sense clean from my brain. I'd have to do what I always did and think on my feet, hoping I hadn't lost my touch completely.

I strained against the darkness. Aside from a clutch of weak strip-lights, there wasn't a lot to go on, certainly not enough to pick out a figure. Instead I stumbled forward, letting my eyes acclimatize, wanting to call to him.

But with my mouth dry after the climb, I didn't have it in me. It was almost a relief when he spoke first, his words slicing through the darkness.

'You're too clever for your own good, you know that?' I had no idea where he was, so turned slowly, the pain in his voice stinging my ears.

'Depends who you talk to,' I croaked. 'And what it is I'm after. Nothing more important than finding you, Jamm, believe me.'

He spoke again, still from the shadows. 'I bet. Must be heavy, carrying all that guilt around with you.'

He wasn't wrong, but I knew bringing Cam up again

wouldn't help either of us. 'Can't be feeling too sprightly yourself, mate. Bit of a mess down there.'

I heard gravel crunch to my left as he appeared at my shoulder. I flinched, couldn't help it. He saw it and smiled.

'Don't worry, bruv, I'm not going to lay you out again. Long as you don't step out of line.'

He walked past me, giving me time to look at him properly, see the state he was in. First thing I saw was his hoodie, left sleeve ripped off at the shoulder, the material now blood-soaked and wrapped tightly around his fist. I was no doctor, but the blood wasn't old. It looked like the material had soaked up every drop it could.

His movements seemed to back this up. He was trying to walk quickly, but clearly wasn't in control. As he came to the edge of the building, his hands reached out and gripped the rail unsteadily, allowing him to stare at the scene below.

He laughed, but there was no pleasure in it. He sounded and looked defeated.

'The crews are loving it down there, you know,' I went on. 'You've given them the excuse to kick off.'

He swayed gently against the railing, silent.

'But what's going on, Jamm? What's this about? We're all worried sick about you.'

'Course you are.'

'We *are*. We've spent the last three hours tearing the place apart looking . . . '

'And the last three months tearing things up with Cam. Must've been a difficult time.'

'Is that really what this is all about? Because I got together with Cam? If it is then I'm sorry. Believe it or not, I didn't do it to wind you up, no matter what you think.'

'At least I do think, Sonny. All you do is stumble blindly about, doing what's best for you and no one else.'

'That's not true.'

'Course it is. You're brilliant at it. You should do it properly, turn pro.'

I knew what he was doing. Riling me, waiting for me to snap, to give him an excuse to start again and blame me. Well, it wasn't going to work.

'You know what, Jamm? I don't think this has got anything to do with me and Cam. Not really.'

He scoffed at me, but I wasn't finished.

'There's no way you'd kick the whole town to bits just because I got it on with her.'

'And you know that, do you? That's fact, is it?'

'No, it's not fact. But you're my brother. I know you, Jamm. I've known it since you decked me that first night back. Something's changed or broken, and all I want to do is help. Put it straight.'

I tried to sound confident, didn't know if it was misplaced.

'I think finding out about Cam and me was just the final straw, and if it's any consolation, it's all over. So there you go. There's your chance. You know full well if she had a choice she'd go for you.'

The words hurt me as they left but I didn't care, I'd say anything to get him off that roof. 'All it takes is a bit of bravery for you to sort it out, and we all know you've got plenty of that.'

He sneered, cutting my attempts dead.

'Because you know all about being brave, don't you, Sonny? You know all about acting like a big man.' The sarcasm poured out of his mouth.

'That's right, I do. What do you think I've been doing the last three months?'

'What, you think robbing a van makes you a man? Are you kidding me? Any idiot could do that.' He was in his stride now, pulling me apart and relishing every word. 'And what about the others? Did you even think what would happen to them if it all went wrong? It wouldn't just be you up in court, you know.'

'But look at us, Jamm. We're all still here, aren't we? Does it bother you that much that we pulled it off without you?'

'No, it doesn't bother me. What bothers me is what happens when you finally do get caught. Cos I'll tell you something, you wouldn't last five minutes inside.'

'Even more reason to let me get on with it, then. Let the coppers do their thing and lock me up. Then I wouldn't be this massive problem to you any more.'

'You think I haven't thought about that? Do you really think that hasn't crossed my mind when I've bailed you out in the past?'

'Then you should've done it. Been as brave as you say you are. Cos from what you just said, you're as big a coward as me.'

'I did it for Mum,' he spat. 'What do you think it would've done to her, to see you banged up?'

'As long as you were around she wouldn't have noticed.'

He yanked me close to him, his face a terrible mixture of anger and anguish.

'And what about me? Did you even think about how I would feel? Did it even occur to you that it would kill me if they put you inside?'

'Course it would,' I answered sarcastically.

'Every day of your life I've looked out for you. EVERY DAY! Even if I didn't want to, even when I wanted to be somewhere else, with someone, anyone, who wouldn't give me the same grief that you do. Did you ever think about that?'

'Then you should've done it!'

He lifted his head skywards, like a volcano set to blow.

'But I couldn't, could I? Because everyone knows that's what I do. Look, there's good old Jamm. Got a problem? Don't worry, dump it on him, he'll sort it out.'

He let me go with a shove and staggered off wildly round the rooftop, arms flailing, voice full of emotion. 'Why do you think I joined up? You think I did it out of choice? I did it because that's all we had left. Mum's behind on the rent, and her benefits had been slashed. It was the only way we could afford to eat.'

I tried to butt in, but he wasn't having it. 'But look. Look how well being a soldier turned out, eh? Look what I did to Tomm. Well that's it! I'm not your dad and I can't do it any more. Any of it. I can't sort it out and I can't bring them back, so it's over. All of it. It's over.'

Tears flooded his face, huge racking sobs bending him double as he stumbled against the railing, pulling a pistol from his waistband as he slid to the floor.

'What are you doing?' I paced towards him, hands outstretched in fear. 'Give me the gun, eh?'

He looked up, grinning through the tears as he pulled his arm away from me.

'What, you think I'm going to do something daft with it? Think I'm going to turn it on myself?' He shook his head. 'That'd be too easy. Know why I've got this?'

I didn't have a clue.

'Because when they find me with it, it's five years inside, no parole. Add that on to the joyriding and the statue and everything else, and we're talking a ten-stretch. Even if I behave myself.'

And without warning, he fired into the air: three rapid shots that had me lunging for the gun.

'WHAT ARE YOU DOING?' I screamed. 'I don't understand, Jamm! Why are you doing this to yourself?'

'Because it's what I deserve. Because I killed them.'

'Who, Jamm? Who did you kill?'

'Tommo. Wayne.'

I still had no idea who Wayne was but it didn't matter.

'But that's not true, mate. You know it's not. We all know what you did. We've seen the reports. You're a hero.'

'Don't call me that.'

'Why? Why be ashamed when it's everything you are?'

'I'm warning you, don't call me that.'

'Then let me help you, Jamm, please?' I meant it. Couldn't bear to see him fall apart when he'd done everything he could for Tomm. 'Let me get you off the roof. If we go now, we can hide you. Get you out of here till it blows over. They don't know it's you up here. Not yet.'

He shook his head firmly and let another three bullets go. A clear message he wasn't going anywhere, that he still wanted to be found.

'LEAVE. ME. ALONE.' He spoke the words with the same rhythm as the shots, but as he finished, I heard his voice crack, saw his shoulders sink as he broke into long gasping sobs.

I didn't know what to do. He'd gone between extremes too quickly for me to work out how to play it. So I stood there, watching my brother fall apart in front of me.

Until it hurt too much to watch.

Slowly I slid down the wall too. The gun shook in his hand until I prised it from him, laying it on the floor next to me, terrified I might set it off again.

'It's all right, Jamm,' I whispered, not knowing if it was at all. 'It's all right. I promise you.'

'It's not.' His words were quiet but strong. 'Can't ever be.'

'It can. Whatever it is that's doing this to you, we can sort it out. You just have to tell me. When have I ever let you down?'

He smiled through the tears at the ridiculousness of what I'd just said.

'Apart from all the time,' I added quickly.

'It's all just so screwed, Sonny. All of it. And there's nothing I can do to change it.'

'There is though, mate. You can talk to me. You can. I might be a nightmare, but I can still help.'

He sighed, a long deep soul-destroying noise that I

thought would be followed by silence. But it wasn't. This was a different brother, a different Jamm.

He didn't do what I expected any more.

Instead he turned his head towards me and began to speak.

JAMMY

My pack felt heavy. Guilt obviously weighed a ton.

I tried to deal with Wayne's death by keeping busy, checking my kit, my rifle, but even as I cleaned, the events of the bombing looped in my head. And as hard as I tried to hide it, well, I failed.

They weren't daft, the officers. They'd seen enough lads like me fall apart before their eyes to know I could fold the same way. So they stuck me in front of the doctor back at the base. Questions followed. Half an hour of them, every one a trap as deadly as anything rigged up in the square.

Regret?

Of course, sir . . . sadness that the boy was killed. That anyone was.

Guilt?

No. Disappointment that it came to this. Though it reminds us why we're here. Sharpens the resolve.

The sentences tumbled out. So many I lost track, too many were lies.

I'm sleeping well. Clean out by ten. Shows my head's at rest.

I watched his pen scratch the pad but had no idea whether

I was being condemned. It made me nervous, led me to ramble.

Home?

I've not thought much about it lately. Hard to when you're focused here. There's so much still to do.

Whatever I said, it worked. Enough to earn a salute and a 'carry on', which led me straight back to Wayne.

I dreamed up so many scenarios, so many ways of avenging him that there were moments where I felt invincible again. Like I'd sucked up some weird superpower that left me immune to any bullet or bomb.

But that's all they were, moments. I never carried them with any confidence once patrols started. No matter how many they threw at us.

Slowly, I followed Tommo through the gate, each of us tapping Davenport's name as we left. The letters were fading. Soon we'd simply be touching a plank, forgetting he had ever been there.

Dusk patrols were the worst. We were at our lowest. Parched from the sun's battering, yet aware that in three hours we'd be prowling in the dark, unaware of which direction footsteps would be echoing from.

That day the sun was setting, winking at us from behind a mountain to our left, a cheeky reminder it'd be back in a few hours for more torment. Everything felt its power, leaving it wilted, lazy, and as a result I couldn't believe our patrol would be anything but routine.

And at first it was. We were circling the perimeter of town, keeping tabs on movement in and out, which for the first couple of hours added up to a procession of the mangiest dogs on the planet. They weren't any kind of breed: it would've been an insult to mongrels to even call them that.

I was wary of them, though. Reckoned they could go a few rounds with the toughest Staffies back on the Ghost, and there was no way I was going home because of a dog bite.

Things only changed when the sun finally gave up. On our third lap, we found an empty truck. On point, I'd spotted it first and felt the danger, fearing a trail of IEDs leading up to it. But none came.

It was more of a van than a truck, I suppose, possibly white before the rust had eaten its body.

Keys in the ignition, but engine off.

Rear passenger tyre blown out: hardly surprising, there was no tread left on any of them.

The windows at the back had long gone, tape and cardboard hugging the space instead. Made the huge padlock below it a bit useless, despite its size. Whatever was inside, they still wanted to protect it.

I called it in; the boss was keen to see for himself, not happy for anyone to blow the lock without him.

'Think about it. Could be anything in there.'

Instead he had us wait for the bomb guys to sweep underneath, checking for wires, pressure pads, anything that screamed IED. I prayed there was nothing, breath easing when they found only what we had: scratchy footprints running from both front doors.

The boss played it straight, set up a perimeter while we waited for tools to cut the lock away. I faced the rear doors full-on, rifle cocked and shaking slightly, on guard in case there was anyone left inside.

There wasn't, but the space wasn't empty, far from it. It was packed with an arsenal that made ours look like a toybox. Pistols, semi-automatic weapons, grenades you could throw, others that demanded to be launched. It was unlike anything I'd ever seen.

As we climbed into the van, two mopeds flashed to our left, each of them carrying two people. Young. Early twenties. Packing pistols of their own. Engines screamed as they powered by, each rear passenger craning to see what we'd found. Their desperation told us it was their haul we'd uncovered.

The boss's rifle flashed beside me, a torrent of bullets eating at the dust around the bikes, but hitting nothing. It was all I needed to tuck my own weapon to my chin and let fly, feeling the butt kick into my shoulder with every release.

But with every bullet, Wayne died again in my head. The pain threatened to tear me up.

All around me bullets sped, puncturing the sky but little else. We were losing range, so, with a deep breath, I squinted hard and focused on the rear tyre of the trailing bike. With a gentle squeeze the bullets left me, the first one clipping the wheel, flipping the rear end high into the air. As the passenger flicked skywards, a dozen bullets ripped into his body, forcing him into a pained dance. He fell harder than the bike, limbs bent and lifeless, as the other moped sped on, disappearing into the edges of town.

We moved on the boss's orders and took only seconds to

reach the blown-out moped, its rider and passenger. I didn't risk even the briefest of glances in their direction, though.

I hadn't washed Wayne off my trembling hands yet, and the fear of seeing his face there instead of the riders was too much to bear.

JAMMY

The second scooter lay on its side, engine whining like a hungry dog.

Small pockets of men stood talking nearby with their backs to it, denying any knowledge of the bike or its riders. Within seconds of our arrival they shuffled from the square, eyes down, never daring to meet ours.

We watched them suspiciously, doubting any of them could be the guys who'd fled from us. They'd be hiding in one of the buildings, tooling up, knowing they'd need every gun they could find.

The twelve of us fanned across the square, hearing the intercom bounce between us.

'Keep talking,' buzzed the boss's voice. 'Anything in those buildings even twitches I want to know.'

I found myself beside Tommo, back to back, packs almost resting against each other. I could hear his breathing, feel his back rising and falling.

'You see anything?' Tommo asked.

'Not a thing, but it's coming.' I was sure of that.

Our concentration couldn't waver despite the fear, not

even when back-up arrived, a further sixty boots kicking dust into the air. My shoulders tensed, remembering how thick the air had been when Wayne's bomb went off.

I saw the boss peel away to the other officers, watched information pass between them quick as an electric current.

'All right, listen up,' barked the boss. 'Our targets exited the square at the south-west corner, which suggests they're holed up in one of the back streets beyond. We will proceed and establish their whereabouts, leaving a presence here in case we drive them back into the open.'

I heard guns click as adrenalin pumped veins wide open.

'Jammy, Tomm, take point.'

I followed his instructions quickly, not wanting to spend a second longer here than I had to; every inch of the square was packed full of Little Wayne.

We marched with purpose, straining for anything: movement, noise, a chance to stamp ourselves all over the situation.

But we came nowhere close, because as our feet hit the side street, the sky was torn apart by a flash of light so bright I thought the world was ending. A second later the ground erupted, spitting each of us to the ground, cowering beneath an avalanche of dust and rubble.

I wasn't hurt, no blood that I could see, just white noise screaming in my ears, scrambling my brain with sickening déjà vu.

At first I lay there motionless, too petrified to open my eyes in case I was confronted with the past. Bricks covering me only toppled when I was finally pulled upright, the terror easing slightly as Tommo appeared above me, alive but coated in dust. I pulled him into me, squeezing so hard that he coughed and told me to let go.

Slowly we clambered over the debris, trying to pick out shapes or faces that we recognized. My heart was going mental, head skidding as the blast played again and again, each boom getting louder, more intense.

'Mortar attack,' the boss winced, looking each of us in the eye, lingering longer with me, I was sure. 'Everyone fit?'

We barked back, me included. Had to shake the fear by ploughing on.

'Let's go.'

We created three banks of four, the boss in the middle, our eyes covering every doorway, window and rooftop that came into view. But nothing moved or twitched: not even a cat dared cross our path. Made me wonder if the blast had taken everyone out but us.

It was a stupid thought, as dumb as they come, for as soon as it flashed into my head a shot rang out, a single piercing crack that sliced between Tommo and me, lifting JC clean off his feet.

He crumpled, eyes glazing before he even hit the ground. A fountain of blood sped from him, and as hard as Giffer tried, he couldn't stem it, or push any life back inside the body. By the time we dragged JC into a doorway, to shield both him and us from more punishment, we'd already lost him.

'MAN DOWN! MAN DOWN!'

With a single phrase, the boss focused us, trained our eyes back to the roof for any sign of the sniper who'd taken JC.

Nothing.

Instead we split up, two men still working on JC as the rest shimmied along the street edge, holding ourselves tightly against the shadows, stupidly hoping it would mask our boot-heavy pacing.

Ten metres became twenty, twenty-five, thirty, but as we approached a single lamp hanging from a shop, everything went biblical again, a torrent of bullets raging from every direction. We scattered through doors, behind bins, or in my case behind a battered car. I fell next to the driver's door, chest pumped full of both adrenalin and fear.

'That's ENOUGH!' I roared. Tommo slid in beside me and reloaded.

'You all right? Not hit, are you?' he whimpered, eyes wider than saucers.

I shook my head, trying to keep my panic from him.

'You were right, Jamm. Stupid idea, joining up. I'm not made for this.'

'We're still breathing. Get out of this and we'll all be heroes.' I couldn't believe how calm I sounded. It surprised me, concentrated my senses.

'We are going to get out, aren't we?'

Bullets shattered the window above us, showering glass on to our helmets, stopping me answering him. I had no idea what I would have said anyway.

'You see anything?' he asked, as I dared to peek around the bumper.

'Two of them. Third floor, two o'clock.'

Tommo shuffled to the other end of the car and craned round, scampering back with a yelp as a volley of bullets snapped past.

'There must be more than two of 'em . . .'

'Probably, but let's start there.'

Resting on my elbows, with rifle poised, I kept low to the ground, and with a deep breath released a stream of bullets that raced away, chipping walls and, hopefully, bone.

But my attack was met by a counter, my head dropping to the ground as bullets whistled past. It left me with a terrifying thought: How long till they get bored and launch a grenade at us instead?

'Tomm, we've got to move.'

'What? Why?'

'We're wide open here.'

'There's a car between us. What are you on about?'

'Trust me, mate.'

Tommo swore loudly, eyes roaming, looking for anything else we could dive through or under.

'We should go separate ways. Divide 'em. Would give us more chance.'

I chewed it over. It might, or they might just choose one of us to chase. The thought pulled at my insides and the promises I'd made to come home safe and united.

'You see something to go for?'

He pointed at a door on the left-hand side of the street. 'Reckon I can barge straight through that. Window should give me a shot back at them too.'

'Right. Let's do it, then. On my word. Don't stop or look, just have it.'

I had no real idea where I was going yet, only that I was going first, to draw the fire, give Tomm a bigger chance. So without warning I broke to the left, only hollering 'NOW!'

after half-a-dozen steps, my rifle flaming as I let a round go. No way could they fire back if they were ducking.

The only thing I hadn't worked out was where to hide. There were no more vehicles, and the doors wore padlocks that I hadn't the time to blast, let alone pick.

So when I spotted a broken window, ten metres ahead, I dived for it, landing inside with a crunching thud and a scream.

But the scream didn't come from me. My rifle followed it to the corner of the room and found three shadows, huddled and trembling. A couple, arms wrapped defensively around a boy, too close to Wayne in age not to be another excrutiating reminder.

The woman spoke, words I didn't understand, but with a fear that was obvious.

Her husband stood in front of me, palms outstretched, making me notice my rifle pointing straight at him. I dropped it to my side, offered a greeting. One of the few words I'd learned.

It did little to settle them.

'We have nothing,' the man said in English, his words clear and matter-of-fact.

His house had given me everything I needed. I told him so.

'I'm sorry. I'll leave as soon as I know where the gunfire is coming from.'

'Then you need more than two eyes.'

'There are many gunmen?'

'Men, women. Some no more than children.' His son picked that moment to cling to his waist, half scared, half interested in me. I flinched.

'You know them?'

He shrugged. 'Of course.'

'And you know where they are?'

'Some. Not all.'

I resisted the urge to lift my rifle instantly.

'So you're prepared to show me?'

'They are no more my friends than you are.'

I had no idea at first if that was a yes or a no, but I followed him as he crept towards the broken window.

JAMMY

He pointed me to a flat about forty metres ahead. Top floor.

At first I saw nothing.

'Be patient,' he whispered, like they could hear him.

So I crouched and squinted into the dark, until two bodies dashed across the space where glass should've been. They were only in view for a second, but there was no mistaking the rifles they were carrying.

We waited a minute more until they struggled by with another piece of kit. The sort that can take out a whole town, never mind a street.

'How long have they been smuggling this stuff in?'

'Weeks.'

'And we didn't see it?'

'It doesn't seem so.'

My cheeks burned at his contempt, and as I had no answer I turned back to the window. 'Is there another way into that block?'

'Not from here. But the building next door to it? There is a back entrance.'

I was on the comms before he could finish, bombarding the boss with intel, the kind he loved.

'You see 'em?' I asked, not sure if he could pick it up from his vantage point.

'I do. We'll have to wait for back-up. No way can we risk driving on with what they're packing.'

The family's eyes were on me. All of them expectant. The boy so reminiscent of Wayne I felt I owed him something immediately.

'No need, boss. There's a back entrance. I can get to it from my position.'

'How do you know all this?'

'Local knowledge. Family whose door I crashed.'

'And you believe them?'

'Well, they haven't kicked me back out into the street, have they? I reckon it's sound, sir. And we can't wait. From the look of it they're shipping the stuff out right now.'

Silence. Only an occasional crackle and the sound of the boss's brain whirring. After an eternity, he came back.

'Right. This is how it works. On my call, we send out some fire from here. Should give enough cover to get you across the street and through the door you need to hit.'

'Got it.'

'But Jammy! Once you locate the back entrance, you wait to engage. Only on my word do you enter that building. Clear?'

'Absolutely.'

'And Tommo goes with you.'

'No need, bo– '

'That's non-negotiable. Now wait for my call.'

I did as he said, though I'd rather have gone alone. It wasn't like Tommo had Wayne to avenge. That was only me.

Keeping below the window I scrabbled back to the family, and shook off my pack.

In the side pocket I found a bundle of pens and boiled sweets that I offered to the boy. He only took them when his father told him to, snatching them from my hands out of fear, not greed. A smile crept over his face as he took in his hoard, and it pumped some steel into me, just when I needed it.

The pack slid on to my back again easily. I barely noticed the weight.

'All right. On my word,' whispered the boss in my ear as I scampered back to the window, taking in a last deep lungful of air. 'GO!'

And with that, it was Guy Fawkes' night, the sky lighting up with a thousand bangers.

Twisting my head in the direction of the enemy, and with bullets of my own to protect me, I tore across the road, back in the direction of the car I'd hidden behind earlier.

It was chaos, the rattling of bullets so confusing that I had no idea where they were coming from. Only when one bounced millimetres from my right boot did I realize they were firing back.

With a despairing dive I rolled behind the car, hearing the sound of bullets tearing into metal. I stared at the bodywork hoping the rust hadn't eaten away its resistance. I couldn't die here. Wouldn't.

Frantically I searched for Tommo, spotting him in a window on the other side of the street, gun raised, bleeding ammo, being a soldier. I yelled at him, taking a dozen attempts and a frantic amount of waving to be heard against the overpowering din.

I pointed in the direction of our target, saw him nod, mouth 'ten seconds' then disappear from sight.

Pulling myself into a crouch, I checked I was good for ammo, then heaved in three deep breaths, hoping that would be enough to see me across the road safely.

With a scream, I hurled myself back into full view. Eyes on the door, but bullets streaming from my nozzle. I didn't care where they hit as long as they kept them at bay. Feeling Tommo's presence behind me, the two of us piled through our target, the wooden door giving like cardboard under my shoulder. With a relieved cry and our lungs on fire, we crashed to the floor, Tommo laughing hysterically. 'What's going on out there? How many guys have they got hidden?'

I slapped his back as we hoisted each other skywards. 'Don't even think about it. You've faced more on the Xbox, haven't you?'

'Aye, but I can pause that, can't I? Can't imagine I can have a break for a beer and a pee now, eh?'

I laughed at the madness of it, craving a can and a bog break more than anything. In that moment, all that mattered was having Tommo with me. The one who'd run with me all my life, the one who ate ketchup with everything, even toast, the one who'd survived endless nights at the wrong end of a drunk dad. My brother. Cam's brother.

I wanted to hug him but couldn't. There was too much kit in the way for starters. Fortunately, whatever was going on, he was feeling it too. His hand stretched out and gripped mine, eyes boring a hole right into the middle of me.

'It'll be all right, Jamm. A week and we'll be back home. It'll seem like a breeze next to this.'

'You reckon pulling Sonny into line'll be easy?'

He chuckled and shrugged. 'Well, it'll be different . . . Only bullets will be the ones leaving his mouth.'

'I'd settle for that right now.'

He looked at me and smiled.

'Me too, pal. Me too.'

JAMMY

The building was like the whole country in miniature: hot and dusty.

We picked our way through the darkness carefully, not wanting to disturb anything, painfully aware they could've laced the entire floor with IEDs to stop us getting close to what they were guarding.

For once, though, there were no surprises, no one waiting for us except for the rats that dashed across our paths, looking for a hole where there were no soldiers, bombs or explosions. Wherever that place was, they weren't going to find it quickly.

I tried to shake the tension from my arms without allowing my guard to drop, but failed. This was it, my chance to try and put things straight.

But as we reached the rear of the building, our ears were pulled back to the street by a ferocious rally of ammo. We raced to the window to see a group of uniforms snaking up towards the car that had sheltered us. Despite their determination, they seemed to move in slow motion, packs dragging their bodies into awkward crouching movements. How had we made it, moving as slowly as them?

Thrusting our rifles into the night air, we looked for someone, anyone, to fire at, but the angles were too sharp, their hiding places too canny for us to reach.

I wanted to scream, as all we could do was watch their bullets trace ever closer to the lads we had promised to fight for, to die for if we had to.

A bullet crashed home, splaying a leg wide open. I strained to see who had taken the impact, but could make out only shadows, two helmeted figures hoisting the body up and towards the car, regardless of the risk to themselves.

Safety catch off, I raced to the door but was yanked back by Tommo.

'Don't be daft, Jamm. There's nothing you can do. Wait for the boss's word.'

But what if it was the boss who'd taken the hit? Where did that leave us?

'Don't give us away. We need this cover.'

He was right, we had no option but to watch, as with a final, huge effort they plunged behind the car's body and out of sight.

I should've been relieved, but as we radioed in for an update, the madness made a return, a mechanical scream ripping at our senses as the car disappeared from view, eaten alive by a monstrous ball of fire.

The impact blew us off our feet and on to the trembling floor. Instinctively we curled into balls, expecting the walls to tumble around us. But apart from a hideous stink of burning metal and flesh, we were left untouched.

This time it was me holding Tommo back as he screamed incoherently, pulling me closer to the street.

'Get back, mate, get back! Look at it. It's too late!'

Tomm yanked his helmet from his head, and pulled at his hair, reminding me of the nervous mess he'd been when we first arrived.

'It's so screwed up, Jamm. All of it!'

He didn't have to tell me. I was feeling everything he was but couldn't let him know, couldn't risk us both being out of control. So I grabbed at his straps and pulled him close. 'Listen, you're breathing, mate. And so am I. We'll be all right.'

'But we won't, will we? Look at that car. That was us five minutes ago. How long till they know we're here? How long till they do the same to us?'

I didn't allow him to look anywhere but in my face, to see that I could make it all OK.

'We won't be here, pal. We're going to do what we planned. Find this back exit and stop them.'

His shoulders stopped shaking for a moment, the tears rolling from his eyes almost stopping too. He'd clearly heard me but wished he hadn't.

'But that's not what we were meant to do. The boss said wa—'

'And now the boss isn't answering. So what other choice have we got? If we wait, they'll have the rest of the weapons out of here and the whole town'll be more volatile than ever.'

'Then let 'em. A week till we go home, Jamm. Think of that.'

'Yeah, but two weeks after that, where will we be? Back here! We have to try, mate. You have to trust me.'

'You really believe we can do it?'

I nodded. I had to believe. The alternative was unbearable. All the guilt, the regret about what had happened in the market square, I couldn't carry it around for another minute, never mind another day. It had to be now. Why lug it home and let it strangle the life out of me, when I had this chance to put it straight?

'And if it looks grim, Jamm, then we'll stand down and wait?'

'Of course. When have I ever let you down?'

With those words I had him, trusting enough to ram the helmet back on to his head and fall in behind me as we sneaked into the alley behind our target.

Out there, though, with the humid air clinging to our skin, I realized I had no real idea of where we were heading. The only lead we had came from a man I'd known for five minutes: was it the sort of intel we could trust?

What I did see as we squinted into the dark was a sturdy-looking reinforced door. Usually they looked as thick as a wafer biscuit, riddled with bullets and rot, but this one had some beef to it, the paint faded but not ancient. Made me reckon it had to be our way in. I pointed it out to Tommo, him nodding in agreement.

'Let's sit back and see what happens,' he whispered, still nervy. 'Let them come to us.'

I didn't share his patience. 'But what if there's another exit? For all we know they could be unloading through another door.'

But Tommo wasn't budging. Instead he turned to face me, blocking the door I was desperate to pile through. 'Jamm, this isn't a five-star hotel. Look at it. It's a mess.

There's no other way out except for the front, and I can't see 'em being ballsy enough to leave that way.'

I tried to reason with him, tell him about surprise being our advantage, our wildcard, but no matter how many times we beat it back to each other, we couldn't reach any kind of agreement.

'I'm not having it,' he moaned, trying to walk past me. 'We can't just bundle in there and expect them to roll over. We should pull back, regroup, wait for the boss.'

My temperature boiled over. We were too close to bail out, so, with my rifle in one hand, I grabbed Tomm by his armour and yanked him in front of me, creating a barrier between him and where he wanted to go.

'What are you doing?' he spat. 'Get your hands off me.'

'You're not thinking straight, mate. We can do thi– '

'Maybe you can. You want to play the hero, then go ahead. I'm not bleeding out just so you can have a medal pinned on.'

That was it. It was the last thing I needed to hear when I was so close to something like revenge. Without thinking, I formed a fist and pulled my arm back.

But I never finished the job, for as I raised my arm, the door behind Tommo flew open and a figure appeared, pistol in hand.

Instinctively I dropped my fist and swung my gun arm, index finger twitching over the trigger. But as it gave beneath the pressure, I felt myself stop.

It was the figure in the doorway. He was packing a gun, pointing it straight at us, but not with menace. Instead he was smiling at me as blood oozed down his cheek.

I couldn't believe it. He was back.

It was Little Wayne, his clothes still tattered and burnt from the bomb, his left arm nothing more than a chewed stump, the rags of his sleeve failing to hide his gangrenous wound.

I resisted the urge to run to him as he slumped against the doorframe, still holding the energy to wave the pistol in our direction.

I've no idea what my expression said, but it was enough for Tommo to crane towards the door, a single word leaving his lips and ripping at my eardrums.

'SHHHOOOOOOOT!'

But I didn't. Why would I, when I was off the hook? Instead I trusted what I'd seen, and in that second the nozzle of Wayne's pistol lit up, launching a stream of bullets straight into Tommo's body, so violent that the impact catapulted him off his feet and into my arms.

My eyes flew back to the door, but there was no Wayne any more, no rotting arm or bloodstained face. Just a kid, my age, my height, a shaking pistol in his hand and two semi-automatic rifles slung across his back.

My head, heart, every muscle in my body wanted to cave in, but as Tommo's weight pushed me towards the dust, my free arm unleashed a torrent of its own that blasted the lad back through the door and on to his back, blood erupting from him like lava.

Our bodies, all three of them, shook. A terrible noise like a witch's cackle crept from Tommo's lips, a vapoury spray of blood pocking my face as he exhaled.

Pinned helplessly to the floor, I had no option but to roll

him to the side; as our bodies parted I couldn't mistake what I'd done.

Small, circular rips littered his armour, but I couldn't make out any blood. It was only when my eyes moved to his head that I saw the claret pumping from his neck with such ferocity that I could see the life flooding out of him.

I screamed as I pressed my hands to the wound, watching in horror as the blood streamed between the creases in my fingers.

'HOLD ON!' I yelled at him, pressing hard with one hand, the other grappling for the intercom.

I had no idea what I was hollering into it, no clue who, if anyone, heard me. All I could see was my best mate bleeding out. The horror consumed me, filled up every sense I owned.

From somewhere, Tomm found the energy to raise his hands, and, with a monumental effort, pulled me back down to him, my ear resting flush against his lips. I wanted to pull away, to stem the blood, to walk over to who did this and riddle every inch of his body with bullets, but I couldn't, as Tommo wouldn't let me, his fists as steady, his will as strong as it had ever been. He wanted to tell me something. He wanted me to listen.

At first, it made no sense: a collection of wheezes and rattles. Frustration bit him hard and he pulled my hair, my ear almost inside his mouth as he forced the sounds into words.

'Is . . . is O . . . is OK.'

'What is, mate?' His blood was swamping us. I swear his lips felt colder, though his grip stayed tight.

'All this . . . You . . . is OK . . . is OK . . . I got . . . I got you.'

As the last word crept out, I swear I heard him drown, the blood pooling in his throat before escaping from his neck.

Every inch of me panicked. My hand pushed back against the wound, ear desperate to pick up any trace of breath leaving his lips.

I felt it once. Again. Then again. Then nothing. His lungs gave out, but somehow his arms didn't. They locked me against him and held me there, and I didn't want to move. Not when a door crashed open behind me, not when the night was full of shouting, not even when the bullets started to rain from all directions.

I didn't care where they were coming from: didn't care if they hit.

Tommo had me, had my back.

What was unforgiveable was that I hadn't watched his.

SONNY

I was shivering by the time Jamm finished, my body stiffening after all the running.

But if I felt ropey, then how was he feeling?

I had no words to match Jamm's, and although he'd laid it all out in bare and graphic detail, I had no answers about how to help either.

Instead I shuffled closer and tried to hug him, but it was like trying to wrap your arms around a fridge.

'I'm sorry, Jamm.' I didn't know what else to say.

'Sorry doesn't help,' he replied, agitated. 'I've had sorry on loop for the past month but it doesn't change anything. I've watched them die a million times, over and over again in my head. And it's killing me, cos every time it's still my fault.'

'But that's just it, mate, it isn't. You've told me yourself, you're not well. All this stuff about the kid that died – that wasn't your doing. The terrorists would've found another way to do the same thing, it had nothing to do with you.'

'You weren't there, Sonny. You don't know.'

'But I know you. No way you'd do anything to hurt anyone on purpose. It's me who does that, remember?'

'Not any more.'

I was starting to feel desperate, needed to find a way to get through to him.

'We could talk to someone in the army. Tell them about Wayne and the flashbacks. They'd understand, mate. It must happen all the time.' I had no idea if it did, no idea if Jamm was even replaying it all now. In his head we could've been sat on top of a tumbling building for all I knew.

'It's too late.'

'Course it's not. How can it be too late . . .?'

'Because they're *dead*. Don't you get that, Sonny? Both of them, Wayne *and* Tomm. And both because of me.'

Our rest was over, he was back on his feet and pacing, eyes searching the floor, and by the time I realized what he wanted it was too late, the gun was back in his hand.

'It's time you went.'

'Are you having a laugh? No way I'm leaving you up here.'

'I said, GO.'

'And I said, NO. After what you told me, do you really think I'm going down those stairs? Not while you're still up here holding that thing.'

He took a step forwards, the gun by his side but his face carrying real menace. However this played out, he wanted it on his terms.

But as he reached me, a piercing light cut through the darkness of the sky, throwing the rooftop into almost burning focus. It must've been Jamm's worst nightmare, further evidence that he was slowly losing his mind.

This was no explosion, though. It was a police chopper: a common sight to anyone living on the Ghost.

Without thinking, I threw myself at Jamm, knocking him to the floor as we rolled in the shadows. It wasn't a surprise that they'd launched an aerial patrol, what with the crew raging downstairs and gunfire from up here, but it focused me beautifully. I had to keep Jamm out of sight to stand any chance of evading the police.

He had other ideas, though, his good arm trying to swat me as I straddled him without wrecking his bleeding fist any further.

'What are you doing?'

I was straining too hard to answer. Knew if I held him for a minute longer the chopper would sweep away towards the other towers. All I had to do was stop him getting the shot off that would give us both away.

'They will find me, so you might as well let go,' he ranted.

But I couldn't let that be an option. Had to get the gun out of his hand before he overpowered me.

So, with my stomach turning at the thought, I dug my knee on to his injured hand and twisted hard. He writhed in pain, the pistol slipping to the floor and into my fingers. Confident that the chopper's beam was moving on, I scrambled away from him, threatening to throw the gun over the side of the building.

I was scared. Terrified. Of what he might do if he got hold of it or me again.

I can't begin to tell you how it felt in my hand, except that it wasn't powerful.

The energy it took to hold it above my head pushed me

to the verge of throwing up. Jamm looked equally distressed.

'Don't!' he shouted, eyes bulging. 'Don't. Think about it. Throw it off there and it'll either go off or cave someone's head in. How will that look with my fingerprints all over it? Yours too.'

I felt the gun shake, my brain telling me to let it fall to my side. But for some reason my arm wouldn't listen, which fed Jammy further.

'Come on, pass it over. You say you want to help me? Then give me the gun. I know what I'm doing. I deserve all this.'

'Shut up, will you? I don't need you telling me what to do.' I meant it this time. This time he didn't have all the answers. This time I did.

'You don't need me? Have you heard yourself? There's not been a day when you haven't needed me. Who taught you to tie your laces, or walked you to school cos Mum was at work? Who picked you up when you took a kicking? I leave you for three months and Hitch ends up a skeleton. Tell me again that you don't need me.'

'All right, I admit it, but right now, Jamm, you need me too.'

'You reckon?'

'I know it. You need me to get you off this roof. You need me to sort your head out. And if you mean what you say, you need me to give you the gun.'

'So give me it. Do as you're told for once.'

I turned the handle of the pistol towards him, but moved no closer. All of a sudden, despite the tiredness, and the confusion and the fear of what was going on, my head cleared and I knew what I had to do.

I had to sort it out before the police arrived, because no matter what I told myself, I knew that they'd find us before I could persuade Jamm down the stairs. And I couldn't let that happen. They couldn't find him.

'Come on, then,' I said, trying to make myself sound broken, like he'd worn me down. 'Come and get it.'

I took a step forward and saw him do the same. I had no idea if this would work, whether I could do it without hurting him badly. But there wasn't time to worry. It was all I had left and was well overdue. It was time to pay him back. To do what he and Mum didn't think I was capable of.

So as he leaned forward to take the gun, I whipped my arm forward, the butt making contact just north of his right eye, a jagged gash tearing his forehead.

I heard a noise as he went down cold, but it didn't come from him, it came from the stairwell behind me. It was faint, but I definitely heard it.

Voices. Police, had to be. They were coming.

There was still so much to do. I fell to the floor beside him, relief flooding over me as I heard him breathing. Without hesitation, I pulled at his hoodie, gingerly removing his bloodied arm before hoisting it over his head, avoiding his newest wound.

A second later, after removing and ripping my own jumper, which I wrapped like a bandage around his head and hand, I was wearing the hoodie myself, tying the drenched dressing from his wrist around my own.

I knew I had minutes, if that, before either he woke up, or the coppers reached me. So I pulled Jamm to a spot on the furthest edge of the roof, out of sight of the doorway. It was shadowy there, full of debris that people had dumped.

I didn't want to do it but had no option, so I pulled everything I could find on top of him. A pram frame, traffic cones, decayed and stinking bin bags. It didn't matter as long as it hid him and bought me time.

I raced back to the centre of the roof with one more thing to do.

Get rid of the gun.

Ditch it before anyone but the two of us saw it.

Carefully, I wiped any trace of prints from the grip and carried it, wrapped in Jamm's hoodie, over to the vents.

Could I hide it inside one of them? No, they were all screwed tight, no time or tools to get the covers off and on.

I spun around, looking for any place I could stash it, but there was nowhere. I heard more shouts from the stairwell, louder, closer, so close I thought again about throwing the pistol over the edge of the tower.

But then I saw it. A bird's nest, wedged on top of a water pipe and caked in years of fossilized droppings. It was perfect. Rank enough to stop people touching it but deep enough to hide something inside. The gun slid in perfectly, holster-like, every bit of it hidden.

There was no way I'd look for a gun there; I hoped no one else would make the leap either. Not until I told one of the lads to get rid of it. But that could come later. Once I'd done what was necessary.

I didn't feel nervous as I paced towards the stairwell, not even when the voices below grew louder.

Instead I thought of Jamm, what he'd seen, what he thought he'd done.

I still had no idea how we could help him or chase the demons away. All I knew was that for now he was safest where he was. He'd find no answers curled up in a cell.

So, with a final deep breath, I stepped off the roof and on to the stairs, making as little noise as I could. I needed to get down as many steps as possible, to keep them away from the roof, Jammy and the gun.

I managed four flights before torchlight found me, voices demanding I stand still, raise my hands, face the wall.

And for once I did as I was told.

I was used to hearing orders. Usually they came from Jamm. And usually I ignored them. But not this time. This was what had to happen. I'd stepped up. It was what brothers did.

SONNY

The stairwell wall was cold against my cheek, especially after fifteen minutes rammed up against it. It wasn't like I had a plan any more. All I'd ever had was knocking Jamm out and taking the blame. Hardly sophisticated. From this point on I was busking it.

I'd hoped they'd pat me down and whisk me away, one more scumbag to lock up while they took control on the ground.

So when they held me on the stairs and dispatched two officers to the roof, my heart started banging again.

Every second was agony. I'd no idea how long Jamm would be out for, or whether I'd dumped nearly enough stuff on him to keep him out of sight.

And as for the gun? Well, if they found that, we were in another league of trouble.

'Are you on your own?' they asked.

I nodded, didn't trust my mouth not to give the game away.

Did that mean the chopper had only spotted one of us? I hoped so.

I imagined them up there, tearing the roof apart,

checking the vents, bins, anything with a lid big enough to hide inside. The thought of them finding him wrecked me, had me grasping wildly at ways to pull them from their search.

'I don't feel well,' I stuttered lamely.

No response. An arm still held me firmly against the wall.

'Did you hear me? I said I don't feel well!' I tried to resist, make enough of a fuss that they'd need all of them to carry me to the ground floor.

It was naive. I know that now. The search didn't end. Instead I was bounced down the stairs by two of the biggest coppers I'd ever seen, cursing them as we went, reinforcing their opinion of what a waster I was.

As we walked outside, though, I could see it wasn't only me acting up. There were plenty of others making life difficult. The statue was only smoking now, but a handful of other fires burned instead. Waste bins had been set alight and in the far corner I could see an emergency crew tackling another blazing car. Sirens, shouts and alarms filled my ears, adding to the terror of what had happened and what was yet to come. They'd make an example of someone for all this and I knew I'd be at the front of the queue, as long as they didn't find Jammy.

They marched me across the square towards a line of riot vans, one of them rocking on its wheels, probably full of angsty Cudas. Knowing my luck I'd be thrown in with them. Still, it'd mean I wouldn't have to face a judge: no point if there was nothing left of me to sentence.

We were only metres from the van when the next complication appeared in my path: Mum and Cam.

Their faces were packed with worry, Mum throwing herself at the copper holding me. 'That's my son!' she yelled.

'My commiserations,' he answered, doing little for any of our moods.

'Well, where are you taking him?'

He looked at her, disbelieving. 'On holiday, clearly. We heard the Caribbean's lovely this time of year.'

'You can't do this,' she screamed, grappling at the cuffs strangling my hands. 'Not without good reason.'

'How about possession of a handgun, madam, or discharging said weapon in a public place?'

Mum let go of me, eyes squinting in disbelief as she asked me if it was true.

'Course it's not. They haven't found any gun, have they? And they won't either. It's not true, Mum. I haven't fired anything.'

The officer tried to take control and march me on, but not before Cam asked a question of her own.

'Did you find him, Sonny? Did you find him?'

I had no idea what to say, not in the time I had or without giving Jamm away. My head scrambled for a cryptic answer as I was pushed into the back of a van, but I came up with nothing but a gabbled: 'It'll be OK. I sorted it.'

I had no idea if the truth in that statement would hold for even the next minute, but right then it was all I had. I hoped it was enough: that she could fill Mum in about Jammy without her going off the deep end.

To my relief the van was empty, and although I could see both Cam and Mum shouting at me through the tinted windows, I couldn't hear what they were saying. Nor could they see the kicks I aimed at the walls, frustration eating me from the inside out.

What was I going to do? How long till the police gave up the search and accepted I was the only one up there?

I had to hope their patience was short, knew full well that Jammy would give himself up if he could. There was no way he'd hide out and wait for them to leave. He wanted to be punished. That's what this was all about.

My head raced, struggling to know where to start, never mind find the answers.

I'd done the right thing, hadn't I? What Jamm had done for me all his life. So why wasn't it sorted?

I replayed what he'd told me, questioned everything I'd said back, whether I'd missed a way to tease him off the roof before he got happy with the gunfire.

My head reeled as sweat pooled on my face, but it was no use. I knew nothing, even by the time the van pulled up outside the police station.

The journey had been slow. It had taken half an hour to crawl off the estate, a hundred fists banging and kicking the van as we left. I tuned the noise out, kept my eyes on the top of Pickard House. It was pointless, no way would I see Jamm from so far away, but it gave me something to focus on, stopped me worrying about what lay ahead.

They marched me into the station with some urgency, bypassing a crowd of rioters who were still trying to wrestle their way free. I didn't put up a fight. I had none left in me. Instead I answered their questions and let them take prints, not bothering to wipe the ink off when they offered me a tissue. Instead I kept my head down and my mouth shut, one eye on the stream of new arrivals.

Jamm's face didn't appear while I was there, and once they'd thrown me into a cell I pressed my face against the peephole, scanning for a glimpse of him.

Minutes passed slowly, torturously edging towards an hour, then two. My calves ached but I refused to sit. If Jamm saw sense and had sneaked away to find the lads, then we had a chance. I could soak up whatever they threw at me as long as it kept him safe and free. There was no way he'd survive this, not when his head was already so tattered.

I thought again about what he'd told me, about the bomb inside the ball and the endless firefights. I wondered how he'd managed to carry it all for so long.

I had no idea how to make his guilt disappear, but we'd find a way between us. We'd beg the army for help, sell everything we had if it gave us the cash for a doctor. There was no way I was coming this far to still end up failing him. It wasn't an option.

The cells filled up around me, complaints bouncing off the walls, demands for phone calls and solicitors. One idiot even asked what time breakfast arrived, though I imagined he already knew the answer. Few of those banged up were strangers to this place.

Within hours the floor was chocker, each door closed, complete with a name scribbled in chalk. None of them read 'James McGann'.

I started timing the gaps between new inmates arriving, feeling hopeful as the intervals got longer. I should've been delighted when half an hour lapsed, but that landmark passed me by. Sleep had grabbed hold of me and only let go when I heard a key scratching at the door. I stumbled backwards as it opened, stifling a groan as Jamm was shoved towards me.

They'd found him. Or he'd found them. The details didn't matter. He was here: my plan was lying on the floor in bits.

'We thought you'd fancy some company,' the copper said. 'Not that you'll get much chat from this one. If you find out his name, give me a yell.'

He locked the door and left, no idea who he'd thrown together or the lifeline it gave us.

Silently I led Jamm to the bunk and sat him down. He was a mess. The gash to his head had been dressed, but he was caked in crusted blood. His clothes were torn and stinking, his hands a collage of bandage, blood and paint. I cringed and rubbed at them but the paint was way too stubborn.

It wasn't good: they might not know his name yet, but the paint would lead the police straight to the graffiti in the town, if they were smart enough to make the leap. I didn't even want to think about how many traces were on the stolen car's steering wheel.

I had to get through to him, find out what they already knew, how we could build a story tight enough to see him march out of here by morning.

'What happened, Jamm?' I whispered. 'Where did they find you?'

He didn't answer, barely managed to blink. I crouched in front of him, my hands warming his. 'Jamm. Come on, mate.

I need you to talk to me. I can help you, you know that, don't you?'

Nothing.

'I know you're mad about what I did up there and I'm sorry, but I can put all of this straight. I just need to know what happened after I left you on the roof.'

Silence.

'Come on, Jamm!' Irritation simmered inside me. I couldn't believe this. We'd been gifted another chance but he was refusing to take it. He must have heard me, was staring straight back as I spoke, but for some reason he wouldn't give me even the vaguest sign.

'You say you can't do this any more, be the one who carries everything around? Well, you don't have to. I listened, you see, to what you told me up there. I can do it for you, mate. I want to. It's time, isn't it? Time I tied your laces for a change!' I hoped a joke might help, but it didn't scratch the surface. His face didn't move or twitch, the rise and fall of his chest so controlled that you had to listen hard to even hear him breathe.

I paced in front of him, feeling myself descend into the kind of anger that always got me into trouble, but I couldn't help it.

'Don't you understand what's going on here? They've taken your prints. They're running them through the computer right now. How long do you think it's going to take them to piece it all together, Jamm? How long till they match them up to the car you wrapped round the statue? And what if they find the gun? Come on, tell me. How long?'

His face didn't change, but I felt my heart break as silent

tears fell down his cheeks. It wasn't my words getting to him. I knew that. My only guess was that he was back in Afghanistan again, watching Tommo die in front of him, guilt swelling every time it happened.

It was pointless even trying to get through. His body might have been in front of me, but tonight had broken him. I closed my eyes and exhaled hard before crouching in front of him again, pulling his head into my chest.

We didn't move or speak for minutes, not even when the door opened again, our friendly officer returning with surprise in his voice.

'You're never going to believe what we've found out.' He laughed, though I knew he wasn't amused. 'You two share the same surname. Would you believe it?'

I ignored him, whispering into Jamm's ear, 'It'll be OK.'

'Not only that,' the copper continued. 'Turns out your address is the same too. Unbelievable, eh?' I heard him get closer, his voice change.

'Now I don't know what's going on here, but I don't like being taken for a mug. So up you get, Sonny, your brother's coming with me.'

I didn't turn round or move my hands from where they rested. 'I meant what I said,' I whispered again. 'It'll all get sorted. All of this. Whatever happens, me, Mum, the lads, we know what you are. Remember that.'

Our friend was getting riled now, his boots louder on the floor. 'I said, on your feet.'

I held my ground.

'This is your last chance, Sonny. Move yourself before I do it for you.'

I squeezed our Jammy harder and held on tight.

The copper could say it as many times as he wanted. Call every officer left in the building. I wasn't doing this for him or anyone else.

I was doing this for my brother.

 SONNY

We stood in a line, all six of us, on the far side of the car park.

It seemed like the best place to wait: we didn't want to smother him as soon as he appeared. If I was nervous, then how was he feeling?

Six months was a long time, and although we'd all visited, I had no idea how he'd react when he was on the outside and confronted by the whole mob.

I knew it wasn't just me who was nervous. Mum and Cam stood on one side of me, squeezing each other's hands so tightly the veins on their arms popped. Den was beside them, trying to hide a tear that had escaped from his eye.

On the other side of me was Wiggs, pulling hungrily on a cig, the smoke drifting straight into Hitch, leaning on his sticks.

'Can't you blow that the other way?' he complained.

'Have a word with the wind, not me,' he answered. They'd been bickering ever since we set off, Hitch upset that he'd had to share the back of the van with his chain-smoking pal.

I didn't tell them to shut up. I welcomed the banter, more evidence that things were getting back to normal. All right,

Hitch wasn't ready to run the marathon, but you could see the strength returning to his stick-thin legs by the day. And as for the gear? He'd been nowhere near it. We'd made sure of that.

My watch told me it was time but the doors remained closed, adding to my agitation. Without shifting my gaze, I bent down to scratch my ankle.

The skin around the tag was chaffed and sore from rubbing against it.

I swear the officer strapped it tightly on purpose, annoyed that I was being let out at all. He'd have locked me up and swallowed the key if he'd had his way.

It had come as a surprise to me too. My solicitor shook his head as we parted on the court steps. 'I'd fart quietly from now on if I were you,' he advised me. Not the advice I'd expected, but I forgave him. He'd done his job.

'Leave that thing alone, will you?' Mum moaned. 'You'll only make it worse.'

'It's doing my head in,' I moaned. But I did as she said. Had made more of a habit of that lately.

'It's better than the alternative though, eh?'

There wasn't much you could say to that. She was bang on.

It had been rough for her. The amount she'd had to deal with would have floored most people, but she hadn't let it. Instead, as the truth about that night and the severity of Jamm's condition became clear, she simply soaked it up and carried it with her from shift to shift. She never complained or tried to share what was going on in her head; she just found another gear and powered on, finding time to visit him at least weekly.

There were times when I saw the strain, but they were quiet moments that I never wanted to disturb, her sat at the table with a shot of vodka, plenty of ice to make it stretch that bit further.

I did what I could. Begged anyone who would listen to give me work. I found a few forgiving souls who let me hump boxes and stack shelves. It wasn't important what I did, as long as I could come home with something to put in the biscuit tin, enough to sort out tea for a couple of days. I always held a bit back, though, had a project that wasn't going to pay for itself: one that had to be ready by today. And it was, sort of.

Mum saw the change in me, but again we didn't dwell on it. It wasn't until we wound up in court that she heard the full truth of what had happened on the roof (well, the full truth minus the gun; there were some things that would never be spoken of).

After the sentencing, she linked her arm in mine and told me we were walking home. I expected a lecture or a final warning but it never came.

She didn't really say anything. We just walked, letting the wind blow us about, each of us soaking up the relief that we'd hoped for but never really expected.

And since then? Well, it's been the same but different between us.

So much had happened on that roof that we couldn't possibly go over it all again. She knew I'd tried to help Jamm and I knew a part of her was proud of me. Didn't matter how big it was. I knew it existed and that was enough.

*

I was the first to spot Jamm as the doors opened. The others were arguing about something – probably Wiggy lighting up yet another smoke. And as soon as I saw him I felt overwhelmingly lucky.

Lucky that he smiled when he saw us, lucky that we hadn't lost him like we had Tommo, and lucky that the glass door behind him slid shut.

It could so easily have been the type made out of reinforced steel: the kind it took half a dozen keys to open.

Because, let's face it, we could easily have lost him to prison. He was staring at serious charges: vandalism, destruction of public property, car theft, joy-riding: an impressive list.

I dread to think what would have happened if they'd found the gun. But they didn't. Den had sorted that three days later, ignoring the police tape and the mess from the birds to make the pistol disappear.

'What did you do with it?' I'd asked. He refused to tell me.

'It's not important. It's gone.'

I had no idea how I was ever going to pay him back, but according to him the slate was clean. End of. And I wasn't about to start arguing with him. I liked my face the way it was.

Aside from Den's favour, it was the thing that had wrecked Jammy in the first place that kept him out of prison. It was the army: the people who had served with him.

Once news broke and the local rag relegated him, in one brutal article, from HERO to PSYCHOPATH, people started queuing up to support him.

His commanding officer arrived at our door, promising the medical help he should've already had. He gave it a name. Post-traumatic stress. Told us it was common now, that the army had a duty of care to Jamm. They wouldn't desert him after what he'd already given back.

Others called or wrote, vowing to be character witnesses, re-filling our heads with things that we already knew. That Jammy was a hero before he was a casualty. That this disorder would pass with the right help from the right people.

These people were good to their word. One hulking squaddie, Giffer, came from Wales to tell the court what he knew. His CO did the same. Cam's mum, Gill, too. She read to the jury a letter she'd had from Tommo, which laid his own struggle bare. Made it clear that without Jamm to lean on he would've died much sooner.

'I might be scared,' it read, 'but I don't regret being here. It's impossible to feel like that with Jamm fighting with me, teaching me to be just like him.'

I don't know how she found the strength to read that note aloud, but we were so glad she did. There was no way they could send him down after that.

Instead they sent him to this clinic, where he's been ever since.

But today was when we finally took him back. All right, there'd be probation officers and counsellors for as long as they saw fit, but at least he'd be home on the Ghost again.

Until my plan comes to fruition.

I watched closely as he walked towards us, looking for reassurance that they'd let the real Jamm out. One that was ready for all the nonsense that living with us brought.

His grin was wide, his strides long and urgent, but I had no idea what was playing out in his head: whether Tommo and Wayne had allowed him enough peace to move forward. I suppose I had to trust the doctors on that one; trust Jammy too. Couldn't imagine he'd want to leave the cocoon of the clinic until he was really ready.

His pace quickened as he approached us, not slowing even when he was metres away. Instead we fanned out around him as he crashed into Mum and me, our arms snaking round each other into one enormous scrum.

Den was the first to crack. He didn't care that he was the biggest. If he wanted to cry then he was having it. We fell in behind him, letting ourselves milk every bit of relief. We'd waited too long for this moment to let it pass any other way.

The bundle held strong, long enough for Jamm to hug each of us in turn. I soaked his embrace up, not flinching as he kissed my forehead, nor feeling jealous when he turned his attention to Cam. As they parted I felt her hand reach around my waist and squeeze.

It was the first time she'd touched me since Jamm went AWOL. It felt better than any kiss we'd ever shared.

'I can't believe you're all here.' He grinned.

'Like any of us would miss it.'

'But it's miles away. How did you afford the fare?'

'It wasn't a problem. We nicked a minibus.'

Cam jabbed me in the ribs.

'No, we came in this.' And I pointed behind me, at the other reason for us standing over here in the first place.

Jamm put his bag down and looked over my shoulder, a look of confusion appearing as he clocked the rusty van.

'Really? That thing has an engine that actually works?'

'Hell, yeah.' I was going to stick up for it after all the work we'd done. 'A good one too. Wiggy's cousin tuned it up. It's er . . . well, it's one of the only things it does have.'

'Why, what's missing?' He walked to it, sticking his finger straight into a rust hole that would've fitted his entire fist.

'Not much, just insurance, MOT and that. It's all in the post.'

'I'm sure it is. I still don't know why you didn't get the train, though.'

'Because we've work to do. So we need the van.'

He looked at me like I was the one with the head problems.

'Have you not read the logo on the side?'

He squinted, trying to be funny. 'That's a logo? I thought someone had sneezed on it.'

I gave him a dig and looked at it again. It was a first attempt. We could start afresh if he liked, though the company name wasn't up for discussion.

'THE ORIGINALS,' it read. 'MOVERS, SHIFTERS. WE'LL TAKE ANYTHING YOU'VE GOT.'

'It makes us sound like burglars,' he said.

'It's a work in progress.'

'That's all right. So am I.' He smiled. 'I didn't even know we were going into business.'

'Well someone has to pay the bills now the SAS won't have you,' I felt another dig from Cam but carried on. 'And anyway, it doesn't have to be forever. Just till we make enough.'

'Enough for what?'

'To let us hang out somewhere other than the Ghost, if

that's what you want? I'm not the ideas man round here, I'm just the one who messes them up, remember?'

I looked into his face as he stared at the van. I knew I had the others onside, but without Jammy it was a non-starter. I was doing this for him, after all.

'So what do you reckon then, bruv? You in or what?' There was no point beating about the bush.

He sighed and looked at the hand I'd offered him, before pulling me roughly into him, squeezing way too hard. I squeezed back, our four arms quickly becoming six, eight, ten and more. They came from every direction, ruffling my hair, patting my back; it felt better than I ever could've imagined.

But it wasn't perfect.

There was still a gap where Tommo should've been.

So, gently and without fuss, I filled it, pulling my brother closer to me, before he noticed it too.

We could stand here a while longer if that's what he wanted, but not for too long.

That van wasn't going to fill itself.

ACKNOWLEDGEMENTS

I am hugely in debt to S. E. Hinton. Without *The Outsiders* I doubt I'd be working with children's books, never mind trying to write them. I only hope that, in some small way, I've done the incredible spirit of her novel justice . . .

Bruce Springsteen needs a thank-you too. I listened to 'Terry's Song' every morning before writing *Heroic*. Don't think I'll ever hear a finer definition of what brotherhood means (go give it a listen).

My thanks go to the people of both Royal Wootton Bassett and Carterton, whose passion and sense of community in honouring those who give their lives in battle moved me massively and planted the seed for this story.

I have also been overwhelmed by the reports of bravery from members of our armed forces fighting in Iraq and Afghanistan. A friend of mine recently travelled on an internal flight in America and saw a returning soldier receive a huge ovation as attendants announced his arrival on the plane. It seems sad to me that, too often, our own armed forces are greeted with indifference or even scepticism. We can never fully understand the horrors they face, or appreciate that, for many, the real battle begins once they return home from active service.

I'm so grateful to all those who offered military advice (even if I didn't get around to taking it), especially to the gentleman that is George Walkley, and to Kingsley Donaldson, Jim Sells, Lara Hancock and Malinda Zerefos.

Huge thanks also to my agent and lunch pal, Jodie Marsh, for her honesty, all-round brilliance and fish finger sarnies (always on white, no granary).

Thank you to the team at Puffin: Katy Finch, Sam Mackintosh, Debbie Hatfield, Sam Combes, Tineke Mollemans, Kirsty Bradbury, Clive Harvey and the sales team who champion my books, and also to Hermione Lawton, who is bloomin' lovely and deserves a medal for pressing my worst-sellers into so many hands.

I must thank Shannon too, for whipping both the script and me into shape, ignoring my grumblings as she did so. Thank you, my friend, you are the business.

Finally, I need to thank my family and friends.

I could never have written a word of this without my mum, dad, in-laws or the friends who have *taught* me what brotherhood means: Matthew Williams, Chris Lowther (my brother next door), Michael Willison, Pee Dee, Bree, Paddy Ritzy, Bobby, Shreev-o, Joseph, Elliiot, Robbie, Mr Bootle, Benton, Burto, Browno, Burb, Will and, of course, Jonny John-Kamen.

I want to thank the Dublin Daves too (O'Callaghan and Maybury) for Scotch eggs, playlists and all-round marvellousness.

I hope Dennis, Matt H and Waggy didn't mind me

borrowing their names. I swear the other character traits are purely fictional, sort of. And thank you, Wagg, for writing the poem for me. It's a thing of beauty. I'll treasure it.

Cheers to my pals in the Palace, especially the newcomer Fred Morgan, but most of all, thank you to Laura, Albert, Elsie and Stanley – I haven't the words apart from these. Stay Golden . . .

November 2012, the X68 bus,
Waterloo Bridge, London

He just wanted a decent book to read …

Not too much to ask, is it? It was in 1935 when Allen Lane, Managing Director of Bodley Head Publishers, stood on a platform at Exeter railway station looking for something good to read on his journey back to London. His choice was limited to popular magazines and poor-quality paperbacks – the same choice faced every day by the vast majority of readers, few of whom could afford hardbacks. Lane's disappointment and subsequent anger at the range of books generally available led him to found a company – and change the world.

'We believed in the existence in this country of a vast reading public for intelligent books at a low price, and staked everything on it'
Sir Allen Lane, 1902–1970, founder of Penguin Books

The quality paperback had arrived – and not just in bookshops. Lane was adamant that his Penguins should appear in chain stores and tobacconists, and should cost no more than a packet of cigarettes.

Reading habits (and cigarette prices) have changed since 1935, but Penguin still believes in publishing the best books for everybody to enjoy. We still believe that good design costs no more than bad design, and we still believe that quality books published passionately and responsibly make the world a better place.

So wherever you see the little bird – whether it's on a piece of prize-winning literary fiction or a celebrity autobiography, political tour de force or historical masterpiece, a serial-killer thriller, reference book, world classic or a piece of pure escapism – you can bet that it represents the very best that the genre has to offer.

Whatever you like to read – trust Penguin.